CAPTAIN COOK'S *Apprentice*

Anthony Hill is a multi-award-winning, bestselling author. His most recent book for adults, *Animal Heroes*, was published in 2017.

His novel *Soldier Boy*, about Australia's youngest-known Anzac, won the 2002 NSW Premier's Literary Award for Books for Young Adults. Alongside *Young Digger* and *For Love of Country*, it's testimony to his remarkable ability to extensively research historical material and, from wide-ranging sources, piece together a moving and exciting story.

He is also the author of two novellas, the beautiful *Shadow Dog*, and the award-winning *The Burnt Stick*, illustrated by Mark Sofilas, as well as the picture book, *Lucy's Cat and the Rainbow Birds*, illustrated by Jane Tanner.

Anthony lives in Canberra with his wife, Gillian. Their daughter, son-in-law and granddaughter, Emily, live in Melbourne.

anthonyhillbooks.com

Also by Anthony Hill

Young Digger
The Story of Billy Young
Soldier Boy
The Burnt Stick
For Love of Country
Animal Heroes

ANTHONY HILL

CAPTAIN COOK'S *Apprentice*

VIKING
an imprint of
PENGUIN BOOKS

VIKING

UK | USA | Canada | Ireland | Australia
India | New Zealand | South Africa | China

Penguin Books is part of the Penguin Random House group of companies whose addresses can be found at global.penguinrandomhouse.com.

Penguin Random House Australia

First published by Penguin Group (Australia), 2008
This revised edition published by Penguin Random House Australia Pty Ltd, 2018

1 3 5 7 9 10 8 6 4 2

Cover design by Alex Ross © Penguin Random House Pty Ltd
Cover images: ship by Gordon Miller; compass, flowers and shark tooth by Shutterstock
Internal maps by Damien Saunder, Demap
Typeset in Sabon by Midland Typesetters, Australia
Colour separation by Splitting Image Colour Studio, Clayton, Victoria
Printed and bound in Australia by Griffin Press, an accredited ISO AS/NZS 14001 Environmental Management Systems printer.

NATIONAL LIBRARY OF AUSTRALIA

A catalogue record for this book is available from the National Library of Australia

ISBN: 978 0 14378 950 5

This project has been assisted by the Commonwealth Government through the Australia Council, its arts funding and advisory body.

Australian Government | Australia Council for the Arts

penguin.com.au

MIX
Paper from responsible sources
FSC® C009448
FSC www.fsc.org

For Jane Tanner,
a fellow voyager

I whose ambition leads me not only farther than any other man has been before me, but as far as I think it possible for man to go . . .

James Cook, 30 January 1774

CONTENTS

THE SHIP'S COMPANY

HM Bark *Endeavour* left Plymouth in August 1768 with ninety-four souls on board. Among them were the following:

Captain Lieutenant James Cook

Lieutenants Zachary Hicks, John Gore

Master Robert Molineux

Master's Mates Richard Pickersgill, Francis Wilkinson, Charles Clerke

Midshipmen John Bootie, Jonathan Monkhouse, Patrick Saunders

Surgeon William Monkhouse

Surgeon's Mate William Perry

Captain's Clerk Richard Orton

Gunner Stephen Forwood

Boatswain John Gathrey

Boatswain's Mates including John Reading, Samuel Evans

Quartermaster Alexander Weir

Carpenter John Satterley

Armourer Robert Taylor

Cook John Thompson

Sailmaker John Ravenhill

Butcher Henry Jeffs

Able Seamen including Isaac Smith (later Midshipman), James Magra (later Midshipman), Forby Sutherland, Peter Flower, Henry Stephens, John Thurman (pressed at Madeira), Archibald Wolf, Francis Haite, Manuel Pereira (from Rio)

Servants, boys including Isaac Manley (later Midshipman), Nick Young, Tom Matthews

Marines Sergeant John Edgcumbe, Corporal John Truslove, eleven Privates including Thomas Dunster, Samuel Gibson, William Greenslade, Thomas Rossiter (drummer), Clement Webb

Supernumeraries Joseph Banks, Charles Green (astronomer), Daniel Solander (naturalist), Herman Spöring (assistant), Alexander Buchan, Sydney Parkinson (artists)

Servants including James Roberts, Peter Briscoe, Thomas Richmond, George Dorlton

Tahitians Tupaia, a priest of *Oro*, Taiata, his attendant

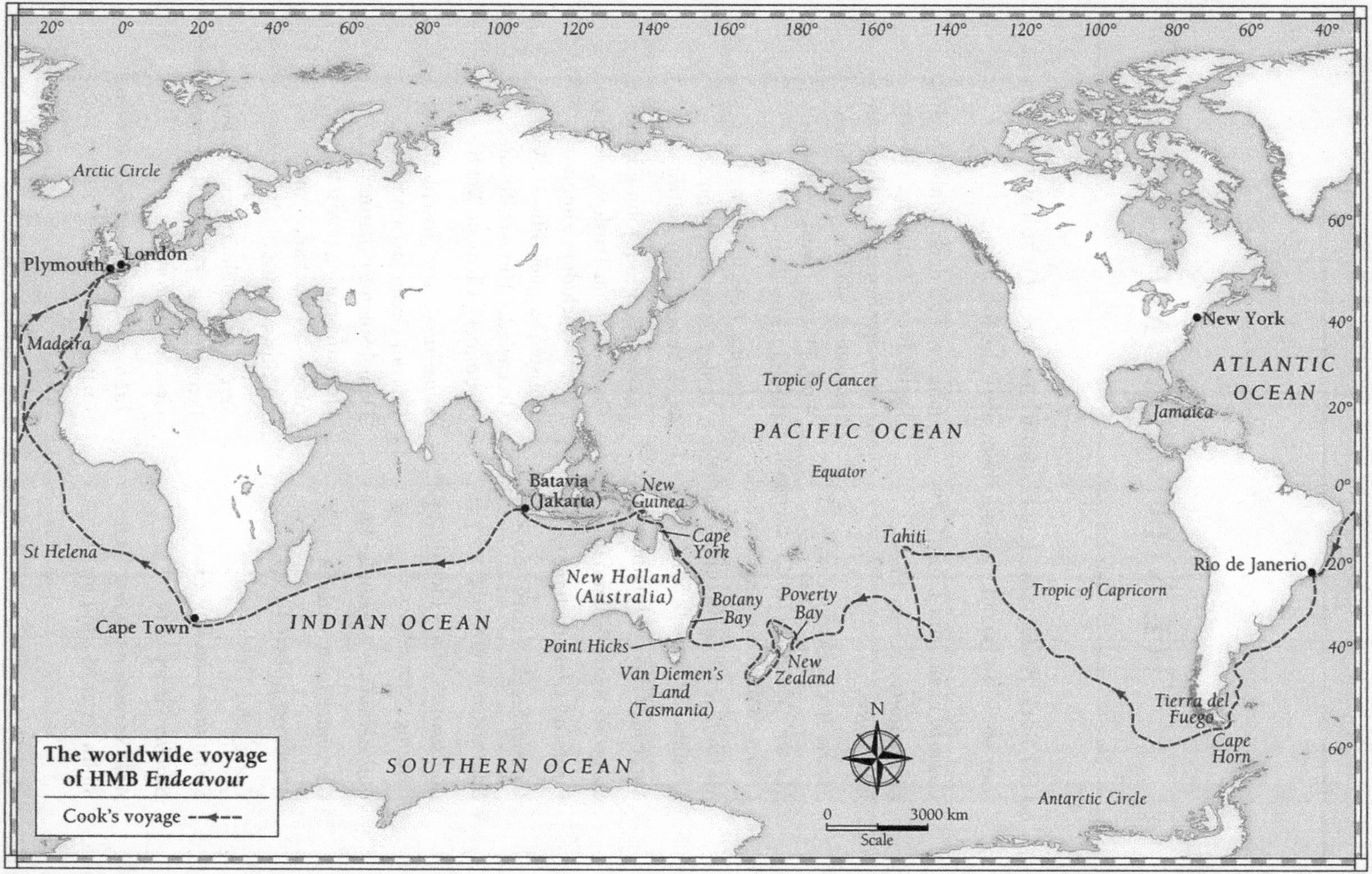

The worldwide voyage of HMB *Endeavour*
Cook's voyage
20°
0°
20°
40°
60°
80°
100°
120°
140°
160°
180°
160°
140°
120°
100°
80°
60°
40°
60°
40°
20°
0°
20°
40°
60°
Arctic Circle
Plymouth
London
Madeira
St Helena
Cape Town
INDIAN OCEAN
Batavia (Jakarta)
New Guinea
Cape York
New Holland (Australia)
Botany Bay
Point Hicks
Van Diemen's Land (Tasmania)
Poverty Bay
New Zealand
Tahiti
PACIFIC OCEAN
Tropic of Cancer
Equator
Tropic of Capricorn
SOUTHERN OCEAN
N
0
3000 km
Scale
Antarctic Circle
New York
ATLANTIC OCEAN
Jamaica
Rio de Janerio
Tierra del Fuego
Cape Horn

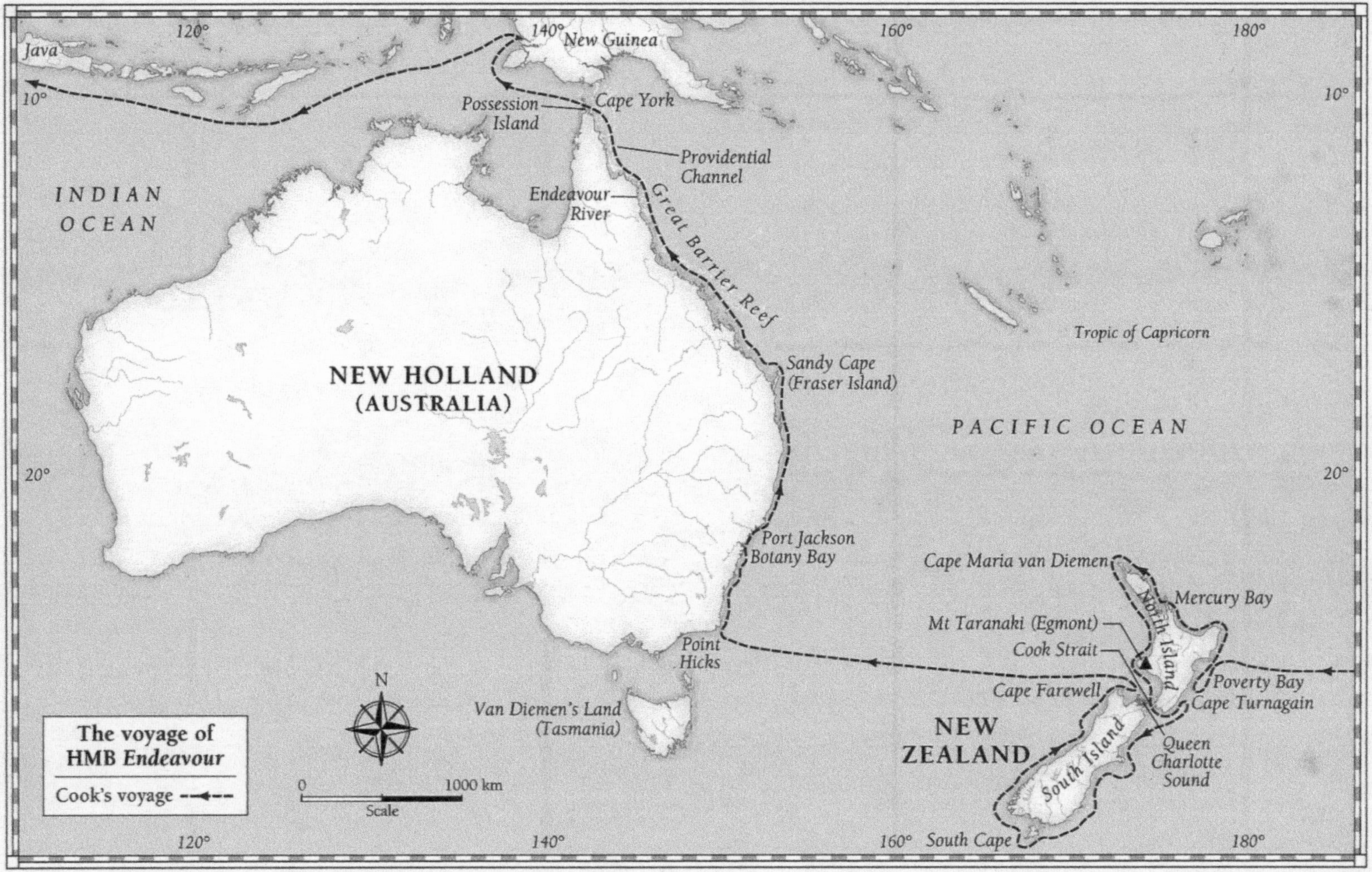
The voyage of
HMB *Endeavour*
Cook's voyage
120°
140°
160°
180°
10°
20°
Java
New Guinea
Possession Island
Cape York
Providential Channel
Endeavour River
Great Barrier Reef
INDIAN OCEAN
NEW HOLLAND
(AUSTRALIA)
Sandy Cape
(Fraser Island)
Tropic of Capricorn
PACIFIC OCEAN
Port Jackson
Botany Bay
Point Hicks
Van Diemen's Land
(Tasmania)
N
0
1000 km
Scale
Cape Maria van Diemen
Mercury Bay
Mt Taranaki (Egmont)
Cook Strait
North Island
Poverty Bay
Cape Turnagain
Cape Farewell
NEW ZEALAND
South Island
Queen Charlotte Sound
South Cape

INTRODUCTION

August 2018 marks the 250th anniversary of the departure from Plymouth of His Majesty's Bark *Endeavour* under its captain, Lieutenant James Cook. Its three-year odyssey is among the most significant voyages of European discovery ever made. And that being so, there could be no better time to bring out this new edition of *Captain Cook's Apprentice* – very much a servant boy's mess-deck view of the great enterprise, which did so much to expand human knowledge in the arts and sciences, and our understanding of the world we inhabit. And for those of us who live in the new nations of the Pacific that arose in Cook's wake, the *Endeavour* voyage and all that followed still resonate in our daily lives.

Beyond all the enduring consequences of the *Endeavour* circumnavigation, however, there remains the sheer adventure of the expedition itself. That intoxicating draught of fear and daring when journeying into the unknown – of sailing into a vast, blank space on the map, and not knowing what might happen. Much, in our own day, as we all felt when humanity first flew with a rocket ship into space.

I'd long wanted to write the *Endeavour* story with the immediacy it would have had to somebody on board at the time, but it wasn't until I was reading J C Beaglehole's *Life of Captain Cook* that I found a way into it. There was a single reference to a young fellow, Isaac Manley, only thirteen at the time they left in August 1768, who rose to become an Admiral, lived to be eighty-two and was the last survivor of the *Endeavour* crew. Here, I thought, was my subject. Isaac had gone on board as servant – more akin to an apprentice in our terms – to the sailing master, Robert Molineux, to learn his ropes; and he must have done well, for Cook made him a midshipman on the way home. It was his first step up the ladder of promotion . . . and gave me a chance to tell the tale through fresh, young eyes, in the dawn of life when everything is new.

Very little had been written about Isaac up to that time. When I began the research project I was privileged to be given four hours with Cook's *Endeavour* journal at the National Library of Australia; he makes no mention of Isaac in it at all, although his name certainly appears in the ship's muster book and in Cook's letter to the Admiralty after the voyage, praising him as one whose 'behaviour merits the best recommendation'. Even during two years of research I could find nothing that Isaac wrote about the voyage, despite his long and prospering life.

Yet all the time I was reading Cook's journal I was conscious of the lad living and growing, darting between the lines as, day by day, the Captain wrote his epic words on the page. During my own sail on the *Endeavour* replica, I made the rounds one night with the watch through the decks of the sleeping ship to ensure that all was well. And I felt very much as Isaac must have done when he did it for the first time after Cook made him a midshipman.

The responsibility was palpable – and it drew me closer to my theme and to all that happened.

I came closer to Isaac Manley, as well. Later in the research journey I stayed for several days in the lovely Georgian 'gothick' mansion he built for his family in Oxfordshire. You can tell a lot about somebody's personality and motivations when you inhabit for a little while the rooms they made for themselves. And by coincidence, a few years ago, I acquired a map signed by Admiral Manley not long before he died. It shows the coastlines of New Zealand and New South Wales that he was among the first Europeans to see as a boy. I must say it was a constant companion while preparing this new edition of *Captain Cook's Apprentice*. I was in direct contact with Manley, as I had been with Cook through his journal.

Having said that, it's important to add that the novel is essentially a literary re-creation: a 'mess-deck view', as I said, of the voyage as I imagine Isaac might have experienced it. The girl Heimata and the pearl, Isaac's thoughts, speech, feelings, and the internals of character are wholly fictional. Yet I have sought to remain true to the externals of the *Endeavour* narrative. The sequence of events as they unfold, and the opinions of Cook, Banks and others, have been based closely on their journals, as documented in the Chapter Notes.

In this, I have tried to keep faith with the many people mentioned in the Acknowledgments who helped with my own journeys in Australia, New Zealand, Tahiti and Britain – as I sought to do justice to the vision I had of the youth who kept appearing in the spaces between Captain Cook's bristling words in the manuscript room at the National Library.

The first edition of *Captain Cook's Apprentice* did well, and received its share of attention. And in thanking Penguin Random

House for deciding to publish this new and expanded edition to coincide with the 250th anniversary of the mighty *Endeavour* enterprise, I rejoice that the tale has been brought before another generation of readers. For truly it touches all our lives.

Anthony Hill
Canberra, 2018

1

BEGINNINGS

England, June to August 1768

The boy knew danger was coming.

He could hear it, sitting at the prow of his ferryboat on the broad River Thames . . . a deep growl of angry water that grew louder as they neared London Bridge.

He could feel it, for the boat began to kick and strain as it caught the edges of the rip, where the pent-up river gushed into narrow channels between the piers.

And then he could see it. A white, foaming cascade as the water swirled through the arches, like a rapids.

Danger. And the boy Isaac knew what he would do.

'Will you get out and walk round, young sir, as I shoot the bridge?' asked the ferryman, rowing towards the riverbank stairs. 'I'll pick ye up on the other side.'

Young Isaac Manley shook his head. 'I'm shooting the bridge with you.'

'Most unwise.' The man squinted. 'Your father wouldn't like it.'

'I don't care.'

'He give me a silver half-crown to deliver you safe down river, to the ship *Endeavour* what's being fitted out for the South Seas. He won't want you drowned before you've even reached Deptford.'

'My father's not here. He'll never know.'

'He's a lawyer, matey. And lawyers know everything.'

'*Please!*' The boy turned to the waterman, seeking his own justice. 'I've never been allowed. It's the first time. Before I board that ship, I must know if I dare . . .'

'You know what they say: London Bridge is for wise men to cross and fools to go under.'

'I can add a sixpence to your fare.' Isaac felt for his purse. 'When we get there.'

'Ah, so that's where the wind lies. How old are ye?'

'Thirteen.'

The man bared his yellow teeth and blinked at Isaac's coin. 'Then I'll be a wise fool and take the young master's money, too.' He spat on his hands. 'I've been a seafaring man myself. Let's see what sort of sailor you'll make.'

And bracing his feet on the boards, he pulled the boat into midstream.

Isaac shivered a little, spray wet on his face, and drew his cloak around him. He hoped he'd be a good sailor and do his father proud, but he didn't know . . .

He looked up river, crowded with boats and barges as it flowed through the great city in the summer morning. Past the towers of Westminster, and the Temple where his father John practised law. He'd just been made a Bencher, and the ancient Manley crest of a black hand on a white shield would be mounted proudly in the Great Hall.

Past the looming dome of Saint Paul's. If Isaac peered hard enough he could see the steeples near Hatton Garden, where lived the family he'd known all his life: Papa and mother Ann, his two brothers and two sisters – and Isaac, in the middle, was the first to leave home. He hoped they'd *all* think well of him . . .

Then he turned to the bridge. Young Master Manley knew it would take more than this to make a seaman of him. But it was a start: a fair beginning to his first voyage.

The Thames moved placidly enough on its own journey to the sea, until it met the barrier of London Bridge. The nineteen piers, protected by massive stone and timber piles, blocked two-thirds of the river. With each tidal change water banked up behind, as if the bridge were a dam wall, and the Thames hurled itself through the narrow arches in violent cataracts. Although they'd widened the middle arch and the bridge itself a few years ago, it still took courage to pass beneath it on a running tide. When the boatman spoke of drownings, he wasn't exaggerating.

'At least they took down the houses on London Bridge!' he called above the torrent. 'We won't have the excitement of people emptying piss pots over us as well, ha ha! Hang on to your cocked hat, matey!'

Isaac removed his hat altogether and clamped it between his knees. He needed both hands to hang on to the boat.

For suddenly they were in the grip of the current. The man had charge of his ferry thus far: now he could only use his oars to steady it as the river swept them into the middle arch. Closer and closer. Like entering a spillway.

Isaac could hear the roar of water as it fell into the whirlpool below. He wished he'd had second thoughts and walked around the bridge as wise men like his father did. But it was too late for that.

The river had seized them and was rushing them forward. Thank God his sea chest was safely roped in the stern!

The sun disappeared. They were under the bridge. Isaac noticed the ferryman had shipped his oars for safety and, looking up, he saw the pointed ribs of the old bridge as they'd been built five hundred years ago. He was about to shout something, when all at once he felt himself tipped backwards and forwards as the boat plunged ten feet down the waterfall and into the white, boiling spume.

Vomit rose in Isaac's throat. Thoughts of drowning, and of the dead found on river mud, flooded his mind. He wished to his gut he'd never wanted to go to sea . . .

There was light. The noise receded. And opening his grey, stinging eyes, Isaac saw the man righting his oars and grinning at him.

'Ye're as green as seaweed, mate. But you'll not reach Deptford floating face down.'

He began to row once more, smooth and easy, for the tide was ebbing and the river carried them quickly downstream. Isaac might not be dead – but he felt half-drowned all the same! A tall, well-built lad, his face and long sandy hair, tied with a ribbon, were by now sopping wet and his cloak was drenched. But they'd soon dry in the morning sun. And having survived the danger, Isaac laughed at it.

Past the Customs House, where Isaac's grandfather John had been a Commissioner and the family first came to know sea captains and navy men; beyond the grim turrets of the Tower, and frantic riverside wharves. Here, in the Pool of London, great ships were all day unloading their cargoes and fitting out for new voyages.

'East Indiamen from Bengal,' the waterman pointed to them. 'Merchantmen from Americky, look ye. Newcastle colliers . . . channel packet boats . . . Gibraltar men-o-war. And crewmen from all parts of the known world – aye, and some parts barely discovered. There's talk up and down river what *Endeavour* will carry men who sailed the South Seas with Captain Wallis and found the island of Tahiti.'

'So my father says,' replied Isaac, his voice kindling with the sounds of ships and such faraway places. Safely through the bridge, the boy's imagination was catching fire again. 'We're supposed to be bound for there. Such an adventure! I was lucky he could get me a berth!'

'And what berth is that?' The man eased his oars and pulled out a pipe. 'Have they made ye captain yet?'

'No, Lieutenant James Cook is Captain. I'm . . .' Isaac realised he was being teased, and his voice fell. 'I'm just one of the officer's servants . . . a cabin boy.'

'No shame in that, not even for a young gentleman whose pa is a rich lawyer. Many an admiral has started just the same way, 'prentice to a officer and studyin' to become a good seaman. It's a hard life, matey. A strict life. But sometimes it's a sweet one. And the sooner ye get started in it, the better. Come on!'

He bent to the oars again.

Swiftly they passed timber yards and shipwrights, bustling warehouses and riverside alehouses, where off-duty seamen caroused with their shore wives. Yes, and the gallows at Execution Dock where pirates hung in chains till their corpses rotted. For the sea could be a cruel life as well.

The river thronged with ships lying at anchor, and the ferryman told Isaac to keep his eyes peeled for loose cables and any other small craft as they threaded among them.

So the boy played lookout as they passed high gilded stern windows, weather-beaten hulls, and above them tall masts and spars swaying like a bare winter forest. Proud thrusting bowsprits supported by carved figureheads – mermaids, sea gods and painted heroes – keeping watch. *Neptune. Admiral Pocock. The Rajah of Calicut.* Such names! Such places they'd seen! Excitement stirred in him again. Soon Isaac would join them and he, too, would sail for Tahiti and parts barely known. If only they could reach his ship . . .

Then, rounding a bend in the river, he saw the domes of Greenwich, the Royal Observatory on its green hill. And before them, the brick clock tower, storehouses and all the swarming activity of the naval dockyard at Deptford.

They rowed about seeking directions for the vessel called *Endeavour*, and at last found her berthed beside the supply tender *Surprize*, getting her spars across. She was a modest little ship – small and tubby in comparison to the men-o-war they'd passed. But to Isaac she was beautiful, and he longed to get aboard.

'She's a coal carrier, no more'n a bark,' remarked the boatman by the ship's ladder. 'Funny thing to take to the South Seas. Still, she's got a good hold and sturdy round bottom, and I dare say her master knows what he's doing.'

A head appeared over the ship's side.

'Permission to come aboard,' cried the ferryman. 'One young gentleman, name o' Manley, with sea chest.'

'Aye aye.'

And turning to Isaac he murmured, 'Up you go, lad.'

Though as he stood, the boy's doubts rose with him. 'Do you think . . .?'

'I reckon they might make something of ye. I'll see to your trunk.'

Isaac gave his promised sixpence, and began to climb.

If ever the time came when Isaac had command of his own ship, he knew he'd be piped aboard with all due naval ceremony.

But on that first morning there was no one to help him as he struggled up the side, not sure where to put his feet, until he sprawled gangling onto the deck. No one except an urchin-faced boy, younger and smaller than himself, lounging on the rigging and watching.

'Landlubber!' the boy laughed. And swinging down as lightly as any cat, he sauntered off to join the body of seamen hauling up the main topsail yard.

Isaac scrambled to join them. But they were far too busy to take notice of a city lad so clearly out of place. Besides, they were shouting a language he barely understood.

'On halyards and tops'l yard lifts! Heave away! Haul away!' And two dozen sweaty men responded.

When Isaac politely tried to ask, 'Please, where's the Captain?' a seaman told him to get out from underfoot. And when he persisted, the sailor hissed that 'Cap'n would nae wanna see *ye*. Go talk to yon one-handed cook.'

'Now, Mr Sutherland, that's none too mannerly,' said a plain Yorkshire voice behind him. 'This Captain's always willing t' oblige if he can, even on busiest days. What is it, lad?'

Isaac turned to a tall man in a blue naval frock coat with brass buttons, dark hair curled and tied behind. A raw, high-cheeked workman's face, perhaps: but his deep brown eyes were shrewd, and he spoke with authority.

'I must find Mr Cook. I've a letter from my father.'

'You've found him. Let me see what he says . . .'

The Captain read quickly.

'He thanks me for having you aboard, and hopes you'll succeed in my service.' Lieutenant Cook folded the letter. 'Ye've already been recommended by the Lordships at t' Admiralty – your father's influence no doubt. And as for success, Mr Manley, that's entirely up to thee. I can only repeat what my Master said when I started on a collier, just like this, out o' Whitby. Show willing. Jump to thee orders. And never stop learning, for t' sea teaches endless lessons.'

The Captain paused a moment, looking at the boy. 'Ye'll find us a strange school at first, with our own ways of doin' things. But wi' time and perseverance it might become your way as well.'

Then he snapped to attention. 'Right. We've a ship to rig, man and store for a long voyage. I've assigned thee as servant to the Master, Mr Molineux. He was with Captain Wallis on the *Dolphin* when they discovered Tahiti. A very useful man. He's just come aboard, and is down below. Seek him out, and follow his orders in all things – after my own orders, of course!'

'I'm sorry, sir, but I don't know the way . . .'

'Nay, thou don't. Hi – you – boy – Young Nick!' Cook called to the scamp who'd laughed at the landlubber. 'Show Isaac to his hammock space, and then take him to t' Master.'

'Aye, Cap'n.'

Lieutenant Cook turned to more urgent matters with the topsail yard.

'It's Nick Young really,' muttered the boy, 'though they all say me name stern abart, just because I'm eleven. Silly joke.' Nimbly he skirted cables, barrels and spars, and shinned down the steep companion steps. Isaac, following awkwardly, almost fell headfirst through the hatch.

'Come down backwards, lubber, and hang on to the knotted man-rope.' It was the voice of experience. But Young Nick spoke more kindly as Isaac stepped from the sun into the half-light of the mess deck where the seamen ate, slept and passed their few hours off duty. 'Don't worry. You'll soon get used to it.'

He sneaked a couple of apples from a barrel near the galley stove and tossed one to Isaac, as the cook – who indeed had only one hand – waved his stump and called them 'a pair of young divils'.

'Truth is, I'm not s'posed to be 'ere at all,' Nick confided. 'No place for me yet on the muster book. But blimey! I'm sailin' anyways.'

Nick dodged mess tables hanging on ropes, with sea chests for benches, until he came to a low bulkhead.

'They've put in a new deck and extra cabins for the scientific gents what are comin' to the South Seas,' he explained. 'Everyfing's a lot more cramped. So watch your 'ead – though I 'spect it will take a few bangs on the noggin afore you remember.'

There was only four and a half foot of headroom, and both boys had to stoop and scuttle crabwise aft to the officers' quarters at the rear of the ship. Nick stopped short, however, and pointed up to a beam.

'We lads sling our hammocks here. Fourteen inches of space between you and me, Issy, and that's home for the next two or three years.'

'It's not very much . . .' Isaac forgot. He stood upright. Whacked his head sharp on the timbers. And Nick Young, laughing at him again, observed that 'At least it ain't far to fall out o' bed at night. Look to, now! Master's cabin is starboard astern.'

'Starboard?' Isaac rubbed the first of many lumps he'd get on his noggin.

'Right-hand side of ship looking for'ard. Larboard is opposite. And don't confuse the two, or you'll wreck your own ship one day.'

There was more headroom aft, where they found the Master, Robert Molineux, unpacking his gear and also complaining at his quarters.

'Look at this, Dicky,' he was saying in a faint Lancashire accent to his Mate, Richard Pickersgill. 'My first day as Master with a brand new warrant in my pocket, expecting a berth up top, only to find meself squeezed out to make way for *botanists* and *artists*.'

Molineux spoke with a navy man's disdain for such lubberly occupations. Pickersgill tried to look sympathetic, for the two were old companions, having sailed as Master's Mates around the world on the *Dolphin*. 'It's not just you, Robert, down here on the half deck, but the two Lieutenants and surgeon as well. And Captain's giving up his own cabin to the head man – name o' Banks.'

'First time I've heard of *scientists* on board a *naval ship*.'

Molineux spoke truly: for a new spirit of scientific enquiry – of reason and human enlightenment – was informing the educated world. Thus the novelty of Pickersgill's response. 'It's a scientific expedition! To observe the Transit of Venus across the sun at Tahiti. That's why *we're* on board. We've been there. Mr Cook wants our advice. And then to make new discoveries in the South Seas.'

'Oh, aye? The great unknown continent. Perhaps.' Molineux smiled. Then, catching sight of the boys in the doorway, he called, 'What do you lads want?'

'I've brung your new servant,' said Young Nick, full of cheek. 'His name's Isaac and he don't know nuffing.' And pinching Isaac on the arm, he darted off up top.

Molineux bestirred himself. 'To work, Dicky. So . . .' casting an eye over Isaac, 'lubber still, are ye? Quite the young gentleman, to be sure. Officer material, d'ye reckon?'

'Maybe. One day.' Isaac was hesitant. 'If I show willing and follow orders, as Mr Cook said.'

'Quite right. Keep your eyes and ears open, mouth shut, and any light fingers to thyself. That's lesson one. Lesson two, you'll attend to my wants without complaint. And lesson three is to start knowing your ship. Mr Pickersgill is about to show me over *Endeavour.* You'll come with us. After you serve our dinner, you'll tidy my cabin. Put away my books and papers. *Don't* touch my navigational instruments, sextant and such like. Make up my cot. Take particular care of my clothes, for I've a new uniform today and silver buckles in my shoes. In short, master Isaac, you'll keep me and my berth shipshape. Oh, and after that I've a dozen cases of good wine to be stored below.' He winked at Richard Pickersgill. 'Understood? Right, then, come along!'

So unfolded the first exhausting day of Isaac's new life. Robert Molineux was a young red-headed gent of only twenty-two, with sharp, intelligent features, and he set a brisk pace. As Master, he was responsible for the stowage and trim of the ship, the rigging, sails and cables, and – under the Captain's direction – their navigation.

Isaac struggled after him. Down to the gloomy hold, smelling of tar, ballast and bilge pumps, where the water barrels were stacked in tiers, and the biscuit, salt beef and other provisions stored safe and dry as they were brought aboard. For'ard to the magazine, where the gunpowder and ammunition were kept (no naked candles there). To the sail room, carpenter's and boatswain's stores on the mess deck. Then back up the steep companionway (Isaac clinging to the man-rope for safety) to the upper deck for Molineux to inspect *Endeavour*'s bewildering array of parts, whose names and purposes had as yet no meaning for Isaac.

Clews and buntlines, stays and tricing lines, timberheads, belaying pins, cat falls and snotters . . .

It was a worn-out boy who sat to his supper of cold meat and beer, wondering why he'd wanted to join the navy, and desiring only sleep. At home, a servant would have drawn the curtains of his feather bed. Here, Isaac *was* the servant, and he had to draw and sling his own hammock.

'Nuffing to it, lubber,' said Young Nick in his nightshirt. 'This long line at each end's called a lanyard, see. Pass it over the beam and through the grommet ring – twice – and then make it off snug with a neat rolling hitch. Easy!'

It wasn't easy. It was a seadog's breakfast, and it took Isaac ages to sling the other end. And when at last he gingerly sat in the middle of the hammock and tried to roll himself on, he almost rolled off the other side again.

Nick thought it funny as a picture. 'I hope you did a good hitch, Issy.'

'Why?'

'You'll find out.'

Isaac lay on his back, scarcely daring to breathe. He felt squeezed like a sausage in its skin. Sleep deserted him. He heard *Endeavour*'s every creak; Nick snoring beside him; the laughter of sailors and their wives drinking in the galley; the ship's bell ringing the half-hours of the watch.

Suddenly he heard the nearer sounds of rope slipping. The hammock jerked. The rolling hitch unravelled. And with all the rush of shooting the bridge again, Isaac was pitched on his arse to the deck.

Nick Young cackled. This was better than a circus.

'I *told* you!'

'Will you sling it for me?' Every part of Isaac ached.

'I'll show you once more. After that, lubber, you'll have to do it over and over till you get it right.'

Isaac picked himself up, hit his noggin again, and fumbled for the end of his hammock.

It took him three nights to sleep in it. That first evening Isaac barely got a wink, and not many more on the second. By the third night, however, Isaac was so weary he'd have slept anywhere. And in time, like any seaman, his hammock became home and heart to him, and he slumbered sweet.

So, as the weeks went by, did Isaac begin to learn his ship. His rolling hitches stayed in place, as did his reef knots, clove hitches and bowlines when he mastered them. He understood starboard from larboard. Remembered to keep his head *down,* below. Could tell the shrouds and ratlines of the standing rigging from the halyards, clews and bunts that worked the sails. Knew where Mr Molineux meant when he called him to the ship's waist or to the quarterdeck. And changed his fine clothes for canvas sea britches as they loaded casks of salt pork, flour and something that smelt awful.

'What's *that*?' he asked Young Nick.

'Fermented cabbage. They calls it sauerkraut. Cap'n says it's good for scurvy.'

'I've never eaten sour cabbage, and won't start now.'

In short, Isaac Manley began to turn into a sailor. Sometimes on Sundays his family came to visit. They went to the seamen's church of Saint Nicholas at Deptford, where the gatepost had a death's symbol of skull and crossbones, adopted by pirates for their flag. And Isaac showed his brothers and sisters over the ship with all the confidence of one who knew a little and thought he knew everything.

'This is the capstan and that's the windlass to bring up the anchor. Maria and Louisa! Go backwards down the companionway hanging onto the man-rope. John! Robert! Watch that low bulkhead or you'll crack your noggins . . .'

Until the morning came for Isaac to say goodbye.

Mamma, somewhat tearfully, said it wasn't too late to reconsider such a dangerous venture. But father disagreed.

'It's all settled, Ann. His elder brother John is down for the army, and Isaac for the navy. He's our second son, and has to make his way in the world. We agreed. Besides, I've already laid out good money.'

Papa laid out a little more by giving Isaac ten gold pieces to add to his purse; and mother unclasped a silver locket set with her miniature portrait.

'Keep it safe, son,' she said, pressing it into his hand. 'We will pray for you every day you're away. One year . . . two years . . .' Mamma began to weep again, 'in the unknown.'

Isaac embraced her for a last time, and Papa too. And when the family had gone ashore, he hid the coins and silver locket in a black velvet bag among the clothes in his sea chest, tears of departure starting to his young eyes, until Mr Molineux called him on deck. For all his apprehensions, Isaac was glad of activity. Lieutenant Cook had given his orders. *Endeavour* was making ready to sail on the next tide.

It was only a short, shakedown run to begin with, along the coast to Plymouth. Here they loaded the last of the provisions; took on a party of red-coated marines; received two months' pay; and had the Articles of War read to them, as a reminder of their duties under naval law.

At length the sails were loosed as a signal to Mr Joseph Banks and his party of scientific gentlemen to come aboard. And with a fair wind on the afternoon of 26 August 1768, *Endeavour* weighed anchor and headed out of harbour.

Isaac stood by the rail and watched as the green headland of Plymouth Hoe faded astern. His voyage had begun. Ahead lay America, the island of Tahiti, and all the wonders – known, and yet to be discovered – of the world beyond.

2

ATLANTIC STORMS

To Madeira, September 1768

Endeavour was a different ship at sea. In port she lay restrained and anxious, like a tethered creature. But once freed from her moorings, the wind filling her sails, she bounded joyfully into the open water. Isaac, climbing the mainmast with Nick Young, could feel all her vigour and tension released. Her bowsprit rose and dipped, flinging high the wild spray. And putting his ear close to the thrumming ropes, the boy could hear the ship sing, *This is what I was made for*.

Going aloft was a different thing, too. In the river, the bark was quiet and stable, and let the lads clamber about her rigging easily enough. Here, bending to the wind and rolling with the swell, it seemed to Isaac that *Endeavour* was constantly trying to throw him into the waves.

He clung to the thick, tarry shrouds, bare feet feeling for the ladder-like rungs of the ratlines. Isaac was giddy and conscious of the strain on the rigging, afraid it might break and that every step upwards would be his last.

'Don't look down!' Nick called from above. 'And climb wiv 'er pitchin'.'

Little by little, Isaac rose one step at a time as the ship rolled away from him. Held fast as she heaved back. Another roll. Another foothold. And up.

Isaac was beginning to feel rather pleased with himself – when suddenly the next step almost *was* his last. Seamen found bare feet better than shoes. They gave a surer grip once the skin toughened. But Isaac's feet were still young and raw, and ached on the thin, biting ratlines. Reaching for the next step, the boy moved too quickly. His foot slipped. His hold slackened. All at once he was dangling over the green, mouthing sea as the ship started to swing back on him.

'*Nick!*'

But Nick was too far ahead to be of use. Isaac could only grab the shrouds with all his strength, silently calling on Mother, until *Endeavour* rolled away on the next wave. He was flung against the rigging. Found a toehold. And the boy stuck there, like a fly in a web, sobbing and vowing not to climb another step.

'Come on!' cried Young Nick, who had seen what happened. 'You can do it. Follow me . . .' For he had run away to sea a year before, and led every time.

Isaac swallowed the salt air. Waited. And seizing the moment, hauled himself up step by painful step, gradually getting used to the ship's motion. He even began to believe he'd mastered it, and that danger was past. Until he came to the worst part of all: climbing over the tops.

On some ships, the rigging passed through an opening called a 'lubber's hole' and onto the mast's platform – the 'fighting tops', where marines could fire down on enemies during a battle. But *Endeavour* didn't have a lubber's hole. To get onto the tops, you had to climb a short section called the 'futtock shrouds', which came at an angle to the outer edge of the platform, and clamber over that way.

Hanging upside down like a monkey from the futtocks, Isaac was sure he'd be hurled into the sea's hungry maw this time. But one of the sailors, Henry Stephens, was waiting for him by the spar with words of encouragement.

'Take it easy, lad. Same as before. Learn from the ship's own rhythm.'

Slowly the boy mounted. Forward and up as the ship swung out. Clinging on for dear life as she returned. Not daring to look down, nor too far above, until at last he felt the iron hand-bar on the platform. Isaac lifted himself. And with a groan he tumbled onto the tops.

'Ye gang well,' said Forby Sutherland from the Orkneys, helping Isaac to his feet. Strange how the crew were different at sea, too. Forby had snarled at Isaac when he first came aboard. Now, in his element, the older man was far more accepting of the boy's attempts to find his own sea legs. 'We'll fear the lubber out o' ye.'

Isaac stood, holding onto a line, listening to the wind playing in the white-bellied sails. Down there, through the canvas clouds, he glimpsed the deck as a sea bird might have done. The ship's boats lashed one inside the other on the 'gallows'; the tiny figure of the helmsman at his wheel; the cocked hat of the officer of the watch moving about the quarterdeck. And looking up, Isaac saw the topsail yards ('*tops'l*, matey') – and higher, the topgallant yards ('*t'gallant*, matey') tracing their wide arcs against the sky as *Endeavour* tossed through the Bay of Biscay.

He thought he might wait a little before climbing the topmast. Young Nick was already halfway up the rigging to the crosstrees, and calling back for Isaac to hurry along.

'Up ye go, laddie,' said Forby Sutherland. Waiting for the ship's roll to larboard, Isaac swung himself out.

His master, Robert Molineux, watching from below, was not pleased to see his servant playing aloft. 'The boy's wanted down here,' he muttered. 'I need him to fetch a spyglass from my cabin.'

Lieutenant Cook was more sympathetic. He'd been a Master himself before given command of *Endeavour*. 'Don't be too hard on the lad, Mr Molineux. It's best to start learning your ropes when young. Better still if it can be a game.'

'Have you *seen* his ropes? A tangled, lubberly mess! He'd be better off learning to do a neat clockwise coil than fooling about up there.'

'Remember thyself at that age, Robert.'

'Aye, sir, indeed. And the boy has his duties to attend.'

They all had their duties, every man jack of the ninety-four souls on board *Endeavour*. Sailor, soldier and civilian alike. Every officer had a servant, much like an apprentice, hoping to become an Able Seaman or even rise higher in his profession, as did Isaac – though few aboard were as young as himself or Nick.

The wealthy naturalist, Mr Joseph Banks, had a whole retinue of staff and servants, among them two negroes – Tom Richmond and George Dorlton – the first black men Isaac had really known. They slept with the boys and marines in the low section of the mess deck; and sometimes before quiet time of an evening, they would tell distant memories of the hot grasslands in Africa where their families had grown up, before being captured and sold into the slave trade.

'A whole line of people, Mr Isaac, men, women and children, chained together and marched down to the coast.'

Isaac, safe in his hammock, could only thank God in his prayers there was no slavery in comfortable England. Unless, as a wry afterthought, it was to become a servant boy on one of His Majesty's ships.

With so many people crowded onto such a small vessel, Isaac's duties brought him into constant contact with the scientific party. Within a short time, in fact, he was familiar with everyone on board.

Thus, when the boy was sent to fetch a pair of compasses to the Great Cabin, where the Master and Captain bent over their charts, he'd see the artist Sydney Parkinson, with a hand to his head, groaning that he could barely hold his pencil. A young man of delicate disposition, Sydney was greatly troubled with seasickness.

Isaac, of course, thought he was well over *that*. Standing at the stern as he fed the pigs and sheep, the hens and the goat kept to provide food and milk for the officers' table, he flattered himself how quickly his body had adapted to the moving ship. Mr Banks and his party were still to find their balance. A platform had been built on the quarterdeck so that they could walk about without being swept off their feet every time the tiller arm moved. Even so, it amused Isaac to see the scientists grab for support whenever they examined their nets scooped up with specimens of small sea creatures.

Interesting, too, how fine gentlemen – even Isaac himself – who would never have spoken to rough sailors in the fashionable streets of London, talked to the crew as they sought to understand this watery world, in which the seamen were at home and the scientists were strangers.

'What do you call that large fish leaping beside us?'

'That be a porpoise, sir.'

'Ah, the *Delphinus* species of Linnaeus,' remarked Banks's Swedish friend and scientific adviser, Dr Daniel Solander.

'And, pray, those birds hovering around the masthead?'

'We call 'em Mother Carey's chickens. And they always foretell a storm.'

So it proved. That afternoon the wind shifted to the west. Thunderclouds blackened the sky. The swell rose and, as the wind hardened into a gale, *Endeavour* pitched and tossed like a bathtub, her decks awash with breaking waves.

It was too much for the gentlemen. Mr Banks retired sick to his cabin, though at six foot three inches he was too tall for his bunk. He lay on the deck and let his two dogs enjoy the comfort of the bed. Sydney Parkinson doubled over the ship's side, pouring his heart into the sea ('*Down* wind, if you please, sir!'). Tom Richmond lay where he was on the deck, vomit all around him and crying, 'I think I'm going to die, Mr Isaac!'

The boy wasn't feeling too well himself. For all the confidence in his new-found sea legs, they became rather unsteady. His stomach began to churn. And watching amidships the seamen aloft furling the topsails as the rain pelted down, Isaac felt hot and flushed.

Backwards and forwards. Up and down. The ship and her reaching yardarms rocked violently from one side to the other. Isaac was determined to weather it out, amazed at the skill of the seamen above as they hauled up the beating canvas, and wondering when *he'd* have the courage to go up in a tempest.

When suddenly it happened.

One of the topmen felt himself about to be sick. And in time-honoured custom he called below, 'Watch under!'

What? Did he want something? Isaac started forward.

''Ch under!' And before he knew it, the boy was covered in a stream of spew raining down on him from above.

It was the end. Isaac's stomach heaved. Breakfast, dinner, and everything he'd ever eaten came emptying out. He lay with Tom

Richmond on deck through the night. Drained. Exhausted. Wishing only that he also might die.

The gale took several days to blow itself out, and it upset more than the sensitive stomachs of men and boys. A boat belonging to the boatswain ('*bo's'n*, matey') was washed overboard. A plate on the main topmast had to be repaired. And several dozen hens were drowned, so no morning eggs for Mr Banks recovering in his cabin.

The sheep and pigs still lived, however – and so did the nanny goat. But then, as one of the Mates, Francis Wilkinson, pointed out to Isaac as he tried to milk her one rough afternoon, the goat had survived worse than this storm.

'She's a good doer, look you. That goat's already been around the world with Captain Wallis on the *Dolphin*. Now she's doing it for a second time, boyo. Take more than a little wind and your clumsiness to finish her off!'

Like the goat, *Endeavour* was a sturdy, heavy-duty little body. And as they left the coast of Portugal and headed into the Atlantic, life aboard resumed its course.

Isaac continued to practise climbing the rigging – and even to venture out along the yards, shuffling precariously along the foot-lines. The old hands were mostly helpful with their advice. 'Just fix your eyes on the horizon boy, because it don't move. And remember that more men die falling from the bowsprit than they do from the tops. There's less to hang on to out for'ard.'

And looking into the sky, they'd observe the signs by which seamen told the weather, and recite the rhymes.

If woolly fleeces bestrew the heavenly way, be sure no rain will come today.

'Means barometer is holding steady, see.'

As the sea calmed and the sun shone, the gentlemen returned to their scientific pursuits. A couple of seabirds, caught in the rigging, were brought down for their examination. One died and was promptly dissected. The other was kept alive by Joseph Banks for six weeks – until it was caught and eaten by the ship's cat.

Mr Banks's boat was out casting for more tiny swimmers to be described and illustrated by Sydney Parkinson in his elegant drawings. Banks was excited, for much was new – though he became angry when Tom Richmond threw the net too wide. The string slipped from his wrist and the net sank, never more to take marine life captive.

'It is too bad,' Banks fumed. 'The other nets are packed in the hold, and here are all these opportunities lost to science until they are fetched. It will *not* do, sir!'

'It's not my fault,' Tom complained to Isaac that night in his hammock. 'For a moment I could smell the scent of Africa on the wind, and I thought of home.'

As well he might. For the easterlies were blowing fresh from the hot interior of the continent, driving *Endeavour* steadily south by west, until at length they came in sight of the island of Madeira, four hundred miles off the coast of Morocco. And there on 13 September the ship anchored in the deep outer harbour – the roads – of Funchal.

Next morning, Captain Cook moved the ship closer to shore and moored with anchors fore and aft. However, the hawser on the small stream anchor astern slipped. One of the Mates, Alexander Weir, was sent with a crew in the longboat to haul up the anchor and take it further astern. Isaac, watching from the rail with Molineux, saw the anchor rise dripping from the deep, Weir coiling its cable and buoy-rope neat and shipshape in the boat, as you'd expect from such a good seaman.

They rowed off a little. But then Mr Weir made a mistake. As he prepared to lower the anchor again, Alex carelessly stepped inside the rope coil attached to the marker-buoy. The anchor dropped beneath the waves. The glistening cable unwound and plunged after it, like a sea serpent chasing its prey. In so doing, the buoy-rope snatched Alex around the ankle, dragging him over the side.

'*Help!*' His one scream before disappearing.

'Man overboard!' shouted the rowers. 'Help us!'

It happened so suddenly that Isaac didn't quite comprehend what his eyes had seen. It was some moments before he, too, took up the cry. 'Man overboard!' But Molineux sprang before him.

'Try to haul up the anchor cable to save him,' he called to the boat crew. 'Sound the bell! Hands for'ard to the windlass!'

Shouts ran through the ship. Feet scuttled up the companionways. Captain Cook and the officers appeared on deck.

'Lieutenant Gore, assist Mr Molineux.'

'Aye, sir.'

The men in the longboat were hauling the cable, but the weight of Weir's body entangled with it was such that they couldn't bring it in. The other end of the line was attached to the windlass, held between two wooden end-posts carved in the form of sailor's heads, near the foredeck. Bit by bit, men winched it in, using wooden bars inserted into the drum slots.

'One . . . two . . . six . . . *heave!* Heave away, bullies!'

Isaac tried to help. Midshipman Saunders shoved him aside. 'This is heavy *men's* work, boy.'

So Isaac and Nick Young observed as the anchor was slowly brought alongside the ship. And as it was hoisted they saw Weir's corpse, his foot still held in the serpent's bite, fished up like one of Mr Banks's specimens. Alexander's pigtail flopped helplessly behind. His face, so alert half an hour ago, was now as lifeless as the windlass heads. And his belt buckle winked wickedly as they reeled him in.

Mr Weir was returned to the sea that afternoon.

Two days later came another terror to initiate young Isaac.

They'd called at Madeira for provisions before crossing the Atlantic Ocean. While Mr Banks and his party were exploring ashore, the *Endeavour* crew were lading her with water and wine (for the beer was running low), fresh beef, greens, onions, more hens, and even a live bullock to be butchered later. For James Cook believed his men should eat fresh food wherever possible.

'It's the best way I know to prevent the horrors of scurvy,' he told Lieutenant Gore. 'You've been round the world twice, John, on the *Dolphin*. You've seen men so weak with disease they cannot move – aye, and die with their gums rotten raw, and skin black as sullage.'

'I surely have, suh.' John Gore was American-born. 'Most of us went down with scurvy at some time on *both* voyages. And many didn't live to get up again.'

'Lord Anson lost three-quarters of his crew to it in '49. I'll not have that on *my* ship. Seamen are set in their ways and don't take easily to change. The sauerkraut, that's been recommended, they can eat as they please. But fresh meat and vegetables I do insist upon.'

The Captain was quite right. Sailors are a conservative lot. When Isaac and Nick Young went to get their dinners of fresh boiled beef from John Thompson, the one-handed cook, they heard many complaints from the mess tables.

'Oi, what's this muck?' called Henry Stephens. 'What's wrong wi' salt beef?'

'Captain's orders,' replied Thompson.

'Let 'im eat it hisself. I want the tack I be used to.'

'That's right,' piped up one of the marines, Tom Dunster. 'And what will I do wiv twenty pounds of onions?'

'Eat 'em. With the fresh beef. Like Captain said.'

'Blast the Captain!' muttered Henry Stephens. 'And damn him,' added silly Tom Dunster.

'Ee! That's mutinous talk,' cried John Thompson, banging the copper boiler with his ladle.

'What is?' enquired Richard Pickersgill, the Master's Mate, passing by.

'These two men,' replied Thompson. 'They won't eat their fresh beef, and they speak against the Captain.'

'Is that right?'

'We just want what we're entitled to,' said Stephens.

'And by God you'll get it!' Pickersgill flared.

'He's let the cat out of the bag now,' murmured Young Nick to Isaac. He spoke literally. For the flogger's whip – the cat-o-nine-tails – hung in a red bag from a beam on the mess deck, as a constant reminder of what happened to insubordinates who broke the strict rule of naval conduct.

Pickersgill told Molineux, who reported to the Great Cabin. The result was that Captain Cook ordered all hands on deck that afternoon to witness punishment at defaulters parade. All hands. No one was excepted.

The officers and Midshipmen stood in their uniforms on the quarterdeck. The red-coated marines paraded on guard with the seamen and servant boys in the waist. A wooden grating was lashed to the rail by the gangway: and Henry Stephens was tied to it, hand and foot, a leather wad between his teeth, bare back pale and tensing.

They waited as Lieutenant Cook read the Articles of War entitling a Captain to summarily order a dozen lashes for breaches of discipline. In fact many exceeded it – though not in this case: 'Mr Reading, do your duty.'

The Boatswain's Mate, John Reading, flexed the whip with its nine heavy thongs.

'He's got room enough to swing his cat out here,' observed Young Nick. Excitement was in his voice. He was fascinated by the spectacle. As was Isaac.

The cat leaped in the air, and with a snarl scratched nine red claws across the man's shoulders. *One.*

Two. The tears deepened.

Three. Skin broke.

Four. Pools of blood welled to the surface.

Five. The blood trickled in small rivulets.

Six. And turned into streams.

Seven. Flooding crimson, like a delta, down Henry's back.

Eight. Bits of gore and torn flesh flecked the air.

Nine. Nick was wide-eyed. But Isaac could bear no more. Henry Stephens had helped him by the yard that first time he climbed the rigging at sea. Now this . . .

Isaac turned to flee. To be sick again. Yet Richard Pickersgill grasped him by the jacket and whispered savagely into his ear, 'You'll stay and watch, boy. Otherwise you'll be tied over a cannon and punished yourself on the bare backside.' Then his voice softened a little, for Richard was only nineteen himself and could remember. 'It's our way. You must understand that.'

So Isaac stayed until Henry was cut down to be carried below, and Tom Dunster tied in his place. But the boy stared beyond them to the cultivated hills above Funchal town, that he might not see what was happening and start to blub.

Nor was that all. Madeira had one more lesson in the navy way to teach him.

When Alexander Weir died, *Endeavour* needed another seaman to replace him; and as no one volunteered from the several merchant ships in port, a press-gang was sent ashore under Midshipman Saunders and Mr Reading.

They searched several taverns after dark, and eventually found young John Thurman, from a New York sloop, straggling in a laneway under the burden of too much liquor.

'How do, bully boys. Come to enjoy yourselves?'

'To be sure we have,' replied Mr Saunders, casually approaching him.

'Let me recommend the Madeira wine to ye, gents. 'Tis good drinkin'.'

'Most kind . . .' As the party closed in and surrounded John Thurman, Saunders's voice suddenly changed. 'In the name of King George, I impress you into service aboard His Majesty's ship *Endeavour.*'

'But . . . but I'm bound for home.'

'Not any more you're not. Seize him!'

Before he could resist, Thurman was grabbed, bound, dragged to the beach and bundled into a boat.

'I'm only twenty!' he struggled. 'I've not seen my family for a twelvemonth.'

'Then they'll have to wait a bit longer for 'ee, matey.'

'Help! Help me!'

'Silence him. Lively now!'

Thurman was hit across the head with a wooden belaying pin. Silent then, he was rowed out to *Endeavour* and kept prisoner below until she sailed.

Madeira! And there was Tom Richmond telling Isaac of a chapel he'd visited with Joseph Banks.

'You should have seen it, lined from floor to ceiling with human bones.'

That only reminded the boy of Saint Nicholas's church at Deptford with a skull and crossbones on the gatepost, and skeletons in the charnel house. The seamen's church. And Isaac wondered why he'd ever wanted to join them.

3

BOUND FOR RIO

Across the Atlantic, October to November 1768

There was no going home. Nor, in truth, did Isaac want to. When he wrote his first letter to Mamma and Papa, the boy spoke only of his continuing health and capital appetite. Doubt and anxiety he dared not mention – for his parents' sake, as well as his own. Indeed, as *Endeavour* left Madeira and headed across the Atlantic for Brazil, she met with fair winds and good, following seas. And in these sunlit tropical waters there were times of languid content to counter, if not erase, more sombre island memories.

One day they saw the volcanic peak of Tenerife far in the distance; and that evening it continued to glow soft pink and golden above the clouds long after sunset, like an ethereal beacon showing their way.

Sometimes, on hot nights, the boys would bring their blankets on deck. They'd lie there happy in their growing friendship – Nick, the ragged dockside imp and Isaac, the well-bred second son – listening to the watchmen singing softly to the plangent music of a fiddler playing a shanty.

Farewell and adieu unto you Spanish ladies,
Farewell and adieu to you ladies of Spain . . .

An awning was stretched amidships. And sometimes when the morning work was done – cabins cleaned, decks swabbed, brass bell polished raw – Isaac would sit in the shade awhile, watching Captain Cook and his officers with their sextants on the quarter-deck reading the midday sun to calculate their position. The young Midshipmen were hard practising at it too. Cook, the navigator, insisted on it.

'There's no point learning to sail a ship,' he explained, 'if you don't know where you're sailing *to,* or can't lay it down rightly on a chart once ye've got there.'

And to the astronomer, Charles Green, sent by the Royal Society to supervise the observations of Venus at Tahiti, Cook added, 'I know the mathematics are not easy, but anything can be mastered with perseverance.'

Isaac knew the time would come when he would also have to master the skills of finding his latitude and longitude at sea. But not yet. The 'prentice boy was still too new, with so much else to learn, to push himself that far forward.

So he would sometimes cast a line with other men of an afternoon, hoping to catch something, though rarely succeeding. More often than not he'd see the flying fish whirring by, silver and black. Some landed on the deck, which saved the trouble of fishing for them. One even flew inside the cabin porthole of Mr Green, who presented it after breakfast for Sydney Parkinson to sketch.

But from time to time the fishermen got a bigger bite than anticipated.

Late one morning, a shark was seen trawling behind the ship. At once a baited hook was thrown, and to Isaac's delight it was taken. But what a fight the shark put up! Thrashing and struggling, it tried to break free: mouth gnashing, blood staining the water.

Yet the men hauling it in were too strong. An iron gaff pierced the flesh. With a final *Heave away, bullies!* the creature was hoisted aboard.

It was only young, not much more than six or seven feet long. But it had the defiance of age. It lay gasping for life in its own crimson pool on the deck, eyes flashing hate to the end, and teeth aimed like knives at its enemies.

Eventually the ship's butcher, Henry Jeffs, killed it with a blow. A number of sucking fish on the body were given to Mr Banks to preserve for science in his spirit jars. The rest of the shark was cut up and – even though it was almost midday and dinner time – cooked by John Thompson into a stew. It was considered excellent fare in the Great Cabin and at the officers' table in the wardroom. The gentlemen, it seemed, would eat anything! But down on the mess deck there were the usual suspicions.

'Eh, 'ave you boys ever eat shark?' asked old John Ravenhill, the sailmaker. At forty-nine, he was one of the most experienced hands aboard – kept afloat, it was said, by his long experience with the rum ration. ''Ave you 'ad such vittles afore?'

'No,' said Isaac. 'First time.'

'Well, there be something to know about sharks.'

'What's that, John?' enquired Nick Young.

'Sharks can smell death followin' in the wake of a ship. They be man-eaters, too. And if a man – or boy – feeds of a shark . . . why, it be almost cannibalism.'

Isaac pushed his wooden trencher aside. So did the others. But the dishes were soon pushed back again. The cat-o-nine-tails hanging in its red bag, and the livid scars on Henry Stephens's back, reminded them of the punishment awaiting people who refused their victuals.

Yet James Cook was learning too. *Endeavour* was his first major command, and he realised he couldn't flog healthy diets into men. A more subtle approach was needed. So, when it came time to open the barrels of sauerkraut, he let it be known it was a delicacy intended for the officers and gentry. Ordinary sailors could have some if they chose – but that was up to them.

'It don't smell too good,' said the Gunner, Stephen Forwood, as Isaac passed by with a bowl of fermented cabbage for the wardroom. 'Stinks, in fact.'

'They like it up top. Say it's delicious. Good against scurvy, too.'

'Well, give us a taste, then.'

'I don't think I'm allowed. It's meant for the Master and Lieutenants. Mr Banks's gents, too.'

'And not for us swabs!' butted in Forwood's mate, Alex Simpson. ''Ere, let me try it.'

Able Seaman Simpson leaned across and grabbed a handful of sauerkraut. He shovelled it into his mouth, chewed awhile, rolled his eyes, and finally pronounced his verdict. 'It ain't up to my old muvver's pickle. But if it's good enough for the wardroom, I say it's good enough for me.'

'Give me some, then,' said Gunner Forwood.

'And *me* along o' ye,' cried Forby Sutherland.

'It would go down better wiv a mug o' rum.'

And so on. Over the next few days most of the mess deck partook of the cabbage. By the end of the week the Quartermaster had to ration it – such value did men place on a dish said to be for their superiors, though they would have despised sauerkraut had it been compulsory.

Thus, they sailed ever sou'-west, through days of calm and sudden squalls. *Mare's tails and mackerel scales make tall ships carry low sails*. 'Long wispy clouds and scaly ones show the barometer's falling. Storms are coming, so reduce canvas.'

Easing sheets and hauling on clews . . . ease away, haul away!

The boys' hands chafing and toughening on the rope.

Come up . . . belay there . . . and make up your lines . . .

Through heat and damp, when iron rusted and leather went mouldy. Through luminous nights, when men drew into themselves, saying nothing, but looking heavenwards as the stars slowly turned and the first constellations of velvet southern skies appeared. For on the morning of 25 October, they crossed the equator. With it came Isaac's next instruction on the lore of the sea.

Lieutenant Gore was in charge of proceedings. Just after dinner he went to the Great Cabin with a petition signed by 'The Ship's Company', requesting permission to examine everyone aboard who'd not crossed the line before – the ship's cat and Mr Banks's two dogs included. The nanny goat, having already once circumnavigated the world, was excused.

'But of course, Mr Gore,' replied the Captain with much good humour. 'And I trust ye'll not overlook myself and the other gentlemen here.'

'I sure won't, suh.'

When all were assembled that afternoon on deck, John Gore produced his Black List and proceeded to trial.

'Sam Jones: is this your first time over the line?'

'Aye, Lieutenant.'

'Will you be ducked in the sea, or pay the forfeit?'

'What that be?'

'You must pay a bottle of rum.'

'Oh, I could never do *that*, sir. I'll have to take my chances wi' the other kind of drink!' And everyone cheered.

True to his word, Mr Gore did not forget Captain Cook or Joseph Banks. But in their case the penalty was willingly paid. They promised a large ration of brandy-wine from their stores: which was what the crew wanted all along.

The boys were given no option. They were ducked as a matter of course. So Isaac and the other youngsters lined up by the rail with twenty men stripped to the waist.

A block had been fixed to the mainsail yard, with a line reeved through it to which three pieces of wood had been fixed. When Isaac's turn came he was told to sit on the lower crosspiece and hold the bar above. The upper timber was to prevent him from hitting the spar as it was raised.

'Try not to struggle,' murmured the chief ducker, as Isaac was tied for safety to the line. 'And hold your breath when you hit the water. Haul away!'

They swung out and Isaac found himself being hoisted forty feet above the ocean. He felt no real apprehension, for the boy had shot the rapids of London Bridge. Why should he fear this placid deep? He was jerked higher, until the line stopped. A pause. Then, 'Let 'er go!'

The rope ran free, propelled by the weight of Isaac's body. He scarcely had time to feel the rush of air and shut his mouth before he hit the surface.

The sea opened to receive him. Down, down, through her turquoise embrace, bubbles strung like diamonds, and into her depths. The boy felt strangely intoxicated, as if wanting to give himself to her cool, liquid caress. When suddenly the line came to.

'Bring 'er up, bully boys!'

Isaac found himself dragged away and returned to the sun, all dripping and spluttering, aware of merriment. But only for a moment, before being plunged back into the dazzling sea.

Three times Isaac was ducked. Then he was reefed in, unbound, and stood somewhat disconsolate – though undoubtedly refreshed – as Young Nick was tied to the ducking seat and the sailors expressed their glee.

'You should see y'self, matey. Seaweed draped over y'r head like King bloody Neptune!'

The gaiety went on late into the night as the ship's company imbibed on the forfeit wine and brandy.

Oddly, Nick didn't enjoy the ceremony. Where Isaac had seen brilliants, Nick saw only the sea's dead shades. He tried to be grown up and nonchalant, as always. Secure in his hammock, however, the little boy whispered, 'I can't swim, Issy. I was scared I might drown or get took by another shark, and go to Davy Jones too soon.'

The needs of friendship ran both ways. And Nick's time was not yet, as *Endeavour* billowed with the trade winds across the aquamarine ocean. At last came the dawn, a fortnight after they crossed the equator, when they heard the lookout cry, 'Land ahoy!' And hurrying on deck, Isaac saw the mountains of South America lifting from the pale horizon.

They coasted south for several days, until one clear morning *Endeavour* stood in for the grand harbour of Rio de Janeiro: deep, and blue, and surrounded by high peaks. The ship eased past a rocky tor standing like a sugarloaf at the entrance. Slid beneath the guns of Santa Cruz castle. And dropped anchor just outside the town.

Captain Cook had sent his First Lieutenant, Zachary Hicks, ahead with a letter for the colonial Governor, requesting permission to replenish his ship. After two months at sea, everyone was anxious to refresh himself in Rio's welcoming delights.

'Oh, the women! Sweet, and ebony-eyed . . .'

'They reckon the rum be pretty good an' all.'

But it was not to be. For the pinnace returned with news that Lieutenant Hicks had been detained. A boatload of Portuguese soldiers arrived to guard *Endeavour*, followed by a party of officers to question her Captain. Where had she come from? Wither was she bound? How many men and guns did she carry?

Cook resented being cross-examined, but he had no choice except to respond. After which the officers said the Governor was looking forward to hearing his account in person. Meantime, Mr Hicks would be returned. Nobody else was allowed to leave the ship. And the guard boat made sure of it.

The Captain went ashore next morning. He returned no better satisfied.

'That damned impudent fellow!' Isaac heard him bellow to Mr Molineux. 'The Governor says we may board provisions – but the only gentlemen permitted ashore are myself and Dr Monkhouse, to buy stores. With the necessary crew, of course. Even then we are to have a military escort everywhere we go. He says anyone else found there without authority will be arrested. It is an affront to the British flag!'

'The men will not take kindly to this,' Molineux remarked.

'We may be sure of that, Robert. No botanising for Mr Banks. No visits by my officers to the gentry of this place. Nay, nor to the low places either, for the crew.'

'What reasons does he give?'

'His Excellency *says* he has orders to treat every foreign ship like this. But the fact is, he doesn't believe a word I say!' Cook paced the Great Cabin in anger. 'He says we don't look like a ship of the Royal Navy. We don't dress as smart British officers. He can't accept that any of His Majesty's fleet would carry a party of scientists around the world to make an astronomical observation. In short, gentlemen, he thinks we're British spies.'

He banged his fist on the table, and Isaac just about prevented an inkpot from spilling over a chart and a sheet of Sydney Parkinson's drawings.

'I shall certainly write a letter protesting in the strongest terms.'

'I should be circumspect,' advised Lieutenant Hicks. 'Those Portuguese were mighty doubtful of me. They could deny us supplies altogether if provoked.'

'Aye, Mr Hicks, I shall be discreet. But His Excellency *will* know my mind.'

A paper war began, in which strongly worded salvos were fired between ship and shore. Like most of these battles it was hot and noisy, but ultimately futile; and Mr Cook was careful not to let any stray shots sink his expedition.

By day the crew worked hard. The ship was scraped, and recaulked with oakum hemp and tar to prepare her for the hazardous voyage around Cape Horn. Rigging was repaired. Water casks renewed. Barrels of rum were purchased. More fresh beef and greens came aboard, eaten without benefit of the lash – though John Thurman, still resentful at being press-ganged from Madeira, was flogged for refusing to help old Ravenhill mend the sails.

But at night men were permitted only to stand by the rail and watch the lights of Rio dance across the water, and listen to her laughter carried on air sultry with temptation. Nor did the city's siren song go unanswered. It was not long before *Endeavour*'s crew began sneaking into Rio for an evening of illicit pleasures.

They grew bolder. Mr Banks sent his people off in broad daylight to collect specimens from the nearby woods. He and Dr Solander even let themselves down by a rope from their cabin window to be rowed ashore. But the two negro servants were reluctant to go with them.

'This is a slave colony, Mr Isaac,' Tom Richmond explained. 'There are thousands of black men here, brought from Africa. Just as our people were.'

'If any soldiers stopped us,' George Dorlton added, 'we'd be put in chains.'

'Yes, and sent to the gold mines until we was dead.'

Their fears were only too real. Crewmen who took Mr Hicks to deliver one of Cook's letters were seized, beaten, and spent the night in a filthy dungeon with dozens of black slaves, shackled and awaiting transportation to the fever-ridden mines of Brazil. Even free men who helped with *Endeavour*'s lading were imprisoned, such were the Governor's arbitrary suspicions.

None of which stopped the crew from infiltrating the city after nightfall to enjoy her guilty charms.

One evening Isaac and Nick begged to join them.

'Get away wi' ye,' exclaimed Forby Sutherland. 'Ye're just wee lads and too young for Rio after dark.'

'Oi! I knows me way around the stews of London well enough,' boasted young Mr Young.

'Can't we have *some* fun . . .?' pleaded Isaac.

'Well . . .' Forby weakened. 'If ye run into trouble wi' soldiers, mind, the young gentleman mun get ye out of it.'

'What trouble?' asked Nick. 'We'll look sharpish.'

They gathered aft, just outside Molineux's cabin, with Forby, Alex Simpson and several other seamen. Tom Matthews, the cook's boy, came along at the last moment.

'I'm boilin' 'ot from that stove,' he exclaimed. 'I need a breaver.'

'Then hoosh ye'r noise!' hissed Forby. 'Or we'll all end up in the stew!'

He stuck his head out a square stern port, through which masts and spars were loaded, and gave a low whistle. It was answered by another from below. 'All clear.' One by one they clambered through, holding onto a knotted rope, and descended to the waiting boat.

Silently they cast off, muffled oars dipping the inky water. The moon hadn't yet risen, but still they kept a keen eye for the guard. The soldiers' sweethearts were visiting, however, and they were too busy with chicken thighs and sweet wine to notice another boat crossing the bay. Furtively. Out of the darkness and into the flaring light.

The risks Isaac and Nick were taking loomed more clearly too. Yet no one wanted to turn back and, as the craft scraped on a beach, its eager passengers jumped out.

'Get ye back here by eleven, mind, when the clock strikes,' warned Forby. 'We must be aboard for the midnight watch, and yon boat won't wait.'

The men disappeared into the nearest tavern, roaring with rum and carousal. The boys wanted to see more than that, however. After all, it was their first time in the New World. And although they weren't supposed to be in Rio, with soldiers everywhere, that only added to the sense of adventure.

'Just don't give ourselves away by talking out loud in English,' whispered Isaac. On foreign soil Master Manley took the lead – and Young Nick, for all his experience of London, was glad to let him.

They set off up the alley and into a thoroughfare jostling with people taking the night air. Fine Portuguese colonists, the gentlemen throwing scented flowers and kisses to young women – *meninas* – leaning from balconies. Merchants and artisans, smelling of garlic and onions, out with their *senhoras*. Sad, dispossessed Indians, wrapped in ponchos, looking in shop windows. Black African slaves in hand-me-downs, attending their masters. Noise and hustle. Lamplight streaming through open doors. And everywhere music! Guitars strumming and raucous singing from the taverns. An organ playing as the lads passed a church. Latin hymns chanted as a procession of choir boys carried a religious image around the sinful town.

It was all so exotic and enticing. Isaac bought ripe scarlet melons with a shilling in his pocket, and felt more than a little drunk on the nectar. The others were just as heady. The lads walked through Rio as if enchanted, all thoughts of lurking danger forgotten. Time passed too quickly, and before they realised it the boys had wandered further than they thought. The street was darker and emptier. In the distance they heard a clock striking. Half past ten.

'Already?' Isaac sounded reluctant to part.

'We'd better go back.'

They tacked about – and at once were jolted from their dream. Coming towards them they saw a patrol of Portuguese soldiers. Five or six soldiers, armed with muskets and led by a corporal with a burning torch. Worse: in the flames they saw the military stop a couple of men just ahead, and shout at them, as if demanding papers and explanations.

Things had suddenly become serious.

'We can't stay here,' muttered Isaac. 'What if they question *us*?'

'Don't be daft,' said Tom Matthews.

'We shouldn't risk it,' Isaac cautioned. As they stood dithering, a quick-witted London imp knew what to do.

'Hurry!' urged Nick Young. 'This way. We'll hide till they've gone past.'

They dodged down a narrow lane, stinking of dung and stale cooking. Squalid houses opened into it, from which came sounds of crying children. Mosquitoes bred in the fetid mud, and they found soft British flesh delectable. Before long the boys were slapping themselves as itchy lumps erupted on bare arms and faces.

'Bloomin' 'ell!' cried Tom. 'I'm out of this.'

The others followed. But their noise roused a drunken beggar asleep in the shadows. As the boys hastened from the lane they stumbled over the man. Hands reached out from the slimy darkness, grabbing and rifling for money.

'*Dinheiro! Dinheiro!*'

The lads ran in sudden fright. And almost collided with the military patrol.

'*Quem são vocês?*' yelled the corporal. Who are you?

'I'm truly sorry, sir,' stuttered Isaac in his native tongue. Forgetting.

'*São ingleses?*' The corporal was astonished. '*Parem!*'

But the English boys had no intention of stopping, and fled up the street to secrete themselves in the promenading crowd. The corporal shouted again, but soon gave it up. The night was too hot for a chase. And *Graças a Deus!* His patrol had the two earlier men in custody, and that would make his captain happy.

Safe in the light again, the boys slowed and breathed, and allowed themselves to feel relief.

'At least we've got rid of the soldiers,' Isaac murmured. 'A lucky escape, I'd say.' He spoke too soon.

It was one thing for the boys to lose the soldiers – but quite another to realise they were themselves lost. Isaac had noted a church near the alley where the boat landed, and a tavern with a ship's sign. But there were several churches in the street. Many taverns by dark alleys. None of them seemed familiar. And if they weren't back by eleven . . .

The lads ventured down endless lanes, desperately searching for the inn where they'd left Forby. Each time they found nothing, except more grasping hands, and they scurried back to the wide street to try again. And again. Becoming ever more confused.

'I don't know where we are!' Isaac confessed. Sweat flowed freely now. 'It all looks the same . . . and different . . .'

Fear swelled like the wind-filled sails of a ship. They heard a bell chime – eleven o'clock, and the boat wouldn't wait! The boys began to rush, blindly bumping into strangers who abused them in a language they didn't understand. There was no one to ask. No one to whom they dared speak for fear of betraying themselves. Look! More soldiers over there. They'd be seized, and thrown into a dungeon, and . . .

The city that had seemed so wondrous became utterly threatening. Sweet melon juice turned to acid in Isaac's gut. He wanted to retch. When across the gulf of his panic he heard a familiar Orkney voice shouting, 'Och, there be the young villains! Come along o' ye, quick now.' And Forby Sutherland took the three adrift lads in tow.

Once safe aboard *Endeavour* again, the boys stuck to her – desiring only Captain Cook's orders to sail.

Isaac finished his letter, for Mr Molineux said his servant could send it with the officers' mail on the next ship home. The shark, sauerkraut and crossing the line were all there; but not a word about terror in the streets of Rio.

'All of us are anxious to leave this place and head for the South Seas,' was the most he could bring himself to write. Indeed there were only a few more days to wait – though whatever Isaac told his parents, they went too soon for some who'd not yet exhausted the joys of Rio. Robert Anderson was flogged for trying to desert ship. So was a marine, Will Judge, for abusing the officer of the watch. Then Cook had the flogger, John Reading, himself flogged for not punishing them hard enough.

The Captain was satisfied with that. And so was almost everyone else on board, as *Endeavour* at last bore down river and set her course southwards . . .

Farewell and adieu unto you Spanish ladies,
And perhaps never more we shall see you again!

4

CAPE HORN

Into the Pacific, December 1768 to April 1769

Isaac stood at the masthead and felt the power of the ship flowing beneath him. Wind glanced off the streaming sea, stinging his face and stretching the canvas like a bow. Nowhere, in that silver expanse of light arching to the horizon where sky and water met, could Isaac see another thing.

'Clear ahead,' he murmured to the lookout.

'Aye.' The sailor lapsed into silence. And Isaac was glad.

Somewhere to the west, South America tapered to the dagger's point of Cape Horn. Rio was far astern. The city had been unkind to the last. Even as they left, Peter Flower had fallen from these very shrouds and drowned. Poor Peter. He'd sailed with Cook for five years: had joined him at only thirteen. Isaac's age.

The boy flinched at the memory. Then dismissed it. He'd be luckier than that, for he was young and invincible. The world flew, and Isaac soared with it. Though, with shades of Peter Flower about, he was careful climbing down.

As *Endeavour* settled again into the rhythm of life at sea, Isaac often took time to be alone with his thoughts. They all did. There was no other solitude, except in the mind. Eating, sleeping and working were crowded with everybody else.

Even going to the lavatory was a communal event. You could always pee over the side or into one of the copper-funnelled 'piss-dales' near the quarterdeck. The other was a different matter. Officers and gentlemen had their own privy chamber pots which the boys, like Isaac, emptied. But ordinary seamen had to lower their britches on the forecastle ('*fo'c's'le*, matey') and take their place on one of the two 'seats of ease' over the bows, near the cat-heads that held the anchor cables. Hence every day Isaac found himself 'going to the heads'. When finished, he washed himself with the frayed end of a rope flushed in the sea. Which was all right in the tropics. But as they sailed further south during December, it became colder and coarser, and Isaac thought it was like wiping himself with sandpaper.

The weather grew sharper. South Atlantic gales bore down, and the ship sometimes ran before them for days under close-reefed sails. *When wind backs and glass falls, be on guard for rain and squalls.* Whenever he could, Isaac willed himself up with the topmen: hands freezing as he hauled the canvas and hitched the gaskets, eyes fixed above the wave mountains to stop himself from vomiting. And all the time his body was becoming more weather-hardened.

He could have stayed below among the so-called 'idlers' – the carpenters and other tradesmen who didn't have to go aloft or stand watch. But it would not have taught Isaac his seamanship; and his readiness to go up stood to his credit. Working the ship became more demanding, and every hand was required.

Cook changed the three-watch system, which gave each man up to eight hours off duty, to two watches. Watch and watch about.

Four hours on and four hours off. It meant more hands were on deck in these heavy seas approaching the Horn – but it gave barely enough time for sleep. On the whole the sailors didn't resent it. This was the discipline of survival. Indeed, men spoke of how well *Endeavour* rode out the storms, and what a tonic they were doing her.

'There's nowt like a good shakin' to loosen her joints,' declared old John Ravenhill over his midday rum. 'She'll settle even better after next one.'

Whatever the ship, Isaac's own joints were stiff and sore. Ice was in the air. Tom Richmond and George Dorlton felt it worse than anyone. The two Africans, huddled in their blankets, still shivered.

'We thought it was supposed to be summer in the south, Mr Isaac, but this is bitter as Christmas in England.'

True. Christmas Day was just like home: braw, though thankfully calm. For it was celebrated in the traditional way, too. Almost everyone got drunk. The Captain and gentlemen in the Great Cabin. Officers in the wardroom. Men and boys around the stove on the mess deck. There was scarcely a sober man to steer the ship.

Rum flowed, mixed with water into grog for the lads. An extra ration of beef and sauerkraut was served. Cheeks reddened. Tongues wagged. And as they edged closer to the tip of America, came tall stories of Patagonia and the terrors of rounding the Horn. These were unknown waters to most sailors, and the few who had sailed them were listened to agog by every man and boy.

'They reckon there be giants in Patagonia,' said a carpenter, Francis Haite, who'd been with Captain Byron on the *Dolphin*'s first voyage in '64. 'Men twice as big as Mr Cook. Though they kept 'emselves well 'idden when we wuz there.'

'We saw a horseman on Tierra del Fuego built like a colossus,' remarked Charles Clerke, one of the Master's Mates. 'Wearing wild animal skins he was, and hideous face paint. I felt like a pigmy.'

'No, *they* were the pigmies,' corrected Francis Wilkinson. 'The Indians we met with Captain Wallis two year ago were small and stank abominably. Ate raw seals and fish caught straight from the water. Head first, look you, like seagulls.'

'Why?' asked Isaac, genuinely interested.

'So the gills won't get stuck in their throats going down backwards. Stands to reason, boyo.'

'Oh, he still don't know nuffing much yet,' Nick teased, until Isaac silenced him with threats of another ducking in icy seas.

'Those waters, where three oceans meet!' mused Richard Pickersgill. 'Worst in the world. Fogs, lightning and tempests, even in the height of summer. It took us nearly four months to get through the Strait of Magellan and into the Pacific. Beaten back each time by storms.'

'And 'ere we are facing 'em ag'in!' cried Francis Haite. 'It'll take stout 'earts and strong stomachs to get through, bullies. Fortified wiv much Christmas rum. So pour out another and give us a song . . .'

We'll rant and we'll roar like true British sailors,
We'll rant and we'll roar across the salt sea . . .

Giants! And four months to round Cape Horn! Isaac's heart quailed. As he mixed himself and Nick another tumbler of grog, he wondered how many other true British sailors were feeling the same?

Cook well knew the risks of the Strait of Magellan, with its myriad small islands and shipwrecked coasts. He decided to sail further south through Strait le Maire between Tierra del Fuego and Staten Island. The Admiralty didn't recommend it: but Cook thought it offered a clearer and safer passage. So as the new year came, every weather eye looked westward for land.

'Look!' cried Isaac from the foremast tops. 'Mountains off the starboard bow!'

'Let's see 'un,' squinted Henry Stephens at the grey, building mass on the horizon. 'No, no, boy . . .' after a long moment. 'They be no more'n cloudbanks. "Cape Flyaway" we calls 'er. You'll find 'un often on a long voyage.'

The weather grew bleaker.

Whales appeared, 'like bloomin' sea monsters on maps!' exclaimed Young Nick to Isaac, clinging to the mizenmast shrouds. 'Who would 'a believed it? I thought they was just stories.'

Antarctic penguins swam about the ship in black-and-white bathing costumes. The crew were issued with thick woollen 'Fearnought' jackets, and even the officers forsook their knee breeches and wore sailcloth trousers. But nothing kept the chill from Tom Richmond, who lay numb in his blanket and cried.

At last in the second week of January came the real shout, 'Land ho!' But *Endeavour* received such another violent shaking from wind and sea that she was some days getting into the Strait and – with her joints thoroughly loosened – anchored in the Bay of Good Success.

Or so they hoped it would prove. But tragedy had berthed there as well.

The Captain went ashore to look for water, and returned with three native visitors. There was no colossus among them, for the men were no taller than the average sailor. Neither did they stink, though their copper skin was smeared with animal grease, and their broad faces painted with red and black streaks.

Isaac watched fascinated as they walked the deck, wearing only guanaco hides like cloaks, and sealskin shoes. At every new thing they saw – the capstan, wheel and binnacle – the chief raised his voice as if, Isaac thought, he were chanting to the gods for protection.

The Indians were friendly enough, having known Europeans before. They wore bead necklaces, loved red cloth, and their arrows were tipped with glass. The visitors were familiar with ship's food too.

'Give 'em a biscuit,' suggested Forby Sutherland. They nibbled the hard tack, laughed, and chewed some more.

'What about salt beef?' said John Thompson, bringing a piece from his galley. The natives seemed to enjoy it – though they kept most of the meat uneaten, to share with their families later.

They wouldn't drink alcohol, however. The crew tempted them with rum, but the men merely sipped it, made faces, and spat it out. Most seamen considered it funny: but those who remembered the lost Indians of Rio staring in tavern windows thought it the best thing they could have done.

Work began next morning. Empty water casks were floated ashore and filled. Men cut wood for the stove. Others harvested wild celery and scurvy grass, for the men who'd sailed the *Dolphin* also knew how valuable fresh herbs were for keeping sickness at bay. The Midshipmen were out in the yawl, mapping the harbour. Isaac and Nick were scrubbing officers' cabins. And, it being a fine day, Mr Banks took a party of gentlemen inland, with his servants, dogs, and two seamen to collect plants and insects.

'It's too cold for botanising,' complained Tom Richmond to Isaac as they left.

'Africa was never like this,' George Dorlton said through chattering teeth.

'Don't worry!' Jim Roberts, one of Banks's young servants from Lincolnshire, tried to cheer them. 'The walk will warm us up, and we'll be back by evening.'

But they weren't.

As the day wore on, chill settled more deeply. Clouds rolled in and snow began to fall. Isaac tried to hide his concern, but others said the party was out enjoying the long twilight! When they'd not returned by nightfall, seamen joked that landlubbers always preferred to camp ashore.

'They've taken provisions and a bottle o' rum to keep 'em happy,' laughed the cook's lad, Tom Matthews.

Isaac, snug in his hammock, didn't share the mirth. He was afraid. It was still snowing, and he wanted only the dawn when his companions would surely return.

There was no sign of them all morning. It wasn't until one o'clock that men on the beach heard shouts, and saw Mr Banks with his friends struggle out of the woods. Of the twelve who'd set out, only ten returned to *Endeavour* – three of them so ill they had to be carried aboard.

Neither of the two negro servants was among them.

'Where are they?' Isaac asked Jim Roberts. 'Where's Tom? Where's George?'

'They're both dead.' Into the sudden silence.

'How? Why?' And Isaac felt ice cut his heart.

'They froze to death in the snow.'

'What happened?' Tears started.

'I'm too exhausted to say,' wept Jim. 'I'll tell you later.'

That night, after a sleep and hot food, the sixteen-year-old felt able to tell the tale to the mess deck.

'We made pretty good going all morning,' Jim began. 'Past the Indian village with their huts like beehives. Uphill through the woods, until mid-afternoon when we came to a plain, and beyond it a peak Mr Banks wanted to climb. Trouble was, the plain turned out to be a bog covered with low, scrubby bushes ripping away at us.

'We were almost there when Alex Buchan fell into one of his fits. You've seen him – the other artist – drop sometimes, shaking with epilepsy. Shouldn't have come at all, I reckon. Anyway, Mr Banks told us to light a fire and look after Alex while his party went to the summit. But it was hard to strike a tinder in that cold damp. And then it started to snow as the gents returned. So once Alex felt a little better, we headed back to the woods.

'But the going was no easier. Dr Solander said he was so cold he couldn't walk another step till he had a sleep. Which he *did!* And Tom Richmond the same.

'"I can't go on no more, Mr Banks, sir."

'"But you'll freeze to death, man, in this weather."

'"Then I'll just have to lay me down and die, sir."

'The woods weren't that far off, so some of the others went with Mr Buchan in the last of the day to light a fire and try to build a wigwam from branches, like the Indians. Eventually Dr Solander woke up and, seeing the firelight ahead, Mr Banks and me helped him into the warmth. George Dorlton stayed behind with one of the dogs to look after Tom, and bring him in when he woke up.

'But they didn't come.' Jim's voice trembled. 'More snow fell, and still no sign of them. At last Mr Banks sent the two seamen to find Tom and George. Then he discovered a bottle of rum was missing from his knapsack.

'Hours went by . . . until someone came yelling, and a seaman reeled out of the darkness to the fire. We knew then what had happened to the rum. They thought it would warm them – but it only made things worse. Mr Banks and a few of us stronger lads went out, and found Tom standing upright, but unable to move or even talk. Rigid as carved marble. And George had collapsed on the snow.

'We did everything to get 'em moving. "Come on Tom! Try to walk, George . . . Wake up . . . *Please!*" But they wouldn't budge. We couldn't even light a fire in the snow. In the end we just had to lay Tom and George on a bed of branches, cover 'em with boughs as a shelter, and leave 'em there till morning with just the dog for company. And drag the second seaman with us back to the fire.

'We went out at first light and removed the boughs. But Tom and George were both dead. Faces frozen grey, and eyes staring blind. There was nothing for it but to cover them up again, decent like. Though the dog survived all right.'

There was stillness on the mess deck, as Jim gathered himself to tell the end.

Mr Banks had shot a vulture, which the ten survivors skinned and cooked for breakfast. Sharing equally. Three mouthfuls apiece. With the weather clearing, they made their way back to the coast – though Alexander Buchan was still sick, and Banks's other servant, Peter Briscoe, almost died of hypothermia too.

As *Endeavour* finished watering over the next few days, Isaac felt some of the light in him had also departed. He was no stranger to death. Two others had already perished during this voyage. But Tom and George were men he knew well. Had laughed with. Messed with. And heard them mumble in their sleep as they dreamed of Africa and home.

Now they were gone, and Isaac mourned them. Even as the ship wore out of the ill-omened Bay of Good Success, his two friends were left to rot under a pyre of snow-covered branches. Unless, of course, the vultures got to them first. Two black Africans – free themselves, but still undeniably two more victims of the slave trade – frozen to death in a land at the very bottom of the world.

Or nearly so. For it was another four days' sail through squalls and foul wind before Isaac saw the round island hummock of Cape Horn itself through a break in the clouds. Even then, they spent almost a week bearing further south, in case the ship ran into uncharted land and was wrecked.

But on the last day of January, when they'd passed latitude sixty degrees south, Captain Cook gave his order to set *Endeavour*'s course north by west. Men cheered and the blood quickened. They were heading into the Pacific! And fortune favoured them in this. The weather moderated. There were sometimes such light winds they set studdingsails ('*stu'n's'ls*, matey') to push the ship along. So that by mid-February, the new boys were boasting to the *Dolphin* hands that, while it had taken Wallis nearly four months to round the Horn, they'd done it in little more than one!

'Don't be too cocky, look you,' Francis Wilkinson checked Isaac. 'We've a long way to go yet, and you never know what may happen at sea.'

Quite. For when Mr Banks shot an albatross and had John Thompson cook it, old Ravenhill thought it shocking.

'Kill a albatross!' he exclaimed. 'That'll bring us the worst kind o' luck. And then to *eat* it! That be worse 'n cannibal sharks. You mark me.'

In the Great Cabin, however, conversation turned on how well the bird ate when served with savoury sauce. On the mess deck, talk quickly moved from superstition to the real delights awaiting in Tahiti to feed other appetites.

'Those girls . . .' sighed Dicky Pickersgill. 'So beautiful. So loving.'

'The whole island is a paradise of love, boyo,' Francis Wilkinson explained. ''Tis the most natural thing in the world to 'em.'

'Though the people know their value. And what they value most of all are iron nails. They don't have metal on Tahiti see, and will do anything to get it.'

'The young men would come down to the river's edge with a twig the size of the nail required, look you. Once agreed, the girls swam across to us like water nymphs in stories . . .' Wilkinson relived the memory.

'It got so as the *Dolphin* was ready to fall apart, so many cleats had been taken from her timbers. Captain Wallis became severe. And when he found Frank Pinkney with a handful of stolen nails, he had to run the gauntlet: three times bare-backed around the deck while we whipped him with nettle ropes.'

'But you know, we were all as guilty as Frankie – and so treated him very gentle. Happiness for an iron hand-spike! If only it were like that at home, in Wales.'

Isaac and Nick listened open-mouthed, pretending to experience beyond their years. They willingly agreed with general opinion that running the gauntlet was a small price to pay; but were not sorry, when Dr Monkhouse examined the crew for venereal disease, they were considered too young to participate.

Molineux and Gore kept discussions with the Captain strictly to business.

'The natives were sure welcoming, suh – after the *Dolphin* fired a few broadsides and killed a number of them, when they attacked us.'

'I'll have none of that, Mr Gore, if I can help it!'

'Once they understood the power of our weapons,' soothed Molineux, 'their queen – Purea by name – was most hospitable. Hogs . . . chickens . . . fruits aplenty. Her people satisfied our every need.'

'So I've heard,' returned Cook, the dour, dry Yorkshireman. 'Generous in all respects. I believe the entire ship's company is anxious to meet them.'

They certainly were. Even the goat began to bleat in anticipation. Last time, she'd butted one of the island men who'd never seen such an animal before; and rearing up to repeat the blow, had so terrified the man that he leaped overboard. Nanny seemed keen to renew the acquaintance.

As *Endeavour* ploughed through the Pacific, the sun grew stronger and the days lengthened. February turned into March and Isaac's fourteenth birthday. The crew went back to the three-watch system. The first tropic birds were sighted, vibrant in red and white plumage. And the evening waters glittered with phosphorescence like starshine, as the ship turned the furrows with her bows.

The earthly paradise of Tahiti was drawing closer. Any bad luck caused by Mr Banks having shot an albatross seemed long past. When suddenly, as Jack Ravenhill knew it would, came another human tragedy to disquiet their journey.

A seaman, William Collett, obtained a length of sealskin in Tierra del Fuego, which he was going to sew into tobacco pouches for some of his friends. A young marine, Billy Greenslade, greatly desired one: but was refused. So when he was asked to look after the skin briefly, on duty outside the Great Cabin, Billy cut off a piece for himself. It seemed an almost malicious provocation – to which the young soldier, unfortunately, succumbed.

Collett was furious when he found out.

'You're no friend of mine, Billy Greenslade, and a damned thief besides. The Captain would have you flogged if he knew!'

'You won't tell him? Please . . .'

'Not this time. But you can be sure your men will find out.' Which they soon did. All that afternoon the marines abused Billy for his wickedness.

'To steal something what's been entrusted to your care! And on duty! That's more than theft. It's cowardly. Despicable. You're a blackguard.'

Isaac could hear them, words striking like snakes, as Billy wretchedly tried to find refuge from shame in a dark corner of the mess deck.

'It's only a bit of sealskin . . .'

'You've disgraced the honour of our whole corps.'

'I never hurt no one.'

'You've tainted each of us in the eyes of the gents.'

It continued for hours, until eventually Sergeant Edgcumbe called Billy up on deck, and said that Captain Cook would have to investigate. It was seven o'clock, just after supper, and night was falling quickly, as it does in the tropics. Few others were about, for a calm had followed the day's squall, and the watch stood easy.

'Excuse me, sir,' said Billy softly, alone before the world in his scarlet uniform of which he'd been so proud. 'I've got to go to the heads, first.'

'As well you might need,' replied the Sergeant. 'Hurry up then, and don't keep the Captain waiting.'

Billy went for'ard to the seats of ease. But the only relief he sought was to his conscience. Overcome by guilt and the taunts of his fellows, Billy looked quickly around – then threw himself into the dark, inviting sea. Down in his blood-red coat through its funeral depths to the waiting arms of Davy Jones and release.

It was some time before Sergeant Edgcumbe realised that Billy had gone and began a search.

'Billy!' Voices calling through the shrouded vessel. 'Have you seen him, boy?'

'No, Sergeant,' said Isaac, coming on deck with a slops bowl from the wardroom. 'Is anything wrong?'

'We can't find him. I'm afeared . . . Billy! Where are ye, man?'

And it was some time after that before Mr Cook was informed. But Private Greenslade was found no more aboard *Endeavour*, and his Captain was distressed.

'I should have been told much earlier,' he said. 'How old was he?'

'Not yet twenty-one, I believe, sir.'

'So young! Such a rash thing to do over so trifling a matter. I might have prevented it, had I known.' Cook sighed. 'It's nigh two months since our last landfall, and I know some minds can lose their proper judgement confined so long at sea. I've hopes we'll sight Captain Wallis's islands before long, and this will be forgotten then. I'm sorry for the lad Greenslade, nonetheless.'

The Captain spoke truly. Within a fortnight of Billy's death, the morning watch spied the first coral island shining on the sapphire sea: small and fringed with palm trees, a white sandy beach enclosing the lagoon.

Isaac and Nick, straining from the rail, felt their pulses beating faster. Was this what paradise looked like?

It seemed people lived there, for Isaac could see smoke. And indeed, as they passed other islands, men were seen running along the shores – bronzed and naked and brandishing spears. Aye, and the crew saw women too through their telescopes, clothed in white skirts and with raven-dark hair.

Sometimes the people would follow *Endeavour* in canoes. But they never came too close, or dared board the strange ship, on which hearts pounded like drums.

'Don't worry, my bully boys. It can't be long now.'

Nor was it. When Isaac went on deck early on 12 April, he saw a high mountain rising from the ocean, its crest garlanded with clouds blushing in the dawn light. The breezes blew warm from the land, carrying the scent of flowers and the promise of good things to come.

The island of Tahiti lay before them.

5

TRANSIT OF VENUS

Tahiti, April to June 1769

All day *Endeavour* glided towards the island, tantalising as a vision before men's eyes. Sometimes Tahiti disappeared behind a rain curtain. Then it lifted, and through a rainbow they saw its peaks lit by sunshine. Surely just a little bit closer!

Out-rigger canoes now crowded about *Endeavour*, filled with men and women of dark, luscious eyes, crying welcome: *Maeva . . . manava!*

Some carried green boughs of the fruitful plantain tree. 'It's their symbol of peace,' Robert Molineux told Isaac. And all of them came ready for market. Coconuts, breadfruit and yams were traded for coloured beads from eager sailors hanging over the ship's side.

One canoe had a fat, black pig, just ready for John Thompson's oven. Nick and Isaac could *taste* the crackling! But while the *Dolphin* men assured Cook that almost anything could be bought for a few iron nails, the natives refused to sell it for less than a hatchet. Which the Captain declined, and the pig returned to the island unsold.

Nor would the supple, brown natives come aboard, despite the seamen's entreaties, until next morning.

Molineux and Pickersgill were out early in the boats, sounding the depths and marking the channel through the reef upon which the Pacific broke in white ruffles, like lace on a gentleman's wrist. *Endeavour* slipped through and came to anchor near the north-east point of Matavai Bay.

A beach of dark volcanic sand met the water. Coconut palms tossed their ragged heads along the fringe, amid thatched longhouses in sheltered groves. Beyond them, unruly hills clothed in green forests climbed to majestic pinnacles.

'They look like pieces of crumpled paper,' said Sydney Parkinson. Isaac could only agree. He'd never seen anything so beautiful. Warm, and verdant, and drenched with perfumes, Tahiti seemed all he imagined it would be.

Once the ship was secure, Captain Cook went ashore with Lieutenant Gore to find Queen Purea, and barter for the hogs and chickens he'd been assured were in plenty. He also issued strict rules of conduct.

'Listen to this,' remarked Private Gibson. 'We have to cultivate the natives' friendship. Well, that's easy, especially with the girls. We'll be charged if we lose our weapons or tools. Only the Cap'n will appoint people to trade for provisions. And no ironware at all can be given except for food. Sounds as if he knows about the *Dolphin*'s nails!'

The rules were put to the test pretty quickly. No sooner was *Endeavour* at anchor than the canoes were emptied of men and women who clambered onto the deck: so beginning that pattern of happy human connection which stayed burnished in the memories of all who were there.

Mr Molineux met an old man with a white beard called Hua, whom he remembered from last time. Friend! *Taio!* The two embraced and wept, and Hua was soon introducing the Master to the pretty young women of his family. Sam Gibson wasn't alone in sneaking down to the carpenter's store to see if an iron spike still retained its purchasing power, whatever the rules. And a more innocent Isaac was entranced by the scene, when a girl wearing a skirt of bark *tapa* cloth and a coronet of fragrant blossoms, offered him a drink of coconut milk.

He held the husky globe to his mouth and drank the cool liquid. The girl's eyes were as clear and deep.

'Heimata,' she said, telling him her name.

'I'm Isaac,' he replied. Yet she found the pronunciation beyond her.

'Tire.' It was the best she could do, and they both laughed. Heimata rapped the coconut sharply. It split and, with the girl's smile upon him, Isaac ate the creamy flesh.

'This,' he thought, 'really *is* paradise.'

But he was wrong. When Captain Cook entered the Garden of Eden, he found it more or less abandoned, and returned to *Endeavour* empty-handed. No Queen Purea. No chiefly palace. Not a hog or a chicken to be found.

'I don't understand it, Robert,' Gore confided to Molineux that evening. 'Everything has changed for the worse. It's as if there'd been a revolution.'

And so there had. Next day two important chiefs or *ari'i* arrived, seated under shelters on their large double canoes – *pahi* – with high curving sterns. The first, Tutaha, was an older man of great authority. The second, Tepau, was younger, but no less stately in his loincloth, cloak and head-dress. Purea was his sister; and whatever power she once had in this part of the island, it was clear she held it no longer.

Clear, too, that the price of pork had risen. When Tutaha brought several hogs to *Endeavour*, he required hatchets and English linen – and this remained the staple price.

'Seems like daylight robbery to me,' observed Mr Molineux to Isaac, remembering the *Dolphin*.

But theft of a more obvious kind exercised the Captain's mind. The natives clambered over *Endeavour* like monkeys, trying to pilfer bits of metal. *Hiro*, the god of thieves, was pleased if you could get away with it. When Cook returned the chiefs' visit, a snuffbox and spyglass were stolen, and only returned after Tepau intervened.

'They're prodigious expert at it,' remarked Cook, who later lost a pair of stockings and Mr Banks his embroidered waistcoat with silver fastenings. Though the extent of the problem only became apparent a few days after their arrival.

The Transit of Venus was to occur on 3 June. Scientists understood that if accurate observations of this rare astronomical event were made around the world, they could calculate the distance of the Earth from the sun. A Pacific location was essential; and since the next Transit wouldn't occur for another hundred years, the Royal Society had persuaded the Admiralty to send *Endeavour* to Tahiti. With nearly two months to prepare for the observation, Cook set up his headquarters on a sandy spit at the head of Matavai Bay: Point Venus, he named it.

The Captain took a party ashore and, to the intense interest of the Tahitians, marked out the site of a stockade – Fort Venus – on the fine black sand. Leaving the marines to guard a small tent, he went for a walk with the gentlemen beside the Vaipopoo River, among the sighing casuarinas and shady breadfruit trees.

Old Hua tried by signs to tell him not to go too far; but it was a pleasant day, and Mr Banks was entertaining everybody by shooting ducks. Cook strolled on. Suddenly, from the point, they heard shots of a different kind. Several shots. And many cries. Cook turned, and hurried back.

Isaac, too, heard the musket fire from aboard *Endeavour*, where Molineux was getting ready to disembark. Quickly the Master ordered an armed crew into the boats.

'Let me come,' pleaded Isaac. 'I can reload the guns.'

'In you get, lad. Sharp now!'

They landed on Point Venus as Cook came running out of the woods, to discover that one of the marines had been knocked down by a Tahitian man, and his musket stolen. Other marines had then fired. The people fled, taking the musket with them, leaving the thief dead on the sand.

Those who had been with Cook ran away too, when they saw the corpse. They knew from the *Dolphin* the power of white men's guns. Only Hua remained. He sought to tell his friend Robert Molineux ('Boba') that he *had* warned the Captain, and would try to reconcile people to the killing. But it took time, and it was some days before the Tahitians again brought their fruits to market.

'This is a bad beginning,' Cook lamented. 'I said we should treat the natives with all humanity. And now look!'

'If we quarrel with these people, we'd never agree with the angels,' cried Banks, visibly upset.

'Nay, sir, there are no angels here, only flawed mankind – white and brown alike.'

And their mortality was universal. A few nights later the artist, Alexander Buchan, took another epileptic fit, and died. It was evident in the heat they'd have to dispose of his body quickly. But not knowing Tahitian custom or wanting to offend more than they had, *Endeavour* boats buried him at sea.

It was as well they did. Some days afterwards Dr Monkhouse came across the body of the man who'd been shot at Point Venus. It was out in the open on a raised bier not far from his house, covered with a cloth, surrounded by his possessions and food for the gods.

'And the stench of his rotting corpse was appalling!' exclaimed the surgeon.

Alex Buchan would not have liked that. But he would approve of what happened next. The Captain at last put Nick Young formally among the ship's company. The boy had been there from the beginning, making himself useful, a good friend to Isaac. Now, Cook entered his name in the muster book: not as one of the crew, but with the passengers – the supernumeraries – in place of Buchan.

For the ship's business had to go on, and all efforts were bent to completing the fort quickly. A sandbank wall protected by a ditch was built at the narrower ends, facing the land and ocean. Another bank topped by a wooden palisade fronted the bay, and a double row of water barrels acted as a breastwork beside the river. It was the most vulnerable part, guarded by two cannons, the whole overlooked by six swivel guns. Cook even warped the ship by its cables closer to shore, where its guns commanded the fort. But even that, he would discover, couldn't prevent theft.

Tents were erected for half the ship's company. John Thompson had a new copper oven. Mr Banks pitched a marquee and moved his party ashore. Outside the stockade old Ravenhill had his sailmaker's workshop, and the armourer set up his forge. He was soon doing brisk trade, repairing not only *Endeavour*'s equipment but also bits of ironware left behind by the *Dolphin* and brought to him by Tahitians.

'There's something else here,' said Molineux, puzzled one day over an axe head he was showing Isaac. 'It don't look a *Dolphin* piece to me. Foreign, I'd say. French perhaps . . .'

As Englishmen and Tahitians came to better understand each other, it was learned two European ships had visited the island after the *Dolphin*. When Tepau looked at a book of flags to identify them, he pointed to the flag of Spain. He was mistaken. Much later in the voyage Cook learned a Frenchman, Louis de Bougainville, commanded the ships. And on board was a woman, Jeanne Baret, disguised as a male 'assistant' to the naturalist: the first known woman to circumnavigate the world.

April lengthened into May, and Fort Venus became a township. Tutaha and Tepau moved nearby with their households. Every crew-man had his *taio* – a male companion – and there was scarcely anyone who didn't also have a girlfriend to ensure the island's reputation did not disappoint.

Whatever their preparations for the Transit of the planet Venus during working hours, it was the earthly Venuses of Tahiti who claimed the attentions of *Endeavour* men at night. In fact Captain Cook complained to his journal that he was the only chaste person aboard: but in this, perhaps, he didn't include the boys.

Nick Young, of course, was soon boasting of his many conquests with the island girls.

'Regular little doxies, they are. Honest!'

But everyone just laughed at him.

Some evenings Isaac went with the crew to a *heiva* at a long-house near the beach. They sat circled in firelight as the earth ovens were opened, and breathed such delicious aromas as the food was lifted from hot ashes wrapped in leaves . . . Roasted sucking-pig, and chickens, and small South Sea dogs which Captain Cook thought tasted like English lamb, but Isaac didn't like the idea of them at all. There were yams and taro roots and baked breadfruits soft as dumplings . . .

Then came the *arioi* – musicians and dancers who travelled the islands, performing at festivals and ceremonies. Their gods were those of peace and fertility; and their dances were often so bold they astounded every sailor who watched.

Nick and Isaac sat goggle-eyed, their souls blazing.

First, the drumming: deep, rhythmic cascades of sound throbbing into the darkness. And into the light leapt men girdled in green leaves, stamping the ground, beating their arms, shaking their legs, and shouting chants of defiance.

After them came the women: beautiful as sunrise, dark hair and bodies reflecting scarlet shadows in the flames. Their graceful, flowing hands were so enticing – and their hips, clothed in *tapa* skirts, swayed and gestured to the music of drums and nose flutes.

Isaac naturally found himself stirred by the spectacle. But when the girl, Heimata, tried to drop food into his mouth in the custom of her people, the boy was overcome by sudden shyness. He laughed. And drew back. And said he wanted something else to eat.

Little wonder that, here on ravishing Tahiti, men from colder cultures felt themselves to be in heaven.

Yet it was a heaven with flaws. There were small irritations. Like flies. They drove Sydney Parkinson mad. He had to do most of the drawings after Alex Buchan died; and Isaac often saw him trying to sketch a fish or a plant, huddled under a mosquito net. Sydney even made a flytrap with a mixture of tar and molasses – until it was stolen by a native as a poultice for a sore on his backside.

There were petty human jealousies. Molineux one day saw the deposed queen Purea sitting in Mr Banks's marquee, ogling the rich scientist. She was a fine, statuesque woman – a 'fat, bouncing, good-looking dame,' Sydney called her – who greeted Robert Molineux as a long-lost friend.

'Boba!'

He insisted on taking Purea's entourage on board to meet Captain Cook: her husband Amo, and her chief adviser Tupaia, who was a priest of the war god *Oro*.

Cook (or 'Toote' as the Tahitians knew him) received Purea with much ceremony, for she still enjoyed prestige if not power. He showed her over the ship, and gave her a little wooden doll dressed in fashionable English costume.

'That, madam, is the very picture of my wife.'

Tupaia translated, and the queen was delighted. Mrs Toote! Purea set such store on the gift that her rival, Tutaha, became jealous and wouldn't be satisfied until Toote gave him a doll of his own. Thereafter, the two constantly vied for the Captain's favour.

There were more serious delinquencies. The ship's butcher, Henry Jeffs, threatened to cut the throat of Tepau's wife if she stopped him taking a stone axe he fancied and sought to buy with an iron nail. They demanded Jeffs be punished. So the couple were invited on board to witness the flogging. All hands were assembled. Jeffs was stripped and tied to the rigging. The Articles of War were read. And Cook made a speech to reiterate his rules.

'Theft *by* anyone and *from* anyone is intolerable, and will be punished accordingly. Mr Reading, do your duty.'

But when the cat-o-nine-tails laid the first stripes on Henry Jeffs's back, the Tahitians were so distressed they begged Toote to stop! The Captain refused. The rules of discipline were inflexible. Yet they sometimes went awry.

With Fort Venus complete, the astronomical instruments were brought ashore to prepare for the observation: the telescopes, clock and the quadrant used to measure the height of a celestial body from the horizon. The brass quadrant in its case, about eighteen inches square, was carefully placed in the Captain's tent. But when the sentry's back was turned, a Tahitian crept inside and stole it.

The theft wasn't discovered until next morning. There was uproar. Nobody owned to any knowledge of the affair – until Tepau told Banks the quadrant had been carried eastward. With astronomer Green they set out in pursuit.

Cook followed with a party of marines, leaving orders that Tutaha should be held at the fort as security for the quadrant's return. He later changed his mind, but it was too late. Alarmed by events, Tutaha made to depart in his *pahi*, and Lieutenant Hicks ordered the longboat to give chase. It soon caught up with the Tahitian canoe and, terrified by seamen armed with muskets, the paddlers jumped out and swam ashore, leaving Tutaha to face his pursuers alone.

The chief was pretty roughly handled by the Boatswain's men as they carried him to Fort Venus where, held under guard, proud Tutaha waited his fate, certain he'd be killed. His people thought so, too. Even before Cook and Banks reached the Fort with the quadrant more or less intact, they were met by crowds protesting at the wrong done to Tutaha. Why had Toote's *taio* deserved this?

Cook tried to mollify them . . . to say it had all been a misunderstanding, and that Tutaha would be freed. But people took much persuading. When Tepau and Tutaha met at Fort Venus, they embraced and wept in a manner truly affecting, and Tutaha gave Cook two pigs as a present for his release.

'What do you say, young man?' Molineux asked Isaac as he served roast pork in the wardroom next day. 'Would you have been as generous, had you been captured and put in fear of your life by those you thought your friends?'

Isaac had to admit he would not.

Still, there was a price to pay. Tutaha was in truth furious, and for some days barely any food was brought to *Endeavour*. It wasn't until Cook visited the chief with a linen shirt and broad-axe that another pig arrived and relations improved. Even then, meat continued in short supply. Although fresh pork was served on most Sundays after prayers, it was still scarce and not what men had expected.

Mutterings began to be heard – not just on the mess deck, but from the Midshipmen's berth as well.

'Those *Dolphin* fellows said we'd be stuffing ourselves with chicken and ham . . . but here we are still on short rations. My belly's always empty.'

'Aye. They was telling us lies.'

'Right about the girls, though!'

'Fings would be better away from this place. If we could slip off wiv 'em to the other side of the island, we'd be kings in a land o' plenty!'

'Keep your voice down! Sounds like mutiny.'

'I don't mean for ever. Just for a little 'oliday . . .'

The murmurings came to the Master's ears. He felt bound to report them to the Captain. Cook was all for punishing the miscreants, but Molineux urged caution.

'I don't think it's too serious, sir. Who wouldn't want to stay here? It's just empty talk on empty stomachs. If I might suggest . . .'

'Well?'

'Our supplies do seem to depend on Tutaha's good humour. If I were to take a boat further round the island, I might find a readier source of hogs and fowls. That would satisfy complaints.'

'If you think so, Robert. You can try. But any disrespectful talk on my ship will stop – whoever it comes from.'

Molineux set out in the pinnace next morning, with Mr Green and young Isaac. It was glorious in the early light, purple shadows turning to blue and dazzling gold as the sun rose. The wind sprang up, stirring coconut palms on the beaches where people came down to meet them.

They were as friendly and welcoming to Boba as always. But Molineux found that Tutaha's power ran further than thought. He saw very few pigs – and they all belonged to Tutaha and couldn't be sold without his permission.

'That fellow seems to own everything!'

After sailing some twenty-five miles along the coast he decided to return, disappointed. Besides, the boat was almost swamped. The wind grew stronger and the waves ran high. Making into a small bay, they got caught in heavy surf and were swept towards the land, foaming water breaking over the gunwales. Isaac thought it was just like shooting the rapids again at London Bridge. Molineux was not amused.

'Don't just sit there, boy. *Do* something! The boat might founder, and our ammunition's wet.'

Isaac began to bail as they headed back to sea. But his attention was elsewhere. Out beyond the reef Tahitian lads were having most wonderful sport in the surf! Standing on the stern of an old canoe, they were skating the waves – carried on rushing crests through the reef opening and in to the beach. Such speed! Such delight! Until the breakers tumbled to shore, and the surfers dived. Only to rise, gasping and dripping, to paddle out again and repeat the game.

Isaac had never seen anything like it. And while he wasn't much of a swimmer, would have given anything to have joined them. The fun of it!

'Come on, boy, put your back into thy work.'

'Look at them!'

'Look to your bailing.'

'Our pinnace couldn't even land in the surf. Yet those fellows are riding the ocean like dolphins.'

They offered nothing to eat, however, and Mr Molineux returned to *Endeavour* empty-handed. Yet nobody could accuse the Master of not caring about the crew's bellies. Often on a late afternoon he'd take his mates Pickersgill, Clerke and Wilkinson to a swamp around the bay to shoot wild ducks, with Isaac along to reload the guns. And they'd return not just with birds, but a new delicacy for the table: rats.

Tahiti swarmed with them. Not the filthy vermin in the ship's bilge – but plump, vegetarian island rats, tasting like young veal. The Tahitians wouldn't eat them, preferring their dogs! *Endeavour* men were not so squeamish.

As dusk fell, the rats crept from their holes. Thousands of them, quite fearless and playing about the hunters waiting in the woods: at least until the shooting started. Even then it was nothing for Isaac's gents to return with several bags full of rats.

Sitting at the mess table with his wooden platter, Isaac wondered what Mamma would say if she could see him eating grilled rats.

But really, they made the most excellent eating – singed, gutted, and crisply fried for breakfast.

There were no breakfast rats on the morning of the Transit. Men were up early for a quick meal of pease porridge and then outside, anxious to see what the day would bring. There'd been showers of late, and Cook sent Lieutenant Hicks to the east and Lieutenant Gore to the island of Mo'orea across the water to make parallel observations, in case his own failed.

As it turned out, the weather on that Saturday was faultless. Not a cloud in the sky. Molineux was to observe at the fort with Cook, Green and Dr Solander. Isaac was there too. There to absorb the tension as the time drew near. There to sense the excitement as Venus first made contact with the sun's disc at twenty-one minutes after nine – as measured by the longcase clock cared for by the ship's carpenter, John Satterley. There for the six hours it took to complete the Transit.

Molineux let Isaac see it for himself – or at least the image projected from the reflecting telescope's mirror onto a screen, for the risk to the eye of observing the sun for too long, even through a dark glass, was well known. The Transit was quite clear: a small, black spot crawling across the glowing orb. And something else. Surrounding the planet was a shimmering grey halo or penumbra – a distortion partly caused by the Earth's atmosphere – which affected the results of the observation.

For Isaac was also there as Cook expressed some disappointment when the Transit was over. Each observer had slightly different times for the precise moments when Venus entered and left the sun's limb. At the point where the two bodies met, a small, dark 'teardrop' seemed to appear. It was an optical illusion, but it affected the timing of the observation – and accurate time was of the essence if exact calculations were to be made.

'There are over forty seconds difference between us – more than could be expected,' the Captain bemoaned. 'The penumbra blurred our vision of the contacts. I can only hope other astronomers had more success than we did.'

But history would prove that Cook was too modest. His results were combined with others from around the world to estimate the

Earth's distance from the sun at ninety-five million miles. Not bad, as two centuries later it's measured at ninety-three million miles.

In any event, the Captain had other things to celebrate. When his Lieutenants returned to Fort Venus, the gentlemen all drank toasts for the King's birthday. And the priest Tupaia, just to show his loyalty, got most enormously drunk.

6

TAHITI

Matavai Bay, June to July 1769

Once the Transit of Venus had been observed, the first purpose of the *Endeavour* voyage was accomplished. Attention now turned to the second.

Everyone knew the Captain had secret orders. And they all guessed what they were: to go continent hunting for the unknown south land *Terra Australis Incognita*. Most people believed it must exist somewhere in the unexplored vastness of the Pacific, to balance the landmass of the northern hemisphere. Cook had his doubts, having discerned no evidence of it from the currents during the sail from Cape Horn. Yet he was not one to shirk his duty. So the Captain had his ship made ready – but not too quickly, for life on Tahiti seemed Arcadian, and there was much to enjoy.

Endeavour was warped inshore to be careened: tilted to each side, her hull scraped, cleaned and recaulked. Her bottom was good, not having been eaten by tropical teredo worm, though her anchor stocks had to be replaced. She was scrubbed with pitch and brimstone, her rigging overhauled, and timbers revarnished.

The gentlemen were busy collecting specimens and learning what they could of the language and customs they hoped would astonish Europe when they returned.

Joseph Banks even participated in island life. When Tepau was once chief mourner at a funeral ceremony, dressed in a costume of *tapa* cloth and pearl shell, disguised beneath a mask and a halo of feathers, Banks acted as one of his attendants. He was naked except for a loincloth, his body smeared black, chasing people away as Tepau strode about wounding stragglers with a staff studded by sharks' teeth.

Isaac found it an amazing spectacle, though no crewman understood what the ritual meant – as always when strangers meet. There was much they didn't comprehend; and those things they thought they knew often turned out to mean the opposite.

Natives, beckoning from the atolls they passed approaching Tahiti, were not welcoming *Endeavour* men as they supposed: they were inviting the crew to come ashore and be killed. The girls who displayed themselves didn't always intend to be provocative: they were showing the beauty of their tattoos. On Tahiti, everyone had a *tatu*. They carried much significance.

Not that the sailors could appreciate that. But they admired the patterns engraved on living flesh, and many wanted one. Banks had a tattoo, as did Sydney Parkinson.

And so would young Isaac Manley – not on the backside, but a small blue leaf on his upper arm. He sat on a palm mat under the trees while a senior man prepared his implements: a bone carved with many small teeth, like needle points, set into a wooden handle; and a coconut dish filled with a purplish-blue dye.

The man dipped the bone and, as an assistant held Isaac's arm, struck it rapidly with a stick. The teeth bit sharply into Isaac's skin, drawing blood. The boy almost cried out with the first blow; but he clenched his teeth and looked away, and held his peace. There were tears in his eyes when it was over, however – though Isaac grinned bravely as the Tahitians congratulated his fortitude, and he bore the pain like a stoic for the days it took the wounds to heal.

Thereafter he wore it as proudly as the family's crest, marking him for everyone to know as a South Seas voyager. For no one in Europe heard of tattoos until *Endeavour*. Isaac even felt as if a part of him had become Tahitian – and certainly the girl Heimata took to him as if he were.

Sometimes on Sunday afternoons, when the crew had free time, the young people would go walking through the woods beside the river, deeper into the hills and a valley where a waterfall dropped to an emerald pool. Many came there, for it seemed the very blissful, sylvan landscape imaged in mythic tales from long ago.

Nick Young demanded to know where they went. But Isaac, who was growing up a lot, told him to stow it. For Heimata would sit on the riverbank stroking his new tattoo, still bruised and hurting, making sounds of admiration.

'Tire . . . Tire . . .'

There came the day, alone with Isaac in a secluded grove by the pool, that Heimata turned to him as a woman, unwinding her bark cloth skirt – her *pareu*. As Isaac reached to touch her smooth skin, Heimata laughed and dived like a mermaid into the stream. The boy followed, holding and caressing her as they rose through cascading water. Kissing the girl's bejewelled mouth – and afterwards, lying in the dappled sunlight – they loved each other. He was awkward and tentative to begin with: Heimata seeming so much more experienced. The youth even felt a little adolescent shame that first time, though exulting in it. And Isaac, an apprentice in love as in life, found his rising assurance led by her guidance each time they went to the forest pool.

They would swim, and laugh, and eat sweet seeded tropical fruit until the juices ran, and they had to dive into the pool again. So that whenever Isaac returned to his ship, he knew he'd been riding the wave of one more tide race through those bridges on the journey to manhood. Discovering that with passion may come tenderness, and a care for the needs of another as well as the claims of the self. He and Heimata together. The boy and the girl, over those golden weeks, learning from each other. For whatever the cultural misunderstandings between Tahitians and Europeans, human attraction everywhere remains a powerful bond.

A sailor, Archibald Wolf, was found sneaking a few spike nails ashore. Indeed, several hundred nails had disappeared from the store – but Archie refused to divulge any names. Cook unjustly decided he should be punished for everyone, and ordered twenty-four lashes. Wolf's back looked like a slab of butcher's meat when John Reading had finished. But Archie kept his silence and the respect of his shipmates.

The same couldn't be said for the other end of the social scale, where Mr Banks and Dr Monkhouse had a severe falling out over a young woman. High words were spoken that sounded like threats; though their friends intervened, and the affair was settled without duelling pistols.

Even so, love in Arcadia still came at a price. Only days after *Endeavour* arrived, symptoms of venereal disease appeared. Men complained of a burning when they peed, and a discharge of pus. They tackled the *Dolphin* crew.

'I thought you said there were no pox in this place?'

'There weren't when we wuz here.'

'Well, there is *now!*'

James Cook was distressed.

'I don't understand it. I had my men examined most carefully, and all but one were free of distemper. Captain Wallis did the same, I know. Yet here we find it as general as anywhere in Europe. In time it will spread through the Pacific, to the eternal reproach of those who brought it.'

Cook found some consolation when Tepau assured him the disease had come from men on Bougainville's ships. But who could say? Wallis and his crew had been there first. And that was of no comfort to the island people who suffered, or half *Endeavour*'s company. Even Isaac examined himself with a secret anxiety.

Still, there were also times of much joy. Of going to a *heiva* in the longhouse at night to watch the *arioi* dance and wrestle and sing into the resounding darkness. One evening they persuaded the seamen to get up and perform: broad, lusty voices and the breaking trebles of the boys, chanting across the lagoon to the reef and beyond to the ocean that would carry them all the way home.

Until we strike soundings in the Channel of old England,
From Ushant to Scilly is thirty-five leagues.

Old England and Scilly were places the people of Tahiti could scarcely imagine. Yet the priest, Tupaia, had already resolved to sail with *Endeavour*, as another Tahitian, Aotourou, had sailed with Bougainville. Tupaia was a man of quick learning. He was soon speaking English quite well, and eating with a knife and fork. Fascinated by Sydney's watercolours, Tupaia even taught himself to paint pictures of island scenes in the English way.

Captain Cook also tried to bridge the divide – to respect Tahitian ways so far as he understood them. He sought permission to cut down trees, for in this age of the poaching laws he knew about property rights. Men who stole from the natives were punished as severely as if they'd looted the ship. John Thurman, press-ganged from Madeira, was flogged again with two dozen lashes for theft of a bow and arrows.

But many matters were beyond Cook, especially things to do with the Tahitian view of the sacred, and were therefore untouchable: *tapu* – taboo – another word that entered the English language from *Endeavour*.

Sometimes, men gave offence unintentionally. Dr Monkhouse visited a *marae*, one of Tahiti's many sacred places – the site enclosed by a coral rock wall, with a high stepped altar like a pyramid, adorned with carved ancestor figures and offerings to the gods. The surgeon stopped to pick a flower from a tree near the wall, not knowing it was *tapu* to do so, and was attacked by a young man. Monkhouse tried to defend himself, but was tackled by two others, who seized him by the hair and brought him down.

Some were just foolish: like the seamen who took rocks from the *marae* for ballast, until the Tahitians complained and the sailors had to collect river stones. Joseph Banks, who should have known better, caused much upset when he lifted the cloth covering a dead woman to inspect the corpse.

And some things were inexplicable. One day Isaac saw Purea arrive at the ship with her husband Amo, and their young son. He was a lad of about seven – already promised in marriage – who was carried everywhere on a man's back. They wouldn't let him stand or walk, though his legs were as strong as Nick's. Only later did Isaac learn that Purea wanted her son to be a high chief. It was the cause of the war that led to her downfall. But the boy was still so revered that, wherever he put his foot, the ground at once became *tapu*. He had to be carried, so that others could walk.

Many other things 'walked' as well, for *Hiro*, god of thieves, was still active. Matters came to a head one morning when Isaac went ashore with Molineux, to find Cook very angry.

'Those damned robbers!' the Captain was shouting. 'They've stolen the iron rake from Mr Thompson's oven.'

'We must get it back, sir.'

'I mean to do more than that, Robert. I intend to make them return everything else they've taken . . . the musket, Mr Banks's pistols – aye, and my stockings, too!'

'How?'

'I've given orders to seize all the large sailing canoes on the beach – I've counted more than twenty *pahi* – and bring them here. I want you to secure them in the river. They won't be returned until the natives restore *our* possessions.'

'And if they don't . . .?'

'I've told Tutaha we'll *burn* their canoes.'

'You wouldn't!'

'Well, of course not, but he doesn't know that.'

'But is this sensible, Captain? Most of the *pahi* belong to people who had nothing to do with stealing.'

'I've made up my mind. The thieving must stop, and seizing their canoes is the only way to achieve it.'

'But sir . . .'

'I *will* be obeyed in this, Mr Molineux!'

So, as the big double canoes were hauled around the point and into the river, there was no option but to make them fast and set a sentry to prevent their owners removing them. Isaac agreed with the

Master, for what that was worth. The exercise seemed both unfair and unwise – and so it proved.

Certainly the oven rake reappeared that afternoon, though none of the other stolen objects did. Nor were they recovered in the days that followed. Despite the protests of the *pahi* owners, Cook refused to return them. Relations turned sour. Tutaha departed in a passion, and fresh food supplies again ran very low.

The chief even exacted his own revenge. One evening a Portuguese sailor, Manuel Pereira, was attacked on the beach by three men. Manuel was a strong fellow, who'd been taken aboard at Rio after Peter Flower drowned, but he was no match for his assailants. He was bound, carried to a canoe, and taken a prisoner to Tutaha.

Next morning a messenger arrived at *Endeavour* with the news. He was offered an axe if he'd go back to Tutaha and return with Pereira. Which he did, by nightfall. No doubt Tutaha wanted an axe all along, as recompense for his canoe.

Still, it was plain that *Endeavour* was beginning to outstay its welcome. Soon it would be time to leave. But before they did, the Captain and Mr Banks made a five-day tour of the island in the ship's pinnace. The crew returned with tales to curdle the blood of every sailor boy.

'We saw this huge *marae* Purea built in the south . . . the biggest one ever!'

'Aye, and we saw the whitened bones of her warriors, scattered where they'd been killed in battle.'

'Crunching 'em underfoot like cockle shells, as we walked up the beach.'

'All except for their jawbones, which had been hacked off and strung up as trophies by the victors.'

'Very pretty!'

Nick and Isaac stroked their own chins. Even on Tahiti, darker streams of human nature ran into the greenwood pools.

So the preparations for departure gathered pace. The ship's biscuit was taken ashore, aired in the sun, and sifted for weevils. The gunpowder was dried. Wood and fresh water taken aboard. The small anchors were stowed, and the sails unbent on the yards.

Fort Venus began to be dismantled. The guns were removed to *Endeavour*, tents taken down, and Mr Banks spent his final evenings ashore. They were all saying farewell. Isaac went for a last time with Heimata to the waterfall. Cook released the canoes to their owners, knowing it had been a futile gesture. And in this atmosphere of fond nostalgia, Purea and Tepau arrived to say goodbye.

The visit, it seemed, would end pleasantly after all.

When something happened to upset everybody again.

On the morning all hands were to come aboard, it was found that two marines – Sam Gibson and Clem Webb – had disappeared from the fort. They'd gone off with their girlfriends into the hills, hoping to start a new life on the island: the first of many who'd seek escape in a Tahitian idyll.

'Those damn young fools have listened to too much idle talk!' said Molineux. But the Captain was more phlegmatic, not wanting to repeat his earlier mistake.

'They'd not have deserted without someone's encouragement – and I dare say Tutaha is that someone. I'll give them another day, before taking steps to find them.'

Gibson and Webb hadn't returned by next morning. With Tupaia as interpreter, Cook asked Purea and her brother Tepau where the men were hiding? They professed ignorance. So the Captain took them hostage for the marines' return: he seized the owners, not their canoes.

'I'm afraid you'll have to stay here in Mr Banks's marquee until my men are recovered,' he said. As he knew that Tutaha carried most political weight, Cook sent Lieutenant Hicks in the longboat to decoy the *ari'i* into his custody.

It wasn't very difficult. Hicks simply said that Toote had a farewell gift, and Tutaha came straight away. Though when he arrived at the fort and found himself a prisoner again, eagerness turned to dismay. Tutaha had been deceived and, for all he knew, his life put in peril once more.

But Tutaha was not one to show fear in front of his enemies. So when the situation was explained, he laughed softly and attempted to make light of it. The missing marines? Was that all? And he spoke briefly to Tupaia.

'What does he say?' asked the Captain.

'If Toote will send two men with the chief's servants, he will ensure the marines are here by nightfall. The *ari'i* is as anxious as you for their safe return.'

Cook at once sent Corporal Truslove and Midshipman Jonathan Monkhouse on foot with four Tahitians to find the deserters. Evening drew on without any sign of them, and the Captain began to get worried. To prevent any surprise attack, Cook had his captives taken out to *Endeavour* and held comfortably enough in the Great Cabin, where the servant boys brought them food and drink.

'You may tell the chiefs that this is for their better safety – and my security,' he advised Tupaia, confident of success.

But it seemed Toote was mistaken. At nine o'clock that night there were shouts from Point Venus. Soon afterwards, a bedraggled Clem Webb was brought aboard. Alone. With news that Truslove and Monkhouse had themselves been taken prisoners, and so had Sam Gibson.

Cook acted decisively.

'Mr Hicks, I want you to take the longboat with a strong party of armed men and native guides to bring those men back.' And turning to Tupaia he added, 'The Corporal and Midshipman Monkhouse are two people I value highly. If any harm comes to them, your chiefs will answer for it.'

Tutaha fully understood the position he was in. Cook, after all, had the guns. He spoke briefly to the priest, and Tupaia replied to the Captain. 'I will go with your men, Toote. They will be here by morning.'

'Thank you. I would appreciate that.'

So it transpired. By breakfast time everybody was safely back aboard: Gibson and Webb confined in irons below, the junior officers and seamen enjoying fried rat, washed down with a warming tot of rum.

Isaac, who was serving in the wardroom, heard what happened as Jon Monkhouse told the tale to his brother the surgeon, and the other officers at table.

'Corporal Truslove and me spent all day searching for those marines in the mountain valleys without finding any trace of them. None of the natives would help us, whatever Tutaha may have said.

'We were giving it up for a bad job and returning to the ship at nightfall, when suddenly we were rushed by a body of men hiding in the woods, armed with spears tipped with our own iron nails, and evil-looking clubs. They surrounded us before we had any chance to use our own weapons, and led us away to a clearing – where we saw Webb and Gibson, prisoners just like ourselves, looking very foolish.

'The warriors kept shouting *Tutaha! Tutaha!* to our faces, and waving their clubs. I began to wonder if *our* jawbones might be strung up as trophies, for plainly we were being held hostage for Tutaha's safe return, as we had taken *him!* They seemed unsure what to do next, and started arguing among themselves. Some were for letting us go, others for keeping us. Before long, words came to blows. They began fighting each other, and left us well alone.

'Finally they agreed that Webb should be taken to the Fort to say what had occurred and secure our release. And I must say I was relieved to see firelight approaching through the darkness, and Mr Hicks with Tupaia and his men enter the clearing. The priest only needed to say a few words and we were released – at least Corporal Truslove and myself were. Gibson was placed into *our* custody!'

Jonathan Monkhouse was only a few years older than Isaac. But the 'prentice boy listened to him with admiration, anticipating the day when *he* might be a Midshipman with responsibilities and a chance to shine in adventures.

In one respect, this adventure ended well enough. Nobody was seriously hurt, and the two marines were recovered. Yet in every other way it was upsetting. With his men aboard, Cook told Tutaha and the other hostages they were free to leave. Although they offered Toote four pigs, they were seething at the insult and Cook refused to accept the gift. He didn't deserve it, and the chiefs departed in fury.

The Captain was as upset as they were at how things had turned out, and he showed it in the severity of the floggings he gave to Webb and Gibson. Two dozen lashes each. And he made them wait several days in irons for punishment, for all hands were occupied getting *Endeavour* ready to leave. Final repairs were completed. Stores brought from the Fort. The last water casks filled. On the night of 12 July, Captain Cook and Mr Banks made a farewell visit to Tutaha.

'We sail in the morning, and wish to leave as friends.'

The *ari'i* was still fuming over the marines, and kept a cool distance. But Purea and her women wept when they heard Toote was to leave. And the high priest, Tupaia, asked the favour he'd been contemplating for weeks.

'I very much wish to travel with Toote on his ship. I can steer by the stars and the currents. I have journeyed many days on this ocean, and know the islands that lie beyond the horizon. Toote is to sail further, and I would like to learn more.'

'I've no doubt you'd be most useful to us. You have been already.'

'I am a priest of *Oro*, and know his language. I can talk to the wind. I can speak to other men across the seas and tell Toote what they say.'

'Assuredly. Still, how could I ever persuade their Lordships at the Admiralty to put you on the pay book?'

'I can solve that difficulty,' Joseph Banks interposed. 'Tupaia can come as one of my party. Other gentlemen collect lions and tigers when they travel abroad. I don't see why I may not come home with a man of Tahiti. He'll create a sensation.'

Banks was unconscious of any offensive implications, and his proposal was agreed. In fact, Tupaia went aboard *Endeavour* that very evening. With him went his servant, a boy priestling called Taiata. And Purea wept again.

There were many more tears on the beach as *Endeavour* men said goodbye to their girls. More sighing, and yearning, and vowing one day to return. As indeed some of them did. Isaac lay in the warm shallows with Heimata making his promises, and watching her surface like his own young Venus from the sea.

'I'll come back to you, one day,' he said. 'I swear I shall never forget you.' But Heimata's name meant 'one crowned with eyes', blessed with foresight. When she looked into her future she could not see Isaac, and her eyes brimmed.

He'd given her a small penknife – a brave thing to do, knowing such a precious gift of tempered steel was against Mr Cook's orders. And in return, Heimata knelt and pressed a grey Tahitian pearl earring into his hand, whispering '*Parahi, nana* . . . stay my dear friend . . .'

'I don't want to go! I just don't want to leave!' Isaac cried, reaching out.

Yet he looked beyond Heimata to the silhouette of *Endeavour*, straining at anchor with her sails half furled. The moon was rising from the island of Mo'orea, shaped like a human heart, casting a silver pathway across the water. And in his own heart Isaac knew he had not spoken the truth.

For he wanted to stay with Heimata, but he also desired to go on with his journey. To remain, and yet to travel further down the moonlit road. Isaac felt as ambivalent and restless as the ship. As he heard the bell summoning the evening watch, Isaac knew there was only one response. The claims of another were not yet enough.

'I must go,' he said quietly. '*Nana*. Goodbye. But come and see me leaving in the morning.'

She was there among the canoes crowding about *Endeavour*, filled with people throwing flowers into the water and crying *Aue!* Alas! Even Purea came – though her rivals Tutaha and Tepau stayed away, still burning with resentment. Which was a pity, but it made no difference.

Men heaved at the capstan bars to an old shanty, and *Endeavour*'s best bower anchor rose dripping from the water. Her sails enfolded the morning breeze. She shied a little at her freedom – then slowly, gracefully turned to the markers and followed the channel through the reef to the sea.

Aue! Aue!

Isaac stood by the rail, waving and calling to Heimata, his own eyes filling and the glistening pearl a weight in his pocket, before Mr Molineux called him to duty. Mr Banks climbed the topmast with Tupaia, and the priest stood on the rigging to stare at Tahiti until the island disappeared into the haze.

Down below, a quarrel between Midshipman John Bootie and Nick Young came to a head. Bootie had reported Nick to the officers for some misdemeanour. But when he opened his journal he found written on the daily page, *Evil communications corrupt good manners*, and signed with a flourish *N Young*. To which name an infuriated Bootie added . . . *is a son of a bitch*. And later tore out the page!

In his own cabin, the Captain unsealed his secret orders and read them. He was to proceed southward as far as forty degrees in search of the unknown continent: and, if it was not found, to sail west until he reached the land called New Zealand, which Abel Tasman had found and marked on his chart almost one hundred and thirty years before.

Exactly as everyone supposed! Mr Cook smiled to himself, closed the paper, then went up to the quarterdeck to breathe deep the freshening wind and give his orders.

INTERLUDE. INTO THE UNKNOWN

South Seas, July to October 1769

Tupaia showed his worth from the beginning.

To help his crew settle to shipboard life again and replenish food stocks, Cook spent several weeks exploring the islands around Tahiti. These were seas Tupaia knew well. He helped Cook produce a map showing more than seventy islands: not drawn to the Captain's precision, but good enough to indicate how the Pacific had been peopled over time by skilled voyagers in their large travelling canoes – *tipairua* – with flexible mat sails that, as Tupaia reminded Toote, sped across the ocean faster than *Endeavour* with all her canvas.

Tupaia called on the god *Tane* to bring them wind. He was usually given a favourable answer – especially when Joseph Banks sensed a breeze was already springing up. And the high priest helped ease tensions with a ceremonial peacemaking whenever they landed on a new island.

On Huahine, Tupaia stripped to the waist and made Dr Monkhouse do the same. He sat before the chiefs in front of the longhouse reciting prayers, before handing over gifts of linen, beads and feathers. He went to the *marae* for more oblations. Was given coconuts and a pig for the gods of *Endeavour* (quickly sacrificed to her crew). And thereafter the strangers were accepted by the islanders.

As it turned out, supplies were not as plentiful as hoped. But things were better on Ra'iatea, where Tupaia had been born – until he was forced to flee after an invasion by warriors from nearby Bora Bora. Ra'iatea was the centre of the *Oro* cult, and perhaps Tupaia hoped Cook would use *Endeavour*'s guns to restore his lands. But the Captain refused to interfere in local disputes: on the contrary, Cook ran up the Union Jack and claimed possession of Ra'iatea for King George! Whatever the islanders thought of *that*, they still welcomed Tupaia's friends, and Robert Molineux was often away in the longboat bartering for food.

He generally took Tupaia's boy, Taiata, with him as interpreter, and Isaac came as well for company. The two were becoming friends. Taiata was only twelve – a softly spoken, chubby lad, with a mass of dark curly hair, who slept near Isaac and Nick Young in the hammock once occupied by the negro servant, Tom Richmond.

The ship was a new world for him, and Isaac and Nick took it upon themselves to help Taiata find his sea legs: to show him the ropes, the rigging, and the whole ritual of mess deck living. Like every islander, Taiata had the sea in his blood; and before long, the boy who could shin up any coconut tree was climbing *Endeavour*'s masts like a topman.

'Look at him!' exclaimed Isaac. 'First time I went aloft I thought the ship would hurl me into the ocean. But Taiata is as much at home up there as if he was born to it.'

'He were,' replied Nick with admiration. 'He climbs even better than me. I don't fink there's ever been a lubberly bone in 'im.'

In return for these compliments, Taiata smoothed their way about the islands. Wherever Molineux landed, the young priest would make ceremony, speak to the people, and the Master usually had his longboat filled with supplies. And sometimes when they went to a *heiva*, Taiata played on his nose flute – soft, fluent notes breathed through one nostril, the other stopped by his thumb – while the *arioi* danced.

Isaac sat there enchanted. Much seemed the same as Tahiti, but there were differences. People on Ra'iatea seemed fairer skinned, almost like Europeans. The women danced in wide cloth dresses, and moved their feet to the drumming in a way that reminded the lad of a ballet he'd seen with his parents in a London theatre. Then he thought of Heimata. And Isaac knew where he'd rather be.

Yet his young mind was still easily distracted. Like the playhouse, dancing was followed by a pantomime – in which the men, dressed as armed warriors, their faces all distorted, showed how the Bora Bora chief Puni had triumphed over the people of Ra'iatea. Love and war together, as always, on the same programme. In fact Isaac saw Puni a while later. He was an old man at that time, half blind and decrepit. Nick Young joked that he wasn't so much Puni as puny! His fighters weren't though. They were known as the Club Men, and would bash out an enemy's brains in a trice. As terrifying as the Maori warriors they would see in New Zealand . . .

For with August, and spring approaching in the south, Cook knew it was time to depart the tropic islands around Tahiti – the Society Islands he called them, in honour of the Royal Society that had sponsored his expedition – and turn *Endeavour*'s bows toward colder latitudes in search of the unknown south land: *Terra Australis Incognita*. And *Incognita* was soon the operative word.

During the first week or so, Tupaia directed them to islands within his knowledge. But there came a time when the priest admitted he didn't know what lay beyond.

'My father told me there are islands two days from here,' Tupaia said. 'But after that I cannot say.'

'Did thy father ever speak of a continent . . . a big land?' asked the Captain.

'No. If Toote were to sail west he would find more islands.'

'Their Lordships have ordered me south. Well, then . . . we will *all* be sailing into the unknown.'

For it was the huge expanse of the southern Pacific that lay beyond the knowledge of European mapmakers. *Endeavour* certainly had her charts – in particular one given to Banks by Cook's rival Alexander Dalrymple, showing the routes taken by Dutch, Spanish and Portuguese navigators in previous centuries, and the discoveries to 1764.

To the east lay the long coastline of the Americas. To the west was the incomplete outline of New Holland, Torres's track below New Guinea, and those fragments of Van Diemen's Land and New Zealand discovered by Tasman and named by the Dutch geographers. Arching across the central Pacific were the points of many islands and 'signs of land'. But to the south was simply a vast blank space on the paper. Here, many people believed, the fabulous continent would be found, with riches to rival the Indies.

The further *Endeavour* sailed into this Incognita, the higher rose the human tensions of those aboard her. By day every weather eye was straining for a sight of land. And at night, no man knew when he'd be called from sleep by the sounds of breakers sweeping the ship onto an unknown shore. Nobody rested easy.

Suspended in their hammocks under the low bulkhead, Nick and Taiata and Isaac never more than half slept. Always, parts of their minds were alert for the bell ringing the half hours of the watch.

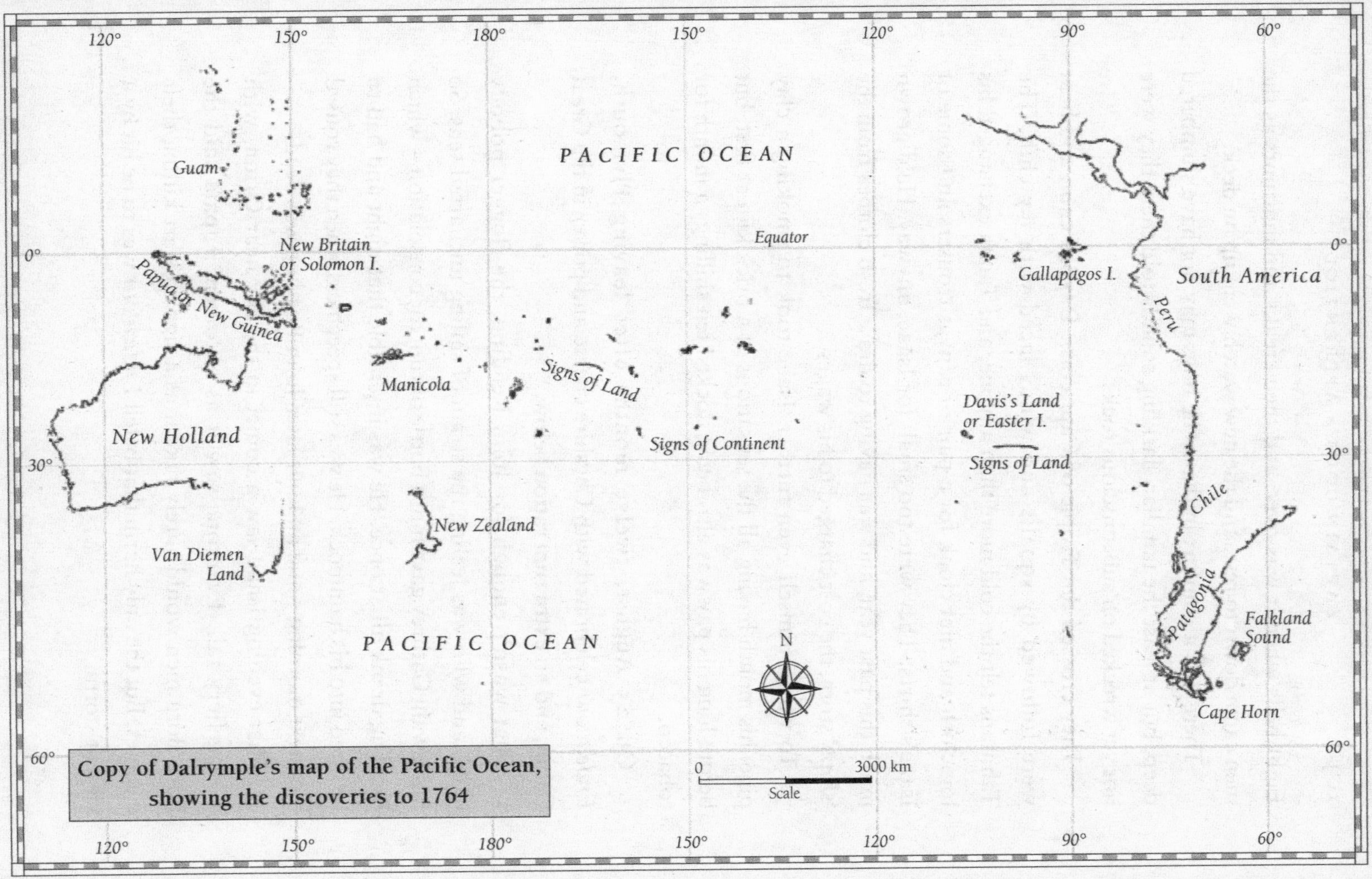

Copy of Dalrymple's map of the Pacific Ocean, showing the discoveries to 1764

Eight bells when it was over; and then creaks and murmurs as the men came down to rest, and the new watch went up on deck.

There was a comfort in that. The boys may not have slumbered deep, but at least the familiar, darkling sounds told them they were not yet wrecked on subconscious rocks.

They crossed the Tropic of Capricorn. Days of calm and heat were followed by squalls and winds laced with icy chill. The Tahitians felt the cold more than anyone, and Taiata exchanged his loincloth and mat cloak for a pair of canvas trousers and some of Isaac's shirts. They were too small for Isaac, anyway. He'd grown much this past year, and was having to draw fresh clothes from the 'slops' store, the cost charged to his wages.

To warm himself even further, Isaac took to smoking a clay pipe: his mouth having all the sensations of a brick kiln at first, but before long his pay was also being docked ten shillings a month for tobacco.

On 25 August, twelve months after leaving Plymouth, *Endeavour* celebrated with Cheshire cheese and porter in the Great Cabin, and an extra rum ration below.

That wasn't enough for John Reading, the flogger nobody liked, and who was feeling the strain of sailing uncharted seas. So Boatswain Gathrey gave him a bottle of rum for consolation – which Reading drank all at once. He was insensible that night and had to be lifted into his hammock. He was still speechless when they roused him next morning – and an hour later John Reading was dead.

That evening Isaac saw a comet in the sky near Orion, with a long fiery tail. Everyone saw it as an omen. Tupaia said the Bora Bora men would surely take it as a sign to start killing their enemies. But the only harm that befell *Endeavour* was to be hit by a violent storm.

She ran before it with just her foresail, the Captain seeming certain by the heavy ocean swell there was no danger of running into land hereabouts. Indeed, when the tempest blew itself out, Cook found he'd passed latitude thirty-nine degrees south. He'd almost reached the Admiralty's limit without any sign of a continent. To go further would risk more damage to his sails and rigging.

First rise after low foretells an even greater blow.

Thus, in early September, he turned north.

The comet continued to appear for the next few nights, and Isaac saw it as a good omen. Time to push himself a little further forward. Finding Mr Molineux in pleasant humour with the change of course, he asked if the Master would show him how to use the sextant.

'Dost want to navigate the ship now, lad?'

'I've got to learn.'

'Still fancy thyself as officer material?'

'I've tried to show willing.'

'Aye,' Molineux nodded at his servant, 'you have that! Well then, you may join the other young gentlemen on the quarterdeck at noon tomorrow.'

Isaac was there long before midday, practising with a brass sextant. Molineux was a willing teacher, but a little short on patience.

'No, no lad! Don't hold the instrument by any of its moving parts! Use the handle or frame. And never look at the sun through the sights without a dark glass shade. You'll burn thy bloody eyes out in fifteen seconds flat! There . . . now bring the sun down to the horizon.'

Bring the sun down? What was he talking about?

Isaac squinted through the lens, but all he could see in the sextant's mirror was a wavering blur of grey sea and sky. It was so difficult to keep the sextant pointed steadily at the sun while trying to keep his balance on a heaving deck.

Then, for a moment, he saw it! The glowing, orange ball of the sun reflected through a dark shade into the mirror.

'I've got it.'

'Now turn the minute knob to adjust the mirror and bring the sun down to the line where sea and sky meet.'

'I've lost it.'

'Don't be daft. Try again.'

And again. At last the boy was able to keep the sun fixed in his sights long enough to tilt the mirror with the knob and bring the sun's reflection down to the horizon.

'Now, when the lower edge of the sun touches the line at midday, you'll be able to work out our latitude. The sextant's arc will show you the degrees, and the adjustment the number of minutes. What does your instrument show?'

'Um . . .' Isaac peered at the markings on the sextant's arc. 'I think twenty-three degrees and forty-six minutes.'

'Good God, lad! You'll have us back in Tahiti. If only . . .' Robert Molineux remembered. As did Isaac. 'Do it once more.'

It took much practice before Isaac became competent with the sextant. Day after day he stood with the officers and Midshipmen on the quarterdeck to get a reading at noon with the sun at its zenith. And eventually his readings began to tally with everyone else's.

'I have thirty-five degrees and seventeen minutes, sir . . . thirty-two degrees and eighteen minutes . . . thirty-seven degrees forty-six, Mr Molineux . . .' as they turned south-west again '. . . thirty-eight degrees twenty-nine . . .'

The Captain looked on and was pleased.

Day after day, veering northward once more, they approached the latitude and longitude where Tasman had marked the few lines on his map he called Cape Maria van Diemen. New Zealand!

Hopes rose. Perhaps it would prove to be part of the unknown continent. After nearly two months at sea, men were longing for the land again.

To be sure, supplies were holding out well. The sauerkraut was as good as ever. There were few signs of scurvy: a remarkable thing for such a voyage. The quarterdeck resembled a farmyard with its sheep, chickens, ducks and pigs, and the goat's milk seemed inexhaustible. Certainly, the ship's biscuit was full of weevils that burned like mustard when you bit them: but hard tack always had weevils. The taro roots from Tahiti went bad, and the plantains ran out. But Taiata was able to remind himself of home whenever John Thompson served yams and sweet potato with salt pork.

Yet it could not be denied that everyone was impatient. Birds clustered around the ship: shearwaters, albatrosses, and some birds that were thought never to fly far from land.

Clumps of seaweed were seen in the water. Then rockweed, and pieces of wood encrusted with barnacles. They passed a seal floating sound asleep. Anticipation rose higher when Captain Cook announced, 'I will name part of the coast after the man who first sights it. Aye, and give him a gallon of rum as reward.'

The competition was really on! Many positive sightings turned into the clouds of 'Cape Flyaway'. Yet the honour went not to a man – but a boy. Nick Young was at the masthead at two o'clock on the afternoon of Saturday, 7 October, when he saw a daub on the painted horizon.

'Land! Land ho!'

'Where away?'

'West by north.'

'Steersman, set your course.'

'Aye, aye, sir.'

By sunset the land was visible from the quarterdeck. At noon next day they saw mountains stretching from sou'-west to nor'-west-by-north. This was no small island like Tahiti.

'It *must* be a continent,' enthused Mr Banks, 'our very Land of Promise.'

Nick Young, at least, got his promised reward. When *Endeavour* entered a large bay two days later, the Captain named the cliffs at its southern point Young Nick's Head. As such it is known to this day. Nick was given his gallon of rum, too. Though in tender consideration of what happened to John Reading, the crew all helped Nick drink it.

Whatever else the country promised, however, the warriors of New Zealand would make them fight for it.

7

MAORI WARRIORS

New Zealand: North Island, October to November 1769

Their first encounters with the Maori were indeed bloody.

Endeavour anchored at the northern end of the bay, and late that afternoon the Captain went ashore with two boats to establish contact and find fresh water. He let Isaac and the other boys come as well.

'Give the young'uns a chance to stretch their legs on dry land again.'

They landed near the east bank of the Turanganui River, at the foot of a high hill called Titirangi, but found nobody. A few men were seen by a stream on the other side, however, and ordering the pinnace to stand off as guard, Cook crossed the river with Mr Banks and the boys in the smaller yawl. Yet the Maori disappeared again behind a sandy ridge.

Deciding to investigate some low, thatched huts not far away, Cook told the boys to tend the yawl – 'And don't stray!'

But it was hard to remain still, when the lads were feeling sand beneath their feet for the first time in months. Before long Nick and Taiata were chasing each other. Isaac and Tom Matthews joined the game, romping along the beach like young colts.

Suddenly there were shouts. A musket fired. And looking up, the boys saw that four fearsome warriors had come out of the woods below Titirangi on the other side of the river, and were running abreast of them.

'Quickly! Back to the yawl!' yelled Coxswain Evans from the pinnace at the river mouth. 'They'll cut you off.'

'Hurry!' cried Isaac, as the boys dashed to the boat, for the river here was only sixty yards wide – a good spear throw – and the Maori could easily swim.

The lads scrambled aboard and pushed out into the swift water, the warriors keeping pace with them on the opposite shore.

'Grab the other oar, Tom!'

The current had the yawl in its grip – like a Thames ferry – and was sweeping them towards a large rock midstream where they might well founder. As the boys struggled to control the boat a second shot was fired over the warriors' heads, but it made no difference. The Maori were closing in.

'Row with all your might!' But even as Isaac and Tom righted the yawl, the river was carrying them beyond the rock to the nearer bank and the waiting Maori.

Their leader, a man called Te Maro, had his spear raised, ready to hurl it at Isaac, when there came a third shot from the pinnace. This one found its mark. The musket ball ripped through Te Maro's ribs and out his shoulder, and he dropped.

His three companions withdrew a few paces, unsure what had felled him. Then, leaving off the chase, they returned to the shot man, carefully gathered his weapons and carried him along the beach. Where, realising Te Maro was dead, his comrades left him and disappeared into woods thick with bright, finger-leaved bushes and tall tree ferns.

Alarmed by the shots, Cook hurried back from the Maori fishing village.

'Are you lads all right?' he called.

'Aye, Captain.'

'Then bring the yawl back to us.'

Isaac and Tom heaved back up river, collected the gentlemen, and landed not far from where Te Maro had been shot. Following the blood trail, they found his body not fifty yards away: a short, stout man, wearing a cloak and loincloth from woven flax, his long black hair tied in a knot on top of his head. What made him look so fierce were the heavy tattoos on the right side of his face: three broad arches above his eye, and intricate spirals etched on his cheek and nose.

Isaac was fascinated. He knew the small blue leaf on his arm, and he remembered every mark on Heimata. But the tattoo on the warrior's face was something else again. The youth stood wondering at the skill and artistry of it – and also at the courage of the man who'd withstood the pain of having it done.

They left him where he'd died, placing some beads and iron nails on the corpse, before returning to the ship.

Cook and the gentlemen went ashore again next morning, taking a stronger force of men and marines. Tupaia went with them, insisting he take Taiata. But after the last escapade, the other lads had to stay aboard.

'It's too dangerous,' said the Captain, 'until we're friends with these people.'

Far from making friends, the day proved even more deadly for the Maori.

Cook landed by the river again. And not far from where Te Maro's body still lay on the beach, he faced some fifty warriors on the opposite shore – all armed and tattooed, with feathers and whalebone combs in their hair. As the Captain began to speak, he was greeted with derision. The Maori began their war dance – a *haka*: rhythmically chanting, stamping, flexing their arms, and poking out their tongues in attitudes of defiance and aggression.

But Cook could not become intimidated. He had Tupaia call to the warriors, hoping they would recognise some words of friendship. To his amazement, they not only understood the priest – their language seemed almost identical. And indeed, he would learn the Maori had come from the same Polynesian homeland centuries before in their mighty double canoes. *Aotearoa* they called this new country, the land of the long white cloud. Tupaia and young Taiata were their first visitors from the ancestral islands for hundreds of years.

The Maori's resistance to the *Endeavour* men was very different to the welcoming Tahitians, however.

'What do they say?' Cook asked Tupaia. 'Did you tell them we need fresh water? That we want to be friends?'

'They say Toote can have water. But as we have already killed one of their men, how can we be friends?'

'It was not my wish. Tell them I will lay down my weapon if they will do the same and come to us. Say we have gifts.'

The Captain laid his musket on the shore – though he had the marines drawn up behind, just in case. Yet the Maori would not disarm themselves, except for one man who eventually stripped and swam across.

He pressed noses with Cook in a *hongi* greeting ceremony. The Captain got a smudge of red paint on his face, and in return gave beads and nails. The warrior called to his companions, and another twenty swam over – although seeing the armed marines, they also brought their weapons.

'Be careful, Toote,' warned Tupaia. 'These people are not your friends.'

'We must establish some contact if we are to trade for supplies.'

Certainly the Maori seemed pleased at first with their gifts. But the warriors were soon more interested in the gentlemen's weapons, especially that object like a short spear – a *tao* – which breathed smoke and killed at a distance.

The Maori began to grab at the muskets held by Mr Banks and Dr Monkhouse. And when astronomer Green turned his back, a man called Te Rakau snatched the short sword from his belt and ran off with it.

'Stop thief!' shouted Joseph Banks. And levelling his gun, the botanist shot the man between the shoulders.

Te Rakau took no notice, but kept on running until Charles Green fired a lead ball, and the Maori fell.

Two comrades rushed to his side. Thinking they'd steal the sword again, Dr Monkhouse faced them with his bayonet. It was Te Rakau's own weapon they wanted: a short, oval-shaped club called a *patu*, made of greenstone hard as steel. They then retreated with the others to the large rock midstream, shouting threats.

Further shots were fired – some by Tupaia – injuring at least three more Maori, who at length were helped across the river and into the woods.

'So much for our friendship,' deplored Mr Cook surveying the slain man, his body not far from Te Maro on the disturbed beach, tattooed face stained with paint like blood, a human tooth hanging in his ear. 'Well . . . t' river is salt water anyway. We'll row further around t' bay and try to find people more amenable to us.'

His next overtures were even more disastrous.

A high surf was running and the boats found nowhere safe to land. They were returning to the ship, when two *waka* – fishing canoes with mat sails – came around Young Nick's Head and into the bay.

'We'll cut them off,' ordered the Captain, 'and persuade them to come aboard to show we mean no harm.'

They gave chase. The canoe paddlers, fearing they were under attack, put on speed and the leading one made it safely ashore. The other couldn't outrun the longboat, however, and as they closed in Cook told Tupaia to call out his friendly intentions. The seven occupants took no notice, and kept trying to escape.

'Fire a musket over their heads, and frighten them into surrender.'

They didn't submit, any more than Cook would have done. On the contrary, the Maori defended themselves by throwing stones, wood and even fish at their pursuers. Thus, the Captain gave a fatal command.

'Fire ball shot!'

The muskets cracked, killing three men and wounding a fourth. The other three – mere boys – leaped into the sea and began swimming for their lives.

'Good God!' cried Joseph Banks, 'What have we done?'

'What we had to,' replied the Captain brusquely. And turning to the Coxswain he added, 'Get those boys into the boat, and say we won't hurt 'em.'

Though why they should believe him, Cook couldn't have explained. Indeed, as the three prisoners were dragged into the boat, they began weeping piteously.

'What are they saying, Tupaia?'

'They are afraid Toote's men will kill and eat them.'

'Kindly tell them we'll do no such barbarous thing.'

'They say that is what their enemies do.'

'We are not savages. We are their friends!'

Assured they wouldn't be eaten, the boys cheered up – surprisingly quickly after what had happened. The eldest was only about eighteen with a tattooed lip, the youngest no more than eleven or twelve. By the time they got aboard *Endeavour* the three were almost merry. They darted about the deck, talking excitedly to Tupaia, eating salt pork and wondering if the weevilly ship's biscuits were yams.

The younger boys dressed in Nick and Isaac's britches and jackets, laughing along with the crew. Though when they came to perform a *haka* they became altogether more serious. Wearing only loincloths, they stamped the Maori's warlike dance. They sang together in harmonies that delighted everyone. And when all was done, the youngsters made a bed on the lockers and slept soundly, with Tupaia keeping watch in case they woke in the night and were afraid.

Others on board were less tranquil. Down on the mess deck, Taiata wept in his hammock as he told Isaac of what he had seen that day. 'Awful . . . awful . . . guns and smoke . . . and three men dead who had done us no harm . . .'

In the Great Cabin, Joseph Banks trembled with emotion.

'This is the blackest day of my life! Heaven forbid I should know another like it. Every instruction from London has been to treat these people with kindness . . . yet already in two days we've killed at least five of them!'

'You may well censure me,' replied the Captain, searching for a justification. 'I would never have chased that canoe if I thought they'd resist us. Once they did, what was I to do? Allow ourselves to be knocked on the head?'

'They were throwing sticks and dead fish!'

'And if I'd turned tail and departed, the Indians would have put the triumph down to *their* superiority and *our* cowardice. We'd be ridiculed in their eyes – and never get anywhere in our future dealings with them. Remember that.'

'They were very brave fellows.'

'Yes. That, too.'

Cook set the boys ashore next day, hoping they'd rejoin their families and say how well they'd been treated by these white strangers . . . these *Pakeha*. But again they grew afraid, pleading that this was enemy territory, and they'd be eaten if discovered.

'Cannibals? I don't believe it. They're just pretending,' said Cook. Though he noticed the lads hid in the bush when the gentlemen went off to shoot ducks.

They reappeared, however, as a body of a hundred and fifty Maori warriors gathered once more by the Turanganui River. The youngsters showed their fine clothes and gifts, and invited their countrymen across. Only one did – who, as soon as he reached them, sat down on the riverbank and embraced the boys. The smallest wept and said the man was his father. Which removed any doubts about cannibalism.

They even performed a ceremony over Te Rakau's body. The eldest boy took off his sailor's jacket and placed it on the corpse, and the man laid a bough of green leaves as a token of peace and sacrifice. The Captain may have hoped the lads would now go home and spread the good news of his friendship. Yet they again pleaded to spend the night aboard *Endeavour*, which he agreed.

'They will depart in the morning, come what may,' Cook added. 'We're leaving this place. There's been nothing for us here. We may find better fortune elsewhere: but this I have named on my chart as Poverty Bay.'

Poor in what it yielded *Endeavour*, though the land is rich. And many of those aboard felt impoverished in spirit by what had happened there.

The three Maori boys were set ashore next day. They came to the water's edge, holding out their hands and crying for the ship to take them. But as *Endeavour* departed, Isaac saw them being ferried across the river in a canoe and go off laughing with some others into the woods. A few days afterwards they heard the boys were safely back with their families. So all was well.

Word spread along the coast of the *Pakeha* in their ship that floated like an island beneath white clouds. As *Endeavour* sailed south, canoes began to come close, and the people exchanged fish and artefacts for Tahitian cloth and European trinkets. It may have been friendship, or curiosity. Perhaps merely respect for their guns, or the fact that *Pakeha* were not cannibals. Nobody could say. For while some Maori traded, others continued to show derision.

In what Cook called Hawke's Bay after Admiral Hawke, the First Lord of the Admiralty, the ship was approached by several war canoes, their prows and stern posts wonderfully carved with spirals and ancestor symbols, eyes glowing with *paua* shell. The warriors jeered, lolling their tongues like the grotesque *hei tiki* figures they wore round their necks. Dr Monkhouse saw some even bare their arses to the strangers in the universal gesture of contempt.

'They behave just like Billingsgate fishwives!'

And he reciprocated by exposing his own arse: which threw the warriors into greater fury. They threatened to use the surgeon's posterior as a spear target – until forced to retire by a round of grapeshot, which the Captain ordered to aim wide.

'No more killings if we can help it,' Cook said.

But more couldn't be prevented a day or two later, near the southern end of Hawke's Bay.

Trade was brisk that morning. Taiata was on the ship's ladder, with Isaac and some of the other boys over the side, handing up the dried (and smelly) fish the Maori were bartering. Suddenly a war canoe paddled towards *Endeavour*, and Cook ordered the marines to prime their muskets. But the warriors didn't seem intent on trouble. Rather had they come to market, and offered to swap their cloaks.

The chief – the *ariki* – was wearing a beautiful garment of a woven design, ornamented with dog's hair. He agreed to exchange it with the Captain for a length of red baize cloth. The deal was struck. Taiata handed it down to the canoe: but instead of passing up his cloak in return, the chief brazenly put both into a basket, and ordered the *waka* to drop astern. Where he stood laughing at Cook's discomfort.

'Hey, you thief! Come back and complete your side of the bargain.'

'Shall I shoot him, suh?' asked Lieutenant Gore too eagerly, his pistol cocked.

'Nay, John. We've shed enough blood. Let it be.'

The fishing canoes returned, and trade resumed.

All at once, however, the chief shouted some orders, and one of the fishermen grabbed Taiata. The boy screamed as he was dragged off the ladder and into the *waka*.

'Tupaia! Master! Help me!'

But his cries were stifled as two men held him down in the prow, and the canoes began paddling quickly away.

Shocked by the speed of events, it took Isaac a moment to realise his friend had been kidnapped – just like John Thurman at Madeira, though here the victim might still be rescued. As the *waka* raced towards shore Isaac shouted urgently, 'Tell the Captain! Tell the Captain!'

'Toote!' cried Tupaia. 'You must stop them!'

'Shall I order the marines to fire *now*, suh?' enquired Lieutenant Gore.

'Aye, John. There is no help for it. But tell them to try and not hit the boy.' Knowing how unreliable muskets were.

'Marines! Take positions!' shouted Sergeant Edgcumbe. 'On my order – fire!'

The muskets spat flame and death. Taiata, lying rigid with fear, heard the man holding him groan and slump, and his grip loosened. As the smoke cleared, Isaac saw that Taiata had wriggled free in the panic and leaped overboard.

'He's swimming towards *Endeavour!*'

'Lower the longboat to pick him up,' commanded Lieutenant Gore.

But as the boat was swinging out, the Maori chief rallied his warriors and ordered the war canoe to go after Taiata. The paddlers bent to the task, chanting their war song. Closer it beat to the floundering boy.

'They're going to get him,' Isaac shouted, hanging out as far as he could from the shrouds. 'Hurry!'

'Another round if you please, Mr Gore. And Gunner, fire ball shot.'

The cannon was primed, loaded, rammed home, and roared. The muskets struck again. This time the *waka* left off the chase and headed for shore, while a very frightened Tahitian boy was hauled aboard the longboat and back to the ship. The Maori carried three of their dead up the beach.

Later, when he'd recovered a little, Taiata went to Tupaia with a fish he had caught that day. 'I wish to offer it to the gods as thanks for my deliverance.'

The priest approved, and said a prayer to his *atua* as Taiata returned the fish to the sea. The Captain celebrated by naming the point Cape Kidnappers, and it's still known as such today.

Isaac often wondered what would have happened to Taiata had he been taken by the Maori. Would he have been killed? Many feared so. Tupaia thought the chief probably wanted the boy priest from the homeland as a valuable addition to his power and prestige . . . his *mana*. Taiata would be worth much more to him alive than dead.

As the days went by, they were all grateful for the Tahitians' presence. Tupaia especially, through his status and knowledge, pacified many a threatening situation.

Endeavour sailed south a little longer, charting the coast of this so-far-inhospitable continent, before Cook headed north once more – at a place he called Cape Turnagain – searching for a suitable anchorage to wood and water.

On the whole, the tribes – the *Iwi* – now seemed friendlier. Canoes frequented the ship bartering for prized Tahitian *tapa* cloth. People sometimes spent the night aboard. At *Uawa* – Tolaga Bay – the crew had their first peaceful days ashore trading for sweet potato and gathering wild celery. The gentlemen explored and botanised with the Maori. And Tupaia spent much time with the priests in the *marae* speaking of the homeland, and receiving many rich gifts.

Some men even claimed to have been with Maori women – but they were few, for the *Iwi* kept wives and daughters close. As for Isaac, his thoughts were still of Heimata and the South Seas pearl she'd given him. He kept it safe in the velvet bag with Mamma's silver locket. And every time Isaac held it to remember, the pearl became as liquid as Heimata's eyes on the grey sands of Matavai Bay.

Maori did not look at the voyagers like that. For even as they continued past the fertile Bay of Plenty there was always an uneasiness: a sense of fragility in relations that could swiftly break into conflict again. Usually Tupaia was able to calm things by speaking as a venerable elder. But sometimes, when taunting from the war canoes became too hostile, or the thieves too barefaced (as when they tried to steal the ship's washing trawling from the stern), *Endeavour* replied with a cannonade or a round of musketry fired wide to scatter them.

'Why do they dislike us so much?' Isaac asked himself, and supplied his own answer. 'They no more welcome us than we would an alien warship sailing up the Thames.'

He was thankful only that there had been no more deaths since Cape Kidnappers.

But that was not to last . . .

In early November the ship breasted into a fine bay, *Te Whitianga a Kupe* – the Crossing Place of Kupe, where the great ancestor had landed after his voyage from the homeland. It certainly suited Captain Cook, who was looking for somewhere sheltered to observe the Transit of Mercury.

High, volcanic tufa cliffs had been sculpted by the sea into coves and inlets scattered with islands and rock pinnacles. A stream of fresh water cascaded into the Purangi River. There was plenty of wood, and the fishing appeared excellent. Atop many headlands were fortified Maori *pa*: small villages sheltering behind ditches and high palisades of sharpened stakes and fighting platforms.

'The inhabitants seem to be constantly at war with their enemies,' Cook observed. And this was very true.

As *Endeavour* anchored, she was surrounded by dugout canoes, *tiwai*, filled with local Ngati Hei tribesmen determined to confront these new intruders under the watchful eye of their chief, Toiawa. Stones were thrown, and a spear which fell harmlessly to the deck. The warriors became less hostile after Tupaia spoke to them, and Toiawa came aboard. Surprisingly, some even agreed to exchange cloth for their weapons: for the Maori, who well understood the terms of fair trade, had hitherto refused to sell their arms except for European muskets – which was forbidden!

Isaac could see why they so prized their weapons. A spear shaft was beautifully carved with an intricate knot of spirals and volutes. And Mr Molineux let him hold a small whalebone club, perfectly balanced in the hand, ready to split skulls.

No skulls were split that day, though a warrior was peppered with small shot when he reneged on a trade. And several men trying to steal the anchor buoy had a musket ball fired through their *tiwai*. They left shouting threats.

'What are they saying?' Isaac asked Taiata.

'They are calling us *tupua* . . . goblins and demons.'

'And what else?'

'They will come back in the morning and kill us all.'

'That is a generous warning,' said Cook, when he heard of it. 'But I suppose they intend to come tonight, hoping to find us off guard. We must disappoint them.'

And the warriors *were* disappointed. Twice their canoes came to the ship in the darkness – but finding the watch doubled, they departed without a word.

Thereafter, under Toiawa's influence, relations generally were very cordial. The Ngati Hei brought so many fish to *Endeavour* there was enough to last them a month. More people came aboard: were given gifts, and salt beef to eat. Many thought it was human flesh, for Maori had no other red meat except rats and the small dogs originally brought from the homeland – together with seals and the occasional beached whale.

For their part, the *tupua* spent much time ashore – astounding the Maori by rowing their boats facing *away* from the direction they were going. They must truly be goblins with eyes in the backs of their heads! But they were mostly harmless ones. The sailors were busy dragging the fishing net; servant boys scrubbing cabins; the Master and officers surveying the bay; gentlemen collecting specimens; and Cook with astronomer Green preparing for the Transit of Mercury.

The observation was important, for the navigator could use it to fix his longitude accurately and thus New Zealand's true position on the globe. Longitude, which involved lunar readings and complex calculations, was always uncertain on a moving ship. Thus Cook set up his telescopes and quadrant with precision on the beach.

It was a warm, clear morning, and the Captain and Mr Green were fully occupied with the Transit, when suddenly came shouting and gunfire from the ship.

A number of large *waka* arrived with warriors from further along the coast or outer islands. They seemed hostile at first: but once they were warned of the *tupua* with their guns, the strangers agreed to trade. Garments and valuable *pounamu* greenstone were exchanged for Tahitian cloth, and all seemed smiles. Until Lieutenant Gore was cheated.

He'd agreed to buy a rare dog-skin cloak worn by a young chief, and passed down a length of cloth. The man took it: but instead of giving up the cloak, he ordered his companions to paddle quickly away, laughing and brandishing his weapons.

Just like Cape Kidnappers! Gore was outraged.

'Hand me your musket!' he ordered a marine. And taking careful aim, Gore shot the Maori in the back. The man staggered even as he shouted a last boast, then dropped among his comrades as they paddled off.

The incident greatly upset the Captain when he came aboard.

'Don't you think that killing the man was excessive punishment for the crime?' he remonstrated. 'Small shot would have been enough.'

'It weren't enough for you in Poverty Bay, suh.' Gore turned the rebuke. 'And they would have been hanged in England.'

'This is not England! We need the friendship of these people.'

Isaac, too, had seen much violent death: but wasn't yet grown indifferent to it.

'Why does it always end in bloodshed?' the boy exclaimed. 'Don't they know we want peace?'

'People only make peace when they know who has the stronger weapons,' Robert Molineux observed.

'Does it *have* to be like that?'

'It usually is.'

To Cook's relief, the death didn't destroy his tenuous friendship with Toiawa and the Ngati Hei. Indeed, they said the young warrior deserved his fate: though whether they really believed this, or were speaking from fear of the *tupua* guns, nobody knew. Even so, the place on the beach where Cook set up his instruments was from then on called *Mahanakino* – 'bad day' – in remembrance of what had happened.

Still, the people continued to show Toote and his men much hospitality during the five more days the ship remained in Mercury Bay, as Cook named it on his chart. Old Toiawa even drew a map in charcoal on *Endeavour*'s deck showing the lands to the north. He took them to visit the *pa* and vegetable gardens on the northern headland. And the oyster beds up the Purangi River were so plentiful, the longboat was almost awash under its load.

In return, Cook gave Toiawa English potatoes to cultivate. The Captain blazoned a tree with *Endeavour 1769*, as a notice to other *tupua* he'd been there first. He ran up the Union Jack and claimed this part of the continent for King George – though he no more sought the consent of Toiawa or the Ngati Hei, than he had Tupaia's people at Ra'iatea. It was other Europeans he wanted to forestall.

Cook gave further things as well.

There was a Maori boy called Te Horeta, who remembered this visit all his life. He was younger than Isaac, and much too afraid of the goblin guns to say very much when he came aboard. But he allowed their great chief Toote to pat his head and give him an iron spike nail.

'*Ka Pai,*' said Horeta. Very good. And he kept the nail on a braided string around his neck.

The boy was more forthcoming with Taiata and the other lads, giving presents in token of the nail. Sometimes they'd go along the coast, and Horeta showed them how to find crayfish – feeling among underwater rocks with bare feet at low tide. It was hazardous, but worth every nip to eat them broiled on an open fire.

Once, Horeta took the boys to the ruins of a *pa* on a rock overlooking the Whitianga River: *Whitianga pa*. Isaac never forgot his steep climb up the path, across the ditch, through a broken gate, and edging along a narrow ridge, only a foot wide, to the inner fort. One slip and he would have plunged down to the sea.

No castle in England could have been better positioned; but like most castles, the *pa* had eventually fallen to its enemies and into decay. It was peaceful enough now: though when they got to the end, Horeta stood on the cliff edge and declared, 'I will be a great warrior myself, when I grow up.'

And so he became. For many years Horeta kept the nail Captain Cook had given him, wearing it like a talisman to bring strength and good fortune. One day, however, his canoe tipped over crossing the bay. The nail slipped from Horeta's neck and sank to the bottom. He dived many times trying to find it, but he never did. At last Horeta had to accept that the charm the goblins gave him had returned to the place it came from.

Well, not quite. For when Toote's men sailed out of the bay, Horeta knew they were going north to where other *Iwi* – and enemies – lived. And he stood on the headland looking at *Endeavour* and wondering the future, until the pennant floating from its masthead disappeared into the morning sun.

8

CANNIBAL BAY

New Zealand: South Island, November 1769 to March 1770

It was some time before Isaac and the *Endeavour* men saw proof positive that the Maori sometimes ate their enemies. They'd first heard such stories from the boys captured at Poverty Bay, but hadn't believed them. Yet tales of cannibalism persisted as the ship sailed up the coast from Whitianga into the Hauraki Gulf. So that, however appalling, most came to think it must be true.

The country here was lush with green and silver ferns clinging to craggy slopes, and open-armed pohutukawa trees now, in early summer, aflame with scarlet flowers.

Further inland, forest giants reached to the sky. When Captain Cook rowed up the stately Waihou River, which reminded him of the Thames, he measured a massive kauri tree with a quadrant: it soared eighty-nine feet without tapering from the ground to its first branch, majestic as a cathedral column.

The land, too, supported many people – and *Endeavour* was met by large numbers of war canoes flying feather streamers, paddles rhythmically drumming the sides, as warriors challenged the strangers.

Come ashore and we will kill you all!

Until the rattle of musketry or a cannonade fired wide persuaded them that the *tupua* wished to be friends!

Certainly the Captain and gentlemen were welcomed at a *pa* they visited on the Waihou. In fact, they thought it would make a site for a future colony. And many *Iwi* came aboard the ship to trade – and even filch a little something.

One man was caught stealing a half-hour sandglass from the binnacle cabinet on the quarterdeck, an important item if the bell was to be rung on time during watch. Lieutenant Hicks was on duty, and decided to punish the thief in the navy way.

'Seize that man!' Zachary Hicks ordered. 'Tie him to the rigging and give him a dozen lashes.'

Other Maori grew threatening. But assured by Tupaia that their companion wouldn't be killed, they watched the flogging in silence. And when the miscreant was released, his chief beat him even harder.

'What was that for?' Isaac asked. 'Stealing? Or for being caught?' Taiata didn't know – probably for both.

The Captain was consistent about punishing those who took other people's property. In the beautiful Bay of Islands, three seamen got a dozen lashes each for pulling up *kumara,* the tasty sweet potatoes, from a Maori garden, when they were supposed to be cutting grass for the animals.

Isaac's friend, Henry Stephens, was one of them. Again. Whipped at Madeira for not eating fresh beef, and now for taking vegetables. His back was quilted with scars. And Gunner Forwood was flogged, with two others, for stealing rum from the quarterdeck cask when he was in charge of the watch. 'The only useless person on board,' the Captain called him, though he later recommended Gunner for promotion. Cook rarely bore a grudge – and many sea captains used the lash a lot more than he did.

The men may have been forgiven for seeking comfort in food and drink. The Bay of Islands might have seemed tranquil and picturesque, but when Cook went ashore with an armed party, they were surrounded on the beach by some two hundred Maori, who began to chant their *haka* as a prelude to attack.

At such moments the Captain showed his coolness. He drew a line in the sand, beyond which the warriors should not pass. They tried to seize the boats, but were repulsed. Some, more daring, attempted to cross the line, though they retreated under a volley of small shot.

An *ariki* rallied them together. Again they began to advance, and again were thrown into confusion by musket fire. But the Maori were growing bolder – until Lieutenant Hicks brought *Endeavour* broadside to the beach and fired a few cannonballs over their heads.

The warriors dispersed. Initial hostilities once more resolved into a cautious amity between Maori and *Pakeha*. There was trade in New Zealand artefacts for paper and Tahitian cloth. There were lessons in geography, Maori saying the land soon turned west and then south, so that this part of the continent seemed to be a promontory. And the Maori again acknowledged they ate their enemies.

The subject of cannibalism was never far from the voyagers' minds – and came rushing to the fore when, on leaving the bay, *Endeavour* struck a submerged rock in front of the anticipating *Iwi*. Fortunately she floated free without damage. Though, as Joseph Banks confided to his journal, *The almost certainty of being eat as soon as you come ashore adds not a little to the terrors of shipwreck.*

*

The sea had other dangers. As the ship headed into December, she ran into squalls and heavy weather, and it took nearly a fortnight just to reach North Cape. Christmas Day was clear enough, and the company celebrated by dining on gannet pie and becoming as drunk as they had off Patagonia a year ago.

Now let every man toss off a full bumper,
And let every man toss off a full bowl . . .

Then the gales returned, like hurricanes. Isaac, who considered himself cured of seasickness, put his queasiness down to Christmas grog. But the storms went on. Although they sighted Cape Maria van Diemen in late December, the winds and currents were such that *Endeavour* didn't round the northland until early new year. Even then, she was blown far off shore, and not for some days was Cook's doughty Whitby collier able to edge back to the dangerous coast 'on a high rowling sea'. It had taken five weeks just to sail fifty leagues – a hundred and fifty miles!

Curiously, at the very time *Endeavour* was sailing west around the cape, she passed the track of the Frenchman Jean de Surville, who was sailing east. Storms kept the ships from sighting each other, though conditions might have turned even more blustery had the rivals met. However, de Surville was in bad shape, with sixty men dead and the rest of his crew so weak with scurvy they could barely handle the boats. Whereas Cook had not one man sick, apart from Lieutenant Hicks and Forby Sutherland, who had both developed consumption. Sutherland, especially, was coughing incessantly, bringing up traces of blood with his phlegm – and Isaac noticed he'd begun to lose weight . . .

Southwards *Endeavour* sailed for the first two weeks of 1770, charting the west coast. The land initially seemed more barren and flatter. Then they sighted the noble volcano *Taranaki* – Mount Egmont, Cook named it – the summit bleached with snow, even in summer.

A few days later *Endeavour* entered what appeared to be a wide, deep bay. Seeing a number of Maori fishing canoes, she steered for an inlet among the tree-covered hills on the southern shore, and hove to in a snug anchorage. *Meretoto* – blood of the fighting club, it was known to the Maori: Cannibal Bay to Cook's men.

It acquired the epithet within a day of their arrival.

The anchor had no sooner dropped, than several canoes came off a nearby island, *Motuara*, and circled the ship. A few stones were thrown; but after Tupaia spoke from the taffrail, their chief agreed to come aboard. He was an old white-haired man called Topaa, and although he didn't stay long he seemed pleased with his presents of paper and *tapa* cloth.

The Captain went ashore and, finding a stream of fresh water, good timber, a sandy beach, and plenty of fish in the nets, he decided to stay awhile: to repair and provision his ship, and to rest his crew before exploring more of the continent.

He could not have known it then, but Cook would return to this place on each of his three voyages to the Pacific. It became his favourite anchorage: a beautiful, sheltered sound of grey-green islands and inlets, like the lochs of Scotland. Every morning Isaac was woken by bellbirds, *korimako*, their silver voices chiming across the water. Nature seeming at her most peaceful and benign . . .

Endeavour was hauled into the shallows and careened: her bottom scrubbed of barnacles and weed, and painted with pitch. With other crew gathering wood, water and celery grass, Cook and the gentlemen went off in the pinnace to visit a nearby cove. They hadn't gone far when they saw a woman's body floating in the water.

'She's been dead for several days,' remarked Dr Solander.

'Drowned, I'd say,' agreed surgeon Monkhouse. 'I see no other wounds on her.'

They left the corpse and rowed ashore, where a fire was burning and a Maori family were preparing their meal. The people ran into the woods as the pinnace beached; but Tupaia called, and all except a boy and an old man crept back to the camp.

A small South Sea dog was cooking in the earth oven, with food baskets close by. Casually looking into one of them, Mr Banks was astonished to find, among the fish and fern roots, two meat bones that were clearly a human arm – both roasted and the flesh picked pretty clean.

'What are these?' he exclaimed, through Tupaia.

'A man.'

'You've eaten him?'

'Yes. Strangers from across the bay paddled by some days ago. We killed five, but two got away and drowned.'

'We saw a dead woman floating off shore.'

'No, not her. She was our relative, who died.'

'Why didn't you eat her?'

'We don't eat friends! Only enemies. It's the worst insult we can give them.'

News of this grisly discovery caused horror when it was narrated on the mess deck – and also fascination, especially among the boys.

'Why can't we see a cannibal feast?' complained Nick.

He was not denied for long.

Next morning, old Topaa came alongside. He was still in good humour; and having heard of the *Pakeha's* interest in his people's dietary habits, had brought along the cooked forearm of one of those killed a few days before.

Isaac and Nick leaned over the rail with the others, eyes and mouths hanging loose, as Topaa gnawed the bone.

'That is a dreadful thing to do!' cried Tupaia, shocked at his fellow Polynesian. While human sacrifice occurred at Tahiti, the victims were not actually eaten. 'It's horrible!'

'No, no, it's very good!' And Topaa drew the arm through his mouth and smacked his lips at the morsel, as Isaac had sucked many a marrowbone.

'But that can't be a man! It's a dog,' Taiata teased.

'Don't be foolish, boy! Look!'

The old man handed the bone to a companion, held up his own forearm to the audience, and made a pantomime show of eating it.

'See. It's excellent eating. The soft upper arm muscles are best!'

Isaac felt ill. He'd heard enough. But it wasn't sufficient for Banks, whose acquisitive mind always wanted more.

'But how can we believe you?' he had Tupaia ask. 'Where are the heads?'

'I don't have any with me. Heads are precious.'

'We'd like to see them.'

'Very well. I will bring some heads to you.'

It was a few days before Topaa returned, for the cycle of death and revenge demanded constant vigilance. A woman in his canoe was cutting herself with shells and weeping for her husband, only recently consumed by enemies. And Topaa's people were alert, the *pa* on its rock in readiness, in case the clan from across the bay came seeking vengeance for the man whose bones he'd just been chewing.

Still, there came a morning when Topaa climbed aboard with a basket, from which he took four freshly dried heads and displayed them to the hypnotic gaze of *Endeavour*'s crew. Three were tattooed adults. The fourth was a boy, only Isaac's age, who'd been killed with a *patu* blow to his temple.

Isaac turned away at the sight of it, his mind beset with images of the fear this lad must have known before his death. Why such violence everywhere? Nick Young was much cooler, content to observe the way things are. So was the indefatigable Mr Banks, who no sooner saw the heads than he wanted to buy one.

'Look . . . *tapa* cloth . . . paper . . . iron nails . . .'

But Topaa was not interested. 'The heads are my treasures, and not for sale.'

Banks had Jim Roberts fetch some clothes.

'I will give you a flannel vest . . . silk stockings . . . my second-best waistcoat . . .'

Topaa was unmoved.

'I do not want these things . . . but what is that?'

'A pair of my white linen under-drawers.'

'What do you do with them?'

'I wear them beneath my breeches, next to the skin.'

'I will exchange the boy's head for your under-drawers.'

'His skull is broken from the *patu* blow.'

'That is why I will trade it – yes, or no?'

Mr Banks handed over his drawers. Even then, Topaa was reluctant to part with the skull, until it was clear he'd otherwise have to return the garment. So he went back to his *pa* the richer for possessing some English underwear. Joseph Banks had the boy's head carried to his cabin.

Isaac lay awake through the night, much troubled by the murdered lad whose head was preserved aboard *Endeavour* in a pickling jar among the thousands of fish, beetles, plants, animals and interesting rocks collected as so many scientific specimens.

Proof of cannibalism introduced a new element of tension among *Endeavour*'s crew. Some became quite jumpy. Mr Molineux, out fishing with his petty officers, fired on two canoes which appeared when he trespassed too close to *Motuara* – wounding several Maori, and perhaps even killing one man.

'I thought we *might* have been under attack,' the Master explained, not very convincingly.

But fears of dismemberment didn't inhibit other men's morbid curiosity, and Topaa's people willingly traded human bones for ribbons and beads, though Isaac declined a souvenir. Indeed, the *Iwi* were friendly and hospitable throughout *Endeavour*'s visit, and Cook made his own expeditions without any concerns for his personal safety.

It was on such a day that he climbed a tall hill with just one companion. And looking seawards, he saw what seemed to be a strait flowing from the eastern ocean to the west coast. Was the 'continent' of New Zealand, then, an island? The Captain looked again on this strait, which was to bear his name, from another mount a few days later. He built a stone cairn, containing some musket balls and lead pellets, to tell other Europeans he'd been there first.

To reinforce his credentials, Cook had the carpenter, John Satterley, make two posts carved with *Endeavour*'s name and the date. The first was set up with a Union Jack on the beach at the watering cove; the other, he took across to *Motuara*, and sought Topaa's permission to erect it on the highest point of the island.

The old *ariki* readily agreed and promised never to pull the sign down. In return for which, he and his senior men were given silver threepences struck with the king's head, and some iron spikes marked with the government's broad arrow.

They went up to the summit together for the ceremony. The signpost was erected; the flag raised; the adjacent lands claimed for King George; the sound named for Queen Charlotte; and their Majesties' health was drunk with a bottle of wine. The empty bottle was given to Topaa, who kept it as another treasure. And he confirmed what Captain Cook had begun to suspect.

'Yes, Toote, there are three *whenuas* – three lands. Two, on this side of the water, you can sail around in maybe four days.'

'What do you call them?' the Captain asked.

'The largest is *Te Wai Pounamu* . . . Greenstone Waters, for here the *Iwi* come to collect precious *pounamu* from the rivers to make adzes, axes, and adornments.'

'And the island over there?' Cook pointed across the strait.

'We call that *Te Ahi no Maui* . . . Maui's Fire . . . to honour the volcanoes.'

'I have heard Tupaia speak of Maui – the god who fished New Zealand from the sea with his magic fish hook.'

'That is so. The land on this side is sometimes called Maui's Canoe. There are many stories . . . Has the priest told you of our ancestor, Kupe?'

'Who brought the people in his great *waka* from the homeland.'

'The same. This sound, which you have named for your Queen *Harlotte*, was made by Kupe. He was chasing a giant octopus across the ocean and caught it in the strait here. He speared it. And as the octopus lay thrashing in its death throes, his tentacles made all these deep bays and inlets. The octopus is still here. See . . . those two little islands at the entrance are his eyes.'

Land and sea can be read in all kinds of ways. And those who claim to discover new countries are never the first to find them. The Polynesians were settling the Pacific when Englishmen were still shore-bound in wicker coracles. Tasman came to New Zealand before Cook. And before that . . . Topaa hinted at Portuguese or Spanish ships whose crews had perished in this very sound.

Unseasonable weather kept *Endeavour* harboured longer than Cook intended. It wasn't until 5 February that they warped into the strait, and ran eastward to the Pacific Ocean. The Captain was content that New Zealand was indeed several islands, but his officers demurred.

'The continent *might* extend south-east, suh, from that point we named Cape Turnagain,' observed Lieutenant Gore.

'But I estimate it's only forty leagues to our north,' replied Cook.

'It *is* possible, sir,' Zachary Hicks added his objection.

'Very well, gentlemen. Never let it be said I failed to resolve such an important question. We'll take advantage of a shift in the wind and set our course northward, if you please.'

Two days later they saw a familiar landmark.

'Cape Turnagain,' said the Captain on his quarterdeck, viewing the land through his spyglass. 'Are you satisfied gentlemen?'

'Aye, sir. We are.'

Having thus circumnavigated the north island, the ship bore about; and passing the entrance to Cook Strait again, they headed south to explore the island of which Topaa had spoken. But the Captain had misunderstood him, because it took much longer than four days to sail around it. In fact they were at sea for three weeks, and still the eastern seaboard extended off the starboard bow.

The country here lifted into high mountains topped with snow; and judging by the fewer smokes seen ashore, it seemed to Issac less populated than the warmer north. The coast was broken into many bays, but they made no landings. And however careful the Captain was with his charting, some things he mistook altogether. An 'island' he named after Joseph Banks turned out to be a peninsula – as a 'promontory' was later discovered to be an island. While Cook got the longitude of North Cape almost exact, he was nearly half a degree out in his reading of the south island.

But for this, the Captain and astronomer Green could not be entirely blamed. *Endeavour* was hit by gales that blew her from sight of land for days on end, and the observations needed to fix longitude were difficult enough at the best of times, let alone on a storm-blown deck.

If this was true for a master navigator like Cook, how much more so for a lad such as Isaac! He was becoming better at reading the sun with his sextant at midday to establish latitude. But longitude . . . that involved taking 'lunars' and understanding the great clock of the heavens. You had to measure the angle between the moon and sun by day, or between the moon and certain known stars at night. You then had to calculate what that angle would be if observed at the same time from Greenwich. The difference between the two gave your longitude east or west of the prime meridian.

The mathematics were horrible! Many a time did young Master Manley wish he'd taken more notice of his tutor in the schoolroom. To be sure, the Astronomer Royal had published tables to help until the end of 1769. After that, each calculation could take four hours to complete; and as he sat agonising over his logarithms in the mess, Isaac wondered if he'd ever understand them.

Some days he appeared to be just off the coast of South America – and on others, near Tahiti: but that may have been wishful thinking. At such times Isaac would unwrap Heimata's pearl and, holding it to the lantern, fancy he could see her face in its soft translucence – until Nick Young came and bumped his elbow, laughed, and told him to get on with his sums!

As it happened, the answer to the longitude problem had already been found. The Yorkshireman John Harrison had invented his chronometer: not much larger than a pocket watch, and able to keep almost perfect time, even in the roughest weather. You can take a reading anywhere on the globe and know exactly what the time is at Greenwich. Every hour's difference is fifteen degrees of longitude.

There was no chronometer on *Endeavour*, for the astronomers were still insisting on 'lunars'. Cook didn't have a chronometer until his next voyage – on *Resolution*. But its accuracy proved its worth to the world. 'Our trusty friend,' Cook called it. And so it became: the seaman's dearest companion. As for *Endeavour* . . . the wonder is not that Cook was slightly wrong about New Zealand's position, but that he was so very nearly correct.

The land continued to fall away southwards, and the few on board who still believed they'd found a continent – among whom was Mr Banks – took heart. They even celebrated a birthday by having Isaac serve them dog pie, a fair indication of how far their minds and stomachs had travelled since leaving Plymouth.

But then the coast trended west; and sailing wide to avoid dangerous rocks, *Endeavour* rounded the southern point of land and, as March gathered apace, turned her head to the north.

'It's the total demolition of my airy fabric called continent,' Joseph Banks admitted. 'New Zealand is undoubtedly two large islands.'

'I shouldn't be too dismayed.' The Captain, born the son of a farmhand, sought to console the gentleman he now counted as a friend. 'A continent might well exist: but if so, 'twould be so far south as to be near Antarctic regions and uninhabitable by mankind.'

Time was to prove him correct in this, too. For certainly the heavy south-west swell spoke of no great landmass nearby, and with favouring winds behind her *Endeavour* made steady progress up the west coast. But this very fact led to some strain in the friendship between Cook and Banks.

Huge alpine peaks rose from the sea, covered with snow and glaciers, carving the land into fiords, like Norway.

'So wild and romantic!' exclaimed Sydney Parkinson, drawing pencil in hand. His mentor, Joseph Banks, agreed, and desperately wanted to sail into one of these fiords to explore for minerals. The Captain refused.

'I understand your desire, Mr Banks. Yet once into such land-locked sounds, the prevailing southerlies could take us a month to get out again.'

'I've put up five thousand pounds to pay for this expedition.'

'That's so. And it's my duty to get you safe home again.'

'Who knows what valuable discoveries we may be passing? I insist!'

'Nay sir, you may not insist. I am the Captain of this ship, and I will decide.'

'But . . .'

'We will continue our present course.'

For the Captain's mind was beginning to turn to other objectives, which he was not quite ready to reveal. And he could not countenance another month's delay.

Even so, it took a fortnight of foul winds and fog before the ship passed through the western entrance of Cook Strait again to complete her circumnavigation of the south island. They didn't return to Cannibal Bay, but anchored outside the Sound not far from what Tasman had graphically called 'Murderer's Bay' on his chart. With *Endeavour*'s crew ashore, to wood and water, and gather greenstuff, the Captain called his officers into the Great Cabin, Isaac pouring the wine, to discuss the matter that exercised his thought.

'We've been away from England for more than eighteen months, gentlemen, and I believe the principal aims of this voyage have been accomplished. It's time to think about heading for home. The question is, by which route?'

'What are your views, sir?' asked Zachary Hicks. His own consumptive coughing was becoming rather worse, and he was in no hurry to return to cold, clammy England.

'Well, my preference would be to return across the Pacific to Cape Horn at a high latitude, to see if a continent really does exist further to the south.'

'But we're heading into winter,' said Molineux. '*Endeavour* is a tough little ship, but her sails and timbers are in no condition to withstand such a stormy passage at this time of year.'

'Quite so, Robert. That is our problem.'

'The simplest thing would be to sail south below Van Diemen's Land,' said Lieutenant Gore, 'and make directly for Africa and the Cape of Good Hope.'

'The same objections apply,' Molineux reminded them. 'Besides, the Dutch and Portuguese have explored those waters, and we can make no new discoveries there.'

'Whereas if we were to head west,' added Cook, 'we must eventually fall in with the east coast of New Holland.'

'The other coasts of that country have largely been mapped,' remarked Hicks, his enthusiasm beginning to rise. 'But the eastern coast is a still an empty gap on our charts. No European's been there, so far as I know, since Tasman.'

'Such a course would enable us to fill in that blank space,' said Cook. 'Not a great discovery, I know, but of some service to navigation and human knowledge.'

'We could follow the coastline north as far as it goes – perhaps even to New Guinea,' observed John Gore with some excitement. 'And return to England by way of the Dutch East Indies.'

'Precisely. My own thinking, exactly.'

So it was agreed. Mr Banks was happy again. On the last day of March 1770, *Endeavour* weighed anchor and turned westward. Isaac climbed the shrouds with Nick and Taiata, the boys staring at the green shores of New Zealand until Cape Farewell vanished into the haze.

They had known terror from the warlike Maori, but at least it had become a familiar fear. Now before them lay the empty sea once more, another void in the map, and whatever dangers the unseen coast of New Holland might bring . . .

9

NEW HOLLAND

To Cape Tribulation, April to June 1770

For eighteen days the ocean lured *Endeavour* westward. Days of brisk winds astern that tore her spritsail into rags fit only for patches, even as they drove the ship forward to the mysterious shores of New Holland. Days of calm and humid heat, when tropic birds were seen and Isaac fancied himself nearing Matavai Bay again – and Heimata.

He'd take her pearl from the bag and caress it in his palm: cool and soothing, and not just a distraction from his struggles with lunars and longitude. For as they sailed further into unmapped seas, everyone's apprehensions rose again. Unspoken, for the most part, but *there*. Like all of them, Isaac turned to the familiar and the loved for resolution to face uncertainty. Thus Heimata, transfigured in the pearl, became not only remembered joy but present strength as well.

When clouds tower like mountains, storms threaten.

And so they did. As *Endeavour* beat under close-reefed topsails, nobody knew when a hazardous coast might suddenly rise out of the wild, expectant deep and dash them asunder. One evening, when the ship was beating against the tempest, Isaac sought to hearten himself by whistling as he tottered with a chamber pot below.

'Stop that!'

A sudden silence descended on the mess deck. Every man ceased what he was doing and tried to touch a piece of cold metal – a nail, a tin plate, a knife – and then turned to stare at Isaac, confused and reddening by the companionway.

'Why? What have I done?'

'Don't you know what dreadful fings can 'appen when you whistle in a storm?' said old Jack Ravenhill at last. 'You be tauntin' the winds, boy, makin' 'em even angrier.'

'Besides,' said Boatswain Gathrey, 'crew couldn't hear me pipe orders with your whistle.'

'Go up on deck and turn around three times,' Ravenhill added. 'Don't cut your fingernails for a month. And never do it ag'in. Whistling! Wiv a unknown coast nigh upon us.'

As indeed it was. Petrels and gannets were sheeting the wind, and a small land bird got caught in the rigging. Captain Cook ordered the leadsmen to take soundings every few hours. No bottom at one hundred and thirty fathoms. He was approaching the longitude where Tasman had left the south-east corner of New Holland in 1642; and even allowing for errors in judging the log-line, sea currents, and old-fashioned methods of 'dead reckoning' sailing distance, he couldn't be far out!

Nor was he. At six o'clock in the dawn of 19 April, Zachary Hicks had charge of the morning watch when, through his telescope, the Second Lieutenant saw a faint smudge on the horizon. Grey on grey, like a thumbprint smeared on glass.

'Land! Land ahoy!'

'Where away, Mr Hicks?'

'Three points off the starboard bow.'

'Helmsman, set your course!'

'Aye, aye sir!'

Putting on all sail, *Endeavour* steered towards it, running before the blustering wind on a swollen sea. The landfall turned to smoky blue by daylight; and as it assumed form and substance to the watching crew, their hearts responded. Any dire consequences of Isaac's whistling seemed averted. For here was a coastline – something tangible – with which practical seamen could deal and navigators trace on paper. Their phantom fears began to evaporate like a sea mist, though the constant need to watch for hidden dangers remained real enough.

The land trended from nor'-east to sou'-west, the furthest point of which the Captain named after Lieutenant Hicks. Beyond that was still a gap on the chart. Cook had hoped to fall in with that part of the coast where Tasman had left it; but the southerly gales forced him further north, and he had to follow that course from Point Hicks. What happened between that and Van Diemen's Land, could be left for future navigators to determine: and it was not until 1798 that Bass and Flinders proved that Tasmania, as it's now called, is separated from the mainland by a strait.

Day by day, *Endeavour* pitched her lonely way up the seaboard, as close inshore as she safely could to let New Holland begin to reveal its secrets. Isaac stood with his pencil among the young gentlemen sketching the features of a coast that, so far as they knew, no other European had seen. Stretches of white sand, and high cliffs; patches of green, like lawn; and tree-covered slopes rising to dusky hills . . .

Mount Dromedary, humped like a camel . . . Pigeon House with its lofty square peak . . . Prosaic enough names the Captain gave them: but important as landmarks for future sailors, and as reference points for the officers who took their bearings from them using the principles of triangulation – and which, with his elegant brass station pointer, ivory scale of sines, and mahogany parallel rule, the Captain translated into the first spider lines on his chart.

'You'll be doing that thyself one day,' said Molineux to his servant. 'You've a nice enough hand at drawing, Mr Manley, but your trigonometry's woeful yet.'

Isaac was too well aware of it. But how could Euclid compete with the exciting prospect of this new country? Smoke rolled from the hinterland and out to sea, carrying the spice of distant dreamings. People were seen walking along a beach: skin dark and naked in the spyglass. But all attempts to land were thwarted by rocky shores and pummelling surf.

It wasn't until Sunday 29 April, that sunrise found *Endeavour* standing off the opening to a large bay into which Cook decided to sail for wood and water, and first meetings with the native inhabitants. The pinnace was lowered for the Master and Mates to sound the entrance and, as recompense for his chiding, Molineux let Isaac come too: for it was the seafarer's tradition to pass knowledge by example from one generation to the next.

'I know you want to be a seaman, not a mathematician,' he said. 'Though ye're finding the one also needs the other.'

''Specially if he fancies himself officer material, look you,' added Francis Wilkinson: a familiar joke, but it showed the boy's measure of acceptance.

A clear, southerly swell carried them through the headlands. The leadsman at the bow cast the heavy lead plummet on its line well ahead with an underarm throw. As the pinnace came abreast the lead found the bottom, with the fathom depths identified by different pieces of leather and coloured cloth tied to the line.

'By the mark seventeen!'

The lead was hauled in, wax on its underside showing if the bottom was sand or shale, and cast forward again.

'Deep twelve!' An estimate, where there was no mark on the line. It required skill and experience; and as the channel revealed itself, empty casks on lines and sinkers were hove as marker buoys to show *Endeavour* the way in.

A group of Aborigines watched the boat from a hill, and as it rounded the point Isaac saw two bark canoes by the beach. The men were armed with spears and what seemed curved wooden scimitars, burnished bright as steel.

He wondered how they'd respond to strangers? But the men neither paddled out to welcome them as at Tahiti, nor to attack as the Maori had done. They just looked on with curiosity. Some people fishing inshore from small canoes barely showed interest, but continued without seeming to notice the pinnace.

Only when the boat approached a cove did two men come to a rock ledge for closer inspection. Both were black bushy bearded and bare as Adam, a thin bone through their noses, their thighs and chests painted with white ochre stripes, like garters or a soldier's crossed belt. They beckoned – but whether with friendly or hostile intent Mr Molineux didn't know, and he wisely returned to the ship.

By noon, *Endeavour* was anchored offshore in a comfortable six fathoms. After dinner, the Captain and a good third of the ship's company went ashore, but following the morning's expedition Molineux told Isaac to stay aboard. 'Give others a chance.' Yet at the last, Isaac sneaked into the stern of the longboat. The opportunity to be among the first Europeans to land on this coast was not to be missed!

A family group was watching from the cove: but as the boats approached, the women, children and all but two men disappeared among the trees. These warriors, armed with spears and throwing sticks – *woomeras* – came down to the sandstone ledge and shouted to the strangers, '*Warra! Warra wai!*' Go away! Go far away!

Neither Tupaia nor Taiata understood what these Gweagal men were saying, for their language was not of Polynesian stock. Nevertheless, the Captain told his men to lay on their oars awhile, as he tried to establish some dialogue and avoid the bloody mistakes of his first encounters with the Maori at Poverty Bay.

He tossed some nails and beads onto the rock. The men picked them up and seemed not displeased with the gifts. They even appeared to beckon again. Cook ordered the boats closer in. At once the warriors took up threatening postures – and this time there could be no doubt they intended to oppose a landing.

Cook raised his musket and fired between them, hoping to establish the power of his weapons without causing injury. Thus was the first shot heard on the tremulous air of *Gamay*: Botany Bay. It had no other effect than to make the Aborigines retire a little to pick up more spears.

The elder of the two hurled a rock at the pinnace, where the Captain waited. Cook fired again, hitting the warrior on the legs with small shot. He was forty yards away, however, and suffered no great hurt. Indeed, the two calmly retreated briefly to some bark shelters – *gunyas* – in the treeline.

The Captain took advantage of the lull to make his landing. The boats pulled to the sandstone outcrop, worn to a flat, pooled stage by the tides. Instead of being the first to step ashore, Cook gave that honour to his wife's cousin, another Isaac – Isaac Smith, who at only eighteen was proving a valuable assistant at the map table. He'd just been promoted, in fact, from Able Seaman to Midshipman.

'You shall go first, Isaac,' the Captain said. And Cook followed after him.

They had no time then to reflect further on the significance of the occasion. *Endeavour*'s men no sooner landed on the rock, than the warriors returned, the elder with a wooden shield, painted white, with two eyeholes.

Warra! Warra wai!

And he threw a spear at the strangers with his *woomera*.

The younger threw a second spear, which landed harmlessly enough between the startled feet of Sydney Parkinson, for the Gweagal also knew how to demonstrate their weapons without intending to kill.

Cook fired a third round of small shot – after which the Aborigines turned their backs and walked into the bush, calling on their families to make themselves scarce.

Isaac Manley, watching from the stern sheets, could only admire the calm bravery of these men in confronting three boat-loads of strangers who must have appeared utterly alien, and who outnumbered them at least fifteen to one.

'They seem so casual we could capture one if we chose,' said Cook.

But Mr Banks urged caution.

'There is some resinous substance on the spear tips which Dr Solander thinks might be a poison. We may be in danger should they attack us *en masse*.'

So the Captain did not go in pursuit of the warriors. Instead he went to the *gunyas* – but found only four or five little children huddled there. And as the bush echoed with the cries of their unseen parents, Cook let them be, leaving a few strings of beads to show he meant no harm.

His party did, however, take all the spears found at the camp – about fifty of them, many were pronged fishing harpoons tipped with stingray spines. The Captain saw their removal as a sensible precaution: but why the natives should interpret stealing their means of livelihood as a friendly act, Cook could not have explained.

As it turned out, the spears were not poisonous – though Robert Molineux *was* with his young servant, when the boats returned to *Endeavour*. The Master was waiting amidships.

'I told you to stay aboard,' he roared as Isaac climbed the ladder, 'and thou's disobeyed me!'

'I only wanted . . .'

'A ship could be lost if every man followed his own wants. Orders are not to be flouted, young man, and you *will* learn discipline. Go aloft now – and stand in the rigging till I tell thee to come down.'

'But I haven't had supper.'

'Be damned! You can stay up there all night. And be thankful I don't get Mr Pickersgill to beat thy backside with his cane.'

So Isaac was forced to climb the mainmast shrouds, clinging like a marmoset, exposed to the gaze and taunts of his shipmates . . .

'Ahoy Issy! Be ye bird watchin'?'

Evening fell, and Isaac's hunger was assailed by cooking smells from below and the native fires ashore. The ship settled to silence, broken only by the half-hour bells and murmurs of the watch. Isaac himself dared not sleep, lest he slip and plunge to the sea.

He fought to stay alert, listening to the harsh cries of night birds calling from the dark land. A heavy dew descended, wetting his clothes and freezing his hands. The boy grew colder and more miserable. His legs ached, and his mind was numb. He tried to cheer himself with thoughts of Heimata . . . but they made him even more aware of his predicament. And any whistling, of course, was forbidden.

Only when the Master came on deck for the morning watch, did he let Isaac descend stiffly from the rigging, and snatch a few hours' sleep in his hammock.

'I hope you've had time to think upon the need to obey orders in future.'

Even then, the boy was not allowed to land again for several days, and his curiosity had to be satisfied by listening to those who were.

When the crew went back on shore, the beads had been left undisturbed in the *gunya* where Cook had put them. A group of Aborigines silently watched the men filling water casks at a small stream. At midday, with the crew aboard ship again for dinner, they approached the barrels on the beach, but did not touch them. Afterwards, when Mr Hicks tried to entice a few men with presents, they desired nothing he offered them.

'They want us only to be gone,' he said. And this set the pattern for the eight days *Endeavour* remained.

Gifts of cloth, nails and trinkets were untouched. When a Midshipman offered a parrot he'd shot to a family he met in the bush, they refused it. The Captain several times tried to speak to the people, but they always moved away. When Lieutenant Gore walked with a companion from the head of the bay to the watering cove, they were followed at a distance by several warriors: but they did not try to attack.

There was little overt hostility – although a native boy, hiding in a tree, once threw a spear at Dr Monkhouse, which missed. For the most part, the Aboriginal family groups moving around the bay just ignored the Europeans. They went on gathering oysters and mussels, or fishing from their simple bark canoes – the ends tied together, kept athwart by sticks – as if these white strangers were not even there.

This reaction was quite different to anything the voyagers had met from other natives. Joseph Banks considered them timid and cowardly, but the first landing showed they didn't lack courage. The Aborigines may have seen the intruders as pale clayed spirits of the dead, best left alone. Perhaps they were just being prudent. Whatever the motives, there could be no doubting their meaning: 'They want us only to be gone.'

Yet *Endeavour* could not go immediately. For one thing, the botanists were vastly excited collecting specimens of trees and shrubs unlike anything they'd seen before. Trees such as Tasman described, oozing thick gum and pungent eucalyptus: dull lozenge leaves rattling, and bark peeling like flayed skin. Bright bottlebrush flowers on spiky plants that were to bear Banks's name. So many new species that Sydney Parkinson laboured through the daylight to capture their colours before they faded and the plants were dried.

Footprints of strange animals were seen. Something like a dog . . . another that seemed to be as large as a grazing deer. None were actually found, although iris-hued parrots, lorikeets and cockatoos winging their way through the bush, were shot down to be painted, classified and stored below.

The ship also had to be replenished: wood and water brought aboard, and fresh food. Fortunately the bay abounded in it. One drag of the seine on the northern shore netted three hundred pounds of fish. Mr Gore caught a stingray that weighed over two hundred and forty pounds – and next day another two that together weighed six hundred pounds. More than enough for everybody.

In fact for months the Captain called the place Stingray Harbour on his chart – until he changed it to Botanist Harbour, and finally to Botany Bay, in honour of the plants collected there.

It was fortunate, too, that almost everyone was in good health. Zachary Hicks still had trouble breathing the cold night air, and Tupaia complained of sore gums: an early sign of scurvy, which Banks treated with lemon concentrate.

But Forby Sutherland was the only seaman really sick. He'd come down with a consumption at Cape Horn, and had been languishing for months. Now, at Stingray Harbour, he lay in his hammock, life ebbing away. The Orkney sailor, once so bonny as he bawled at Isaac that first day he came aboard, had shrunk gaunt and hollow in the canvas that enclosed him like a shroud already.

Forby had encouraged the boy aloft at sea, had rescued him adrift on the streets of Rio. Now, Isaac held the basin as the man retched and spat blood. Brought water to soothe his gasping lungs, and spooned warm gruel into his mouth.

'It will do you good, Forby.'

'Nae, laddie. Nae good at all. I'm done for.'

And Isaac grieved more than most when Forby was found dead on May Day morning, and helped stitch him into his hammock for a last sleep. Mr Molineux let the lad go ashore with the funeral party, for he knew the two were close, and understood the need sometimes to ease the reins of discipline.

A grave had been dug in the sandy soil not far from the freshwater stream. They laid Forby in it, the first European to be buried on this coast, which the Captain acknowledged by calling the head of the cove Point Sutherland.

His name is still remembered in the Shire of Sutherland – though no one aboard *Endeavour* could have guessed the great city of

Sydney would one day grow and spread over this land from a convict settlement planted eighteen years later at Port Jackson.

'The finest harbour in the world,' Governor Phillip called it when he arrived with the First Fleet in 1788: though curiously Cook never saw it. Not long before *Endeavour* left Botany Bay he went walking on the heath across the cliff tops, but not far enough to sight the sparkling harbour. While he spied the entrance as they sailed north – marked and named it on his chart, reckoning it would give safe anchorage – he didn't go through the heads. And Isaac always felt the Captain would have regretted that, had he known.

Regretted, too, what befell the Aborigines who faced them that first day with shield and fighting spear on the sandstone littoral. Within decades of European settlement, the Gweagal had almost disappeared from the shores of Gamay. Drink, and disease, and the power of the white man's weapons saw to their destruction. It was much the same story everywhere *Endeavour* went, and the ships that followed her across the South Seas. And they *were* brave men.

Warra! Warra wai!

Northwards *Endeavour* men sailed through May, towards nightmare visions of their own destruction. Northwards, as day by day the outline of the land was fished from the sea: caught in their nets of compass bearings and mapping grids, tagged with names that still fringe the charts . . .

Port Stephens – named for the secretary of the Admiralty, a friend of Isaac's father . . . Cape Byron and Mount Warning where New Holland swings nor'-nor'-west, as if on a needle point. Moreton Bay . . . the jutting promontory of Sandy Cape, where they found shoal water – and not long after that, the first of the coral reefs.

Now, in tropical seas, the boats were out all day sounding a passage for the ship through a maze of shallows and coral outcrops hidden just below the surface. Leadsmen cast from the 'chains' – the channel platforms which secured the rigging on either side of *Endeavour*'s bow – and the sweating air rang with their calls . . .

By the mark thirteen!

Deep nine!

At night they usually anchored safely offshore. Sometimes they sought refuge in sheltered bays – but mosquitoes, mangrove swamps, and lack of fresh water made them inhospitable places to stay.

Heat, and the slow-going strain of feeling their way along the coast, began to tell on men's nerves – sailors and officers alike. Isaac noticed they drank more heavily, became more quarrelsome, jostled to assert themselves in cramped, confined spaces. And at a place called Bustard Bay, named for a bird that Mr Banks shot and had cooked into a pie, animosities erupted in an act of violence that threatened the Captain's authority.

His clerk, Richard Orton, had been drinking all evening in the Midshipmen's quarters below the foredeck. He was a rather vain young man, and a fractious drunk. The drunker he got, the more he argued with his companions – especially the American, James Magra, and his mate Patrick Saunders. Midshipman Magra had once cut the clothes off Orton's back in their drunken frolics, and had been heard boozily to say that he'd murder Dick Orton – 'if Ah weren't afeared of hangin' fer it.'

Awake in their hammocks, Isaac and Nick were distantly aware of them quarrelling again in the forecastle. Eight bells had sounded and the middle watch gone on deck, before the lads heard Orton stumbling down the companionway and into his cabin aft to sleep off the grog.

But oh! the shrieks next morning when Orton woke to find not only had his clothes been cut off again, but that someone had also sliced into both his ears. Blood had spurted from the lobes and down his neck, staining the blanket. Half-conscious with pain and a hangover, this time Orton thought he really had been murdered.

The Captain was furious when he heard about it.

'Mr Orton is not a man without his faults!' he exclaimed, 'and his injuries are more apparent than real. But this breach of discipline is a direct challenge to me as commander of this ship. It could undermine our whole expedition!'

Cook had the Master bring in the men, and he questioned them closely. But apart from Orton's accusations, he obtained no admissions from either Magra or Saunders. He suspected their involvement, but in justice this wasn't enough to press charges. Still, the Captain took advantage of their acknowledged drunkenness to demote them: Saunders was disrated from Midshipman back to Able Seaman, and Magra was denied the quarterdeck for three weeks: suspended from any duty aboard.

'He's one of those young gentlemen frequently found on board the King's ships that can well be spared,' Cook raged into his journal. 'Or to speak plainer, good for nothing.'

And the matter brooded on his mind for months.

Certainly, whenever Isaac thought of his own humiliation at being made to stand in the shrouds at Stingray Harbour, he knew how much worse his punishment might have been. Not that he could have been demoted lower than a ship's servant: but all hopes of his further advancement in the navy might have been blocked for ever.

So he made himself as useful as possible to the Master: being on hand whenever wanted, and applying himself by study and practice to better understand the principles of navigation. Molineux saw, and approved, and once again shared with the boy the knowledge of his own seamanship. He even had Isaac in the boats to help with the sounding, for it was strenuous and time-consuming work as *Endeavour* threaded her way ever northward among the shoals . . .

Across the Tropic of Capricorn and into June . . . past the lovely islands they discovered on Whitsunday rising from the deceptive sea . . . Magnetic Island, where the compasses acted very strangely . . .

'See here, boy,' Molineux pointed it out to Isaac. 'We know there's always a difference between true north and magnetic north, because the earth or even a metal object nearby can cause the compass to deviate from magnetic north. How do we correct for it?'

'By reading the sun or moon with the azimuth compass.'

'Quite true. Look at this . . . the sea compass is swinging all over the place like a cock on a weathervane. Yon island must be a veritable magnet.'

Isaac saw smoke from the land, where the Aborigines still mostly ignored them . . . and to seaward, a small green atoll – the first true coral island he'd seen off New Holland.

Ever northward. Ever more dangerous. All unbeknown, *Endeavour* had entered that zone where the Barrier Reef narrows towards the coast, squeezing the ship into a tapering funnel between the land and the perils of the coral.

From a height it is easy enough to see the reliable, ultramarine blue of the deepwater channel weaving between the coward yellow shoals. But from the surface – even from a masthead – the ever-changing sea, like a chameleon, is glassy and deceitful, reflecting the shadows of passing clouds as well as sunken rocks. The wonder is the ship had sailed as far as she had without disaster. But that was due to the fine judgement of her Captain and the skill of his crew.

Until Monday 11 June, when they were abreast a point on the mainland that Cook was to name Cape Tribulation, 'Because here began all our troubles.'

That night, *Endeavour* struck the reef.

10

AGROUND!

Endeavour Reef, June 1770

It was just before eleven o'clock, and the ship was burdened with sleep: the Captain yawning over his journal notes, Mr Banks undressing for bed. The mess deck was already snoring, though the wind still carried the leadsman's chant to the furthermost corners of sailors' dreams.

Deep twenty!

On deck, the watch looked out to a calm, moon-shimmering sea. Thoughts turned to their own hammocks at the end of the next hour. For Mr Cook had decided to sail through the night. He meant to anchor at sunset: yet *Endeavour* had found deep water, and as the evening shone clear he thought there could be no danger.

By the mark seventeen!

But before the lead could make another cast, there was a hideous jolting and scraping. The ship convulsed. Her masts jerked in a whiplash. The wheel spun in the helmsman's hands. Men and boys were flung off their feet and out of their slumber shouting, 'She's aground! We've hit the reef!'

'All hands on deck!'

The brass bell rang. Feet bounded up the companionways. The Captain rushed to the quarterdeck in his shirt and stockings.

'Bring in all sails! Lower the boats! Mr Molineux, you'll inspect the damage.'

'Aye sir.'

Hands were already climbing aloft. They knew without orders the need to stop the ship driving further onto the coral.

'Where's Mr Satterley?'

'Down in the hold to see what water we're taking.'

'Well done. And Master . . . when the boats are out, we'll strike topmasts and yards to ease the weight on t' ship.'

'Mr Pickersgill, you'll take the call.'

Mr Banks and the gentlemen appeared with a lantern: white of face, hair loose, and breeches unbuttoned.

'What's happened, Captain? Are we sinking?'

Cook at first seemed to take no notice.

'Mr Satterley,' as the carpenter's head appeared at the hatch, 'what's below?'

'Holding fast, sir, and taking little water at present.'

Cook turned to his passengers.

'Nay, Mr Banks, we are not sinking. Not yet. But you may get a few things ready in case we do. Oh, and Mr Banks . . .' as the botanist was about to go below.

'Captain?'

'No more lights on deck, if you please. They ruin our night vision as we work. Eyes get used to t' darkness.'

Isaac knew this was very true. Even without starlight the night was never really black, merely shades of grey on deeper grey, to which his eyes quickly adjusted. And tonight they had the moon.

'Mr Hicks!' The Captain gave his full attention to saving the ship. 'When the longboat is clear, we'll take out t' stream and coasting anchors. We may be able to heave her off – if not, they'll hold her until we can!'

'Aye, aye.'

Nick and Isaac shared the same terrors of shipwreck as Mr Banks. Beneath their feet they could hear coral grinding the timbers as *Endeavour* shuddered on the reef – and they all knew there wasn't enough room in the boats for everyone. Most would drown miles from shore, and become food for the sharks!

Isaac could feel panic welling deep inside. Was this the sea's revenge for his whistling in the storm those months ago? He dared not ask, for fear of shaming himself in front of others. So Isaac struggled to force it back. Everyone knew the dangers they faced: yet men in the rigging or at the boats worked with controlled determination, in which barely a seaman's curse was heard.

They took their cue from the Captain. And when Molineux passed on his way to the yawl, he stopped and said, 'Stand fast, lads. Don't give way to thy fancies.'

'I want to come with you,' Isaac murmured.

'Nay, not this time. We shall be working by moonshine, and need only experienced hands. There's more than enough to do on board. Attend to Mr Pickersgill and your duty.'

For all his disappointment, Isaac knew that Molineux was right. The topmen furling the sails, preparing to cast off the network of lines to lower the yards and masts – and as neatly made good, ready to raise them again – threaded their way aloft in the silvery shadows as deftly as spiders in gossamer. Much better for the boys to give their strength where it could do most good: at the end of a rope on deck.

Standby on halyards and lifts . . . haul away . . . ease away . . . come up, come up . . . belay, and make fast your lines!

Orders were given as necessary; but mostly men kept their voices low to hear news from elsewhere on the ship.

'What's to report, Mr Molineux?'

'We've hit the edge of the coral, sir. Deep water . . . eight to twelve fathom astern and to starboard . . . a mere few feet for'ard.'

'Damage to the hull?'

'A few broken planks – strakes – afloat . . . and part of the false keel.'

'So the main keel may be unharmed?'

'God willing, Captain.'

'To be sure, Mr Molineux.'

The ship had gone aground close to high tide. With three smaller anchors out, all available deckhands strained upon the capstan and windlass, trying to heave *Endeavour* off the reef.

Two . . . six . . . HEAVE bully boys . . . HEAVE away . . .

But to no avail. The ship was caught fast. Six hours . . . the tide was dropping as dawn approached; and with spars and masts stowed, Captain Cook gave orders to lighten the ship by all means possible.

'We'll try to refloat again at noon.'

They went down to the hold. Stone ballast and iron ingots were lifted through a hatch aft by the officers' cabins, and man-and-boy-handled to the stern ports and cast into the sea. Lads scurried to the stores, and anything not immediately required was likewise carried up and heaved overboard.

Decayed food, iron barrel hoops, oil jars . . . all went into the sea. Marines seized the capstan bars and, as if they were undertakers, lifted the six deck cannons and tipped them corpse-like into the deep. The gun carriages followed.

There was a moment when Isaac – everyone – feared they'd soon join them.

As the water receded, the coral rock was exposed. And with a sickening lurch, *Endeavour* heeled several degrees to starboard. She lay with her deck angled, three or four strakes further into the water, her topmasts down, as if she were a wreck already. Her crew could only cling to the hope that, if the ship did start to break up, the sea would stay quiet.

Please God! They'd have time to make rafts and paddle to two small islands – Hope Islands, the Captain named them – visible a few miles away in the morning sun. For everybody knew the boats could carry at most only one-third of their company.

The midday tide flooded in, covering the reef again. Higher it rose around the stranded ship – but not high enough. For all that they'd heaved fifty tons overboard, and every heart and sinew was striving on the cables, *Endeavour* remained trapped.

Isaac could hear more coral ripping as the ship ground and rasped upon it. More timbers floated to the surface. And as the tide receded, water began to flow greedily into the ship. She'd been holding well until now. But as the afternoon wore on, it took two pumps to keep her clear.

The two bower anchors were carried out by the longboat – the best bower to starboard, the other astern – and hove taut with block and tackle.

'The evening tide is usually higher,' the Captain observed to a worried Mr Banks. 'I've hopes the big anchors will bring us off.'

So did they all. For every seaman knew the ship could not withstand this much longer. It was a mercy the weather had been so kind these twenty-four hours. But when a wind blew up and the sea roughened . . .

Don't think about it and give way to thy fancies!

Men ate cold meat and biscuit and drank their grog, to keep up strength and spirits, as evening gathered and the tide began to turn . . . dark fingers of water feeling about *Endeavour's* hull. They found her weakness – and the sea gushed even more quickly through the breach, so that two pumps were no longer enough.

The Captain ordered hands to all four pumps – long, hollowed elm trees, worked with handle and plunger, that descended from the upper deck near the mainmast to the well in the deepest part of the hold. It was gruelling labour, especially as only three pumps would work . . . and even more especially when, at nine o'clock in the darkness, *Endeavour* suddenly righted herself with a stagger, and the predatory waves – as if sensing another victim – rushed further in.

'The water is gaining on us, Captain!' the carpenter reported, coming up from the hold. Everyone knew what danger that posed to the ship when they got afloat. Still they held fast, conscious that Mr Cook had only one option when he replied, 'Thank you, Mr Satterley. But we must risk all, and try to heave her off if we can.'

The flood tide swelled. As many hands as possible went to the windlass and capstan, their turn at the pumps taken by the gentlemen. In this emergency there was no place for idlers and supernumeraries: all were souls in peril on the deep.

HEAVE bullies . . . HEAVE away for your lives . . .

And not long after ten o'clock, with a sighing, wrenching sound, *Endeavour* finally floated free. Quickly she was hauled astern, the boats out ready to bring up the stream anchor and make her fast in deep water for the night.

Cracked, exhausted voices cheered their release. At last, there really was a chance they might reach Hope Islands!

But elation didn't last long. Once afloat, the leak increased as feared, and every hand aboard took his turn at the pumps – the boys, the Captain and Mr Banks included – working in fifteen-minute spells. Muscles stretched and ached . . . and as the black water was sucked up from the bilge and spilled across the deck, all felt they must surely be making some progress!

Mr Satterley reported the water measured three feet nine inches in the hold. Shortly afterwards, however, the Carpenter's Mate came up to say he'd taken another reading, and the sea had gained a further eighteen inches.

Their chances of survival seemed lost. Only room in the boats for a few . . . and even they would be marooned as castaways on a barren coast. Better, perhaps, to drown quickly and plunge with the ship to Davy Jones!

Isaac knew a servant boy would be the last to be saved. And into his mind came the picture in his mother's locket, and remembrance of Heimata's shining pearl.

Yet the bonds of that naval discipline Mr Molineux sought to instil stayed firm. Whatever their private alarms, men didn't yield to them, but redirected their minds to the pump handles and the release of physical exertion.

Don't give way to thy fancies!

Indeed not. For Mr Satterley went down to the hold again. Remeasured the depth. And returned to the quarterdeck saying, 'Captain, there has been a mistake. I measured from the floor of the hold, the Mate from the outside plank of the hull – eighteen inches lower. We are keeping the water steady.'

The lightning words, as they flashed through the ship, worked like a charm. They might all live! Every man jack redoubled his efforts at the pumps to stay afloat until dawn.

Daylight brought more hope. Midshipman Jonathan Monkhouse, the surgeon's younger brother, had once sailed on a merchantman that sprang a leak crossing the Atlantic. The ship was saved by 'fothering' her with a sail, slung beneath the keel like a tourniquet, where water suction forced the canvas into the hole. It stopped the inflow, and was held in place by the pressure of the sea.

'We completed our voyage safely, Captain.'

'You remember how this was done, Mr Monkhouse?'

'I believe so.'

'And you think it will help us?'

'I see no reason why not. The breach cannot be so great, or the pumps wouldn't be holding the water.'

'Very well, Mr Monkhouse. I place you in charge of the operation.'

So, while some hands were raising the foretopmast and yard, and others lifting the bower anchors, Jon Monkhouse got a lower studdingsail ('*stu'n's'l,* matey') ready to fother the ship. Onto the canvas, sailmakers stitched handfuls of frayed old rope, teased out into what sailors called 'junk' and mainly used to caulk the ship's timbers. Wool and hair from the sheep and goat were also sewn onto the sail; and on top, the boys spread manure scooped from the pig pens.

It seemed *Endeavour* suffered the worst damage near her bows, below the starboard chains. When the studdingsail was ready, it was carried for'ard, weighted and carefully lowered over the bows on ropes into the sea. Once the sail's lower edge had slipped below the keel, men started to haul it aft. Hearts and eyes strained to see what would happen as the canvas slipped along the wooden hull . . .

Suddenly, a rush of water snatched the sail and dragged it into the leak. Scraps of wool and oakum junk were forced into the smaller gaps, the manure acting as a kind of caulking pitch. The main breach was stopped like a gag by the canvas – the studdingsail plugging the ship, even as it fothered Isaac's nightmares. And within minutes the flow into *Endeavour*'s hold was reduced to a runnel, with only one pump needed to keep her clear.

How Isaac's 'prentice soul soared! He'd been staring at death on the reef for twenty-four hours. Now, he'd not only been given back his life, but also offered the chance of salvation. At best, men had been hoping for an island where they might build a boat from *Endeavour*'s wreck to carry them to the East Indies. But with Jon Monkhouse's help, they had the prospect of repairing and sailing their ship all the way home. There wasn't one of them who did not offer silent thanks for deliverance.

Yes, and not so silent either when Mr Cook gave orders later that morning to make ready for sail. The anchors were hoisted – all except for the second bower, which stuck fast in the coral rock and had to be cut away. The forecourse was set. The longboat out sounding. And with a light breeze and a rousing crew behind her, *Endeavour* stood in for the mainland nine miles off her bows.

With the ship under way, the Master and Mates went ahead to find a suitable bay where she could be laid up. Acknowledging Isaac's own self-discipline during the crisis, Mr Molineux let him come in the pinnace to help with the buoys.

The lad revelled in the freedom and sweetness of it: scudding across the waves, the Hope Islands already behind him, wind in his hair, salt flecking his face, as the living sun danced on the water and played with the rollicking coastline.

They looked at one possible harbour, yet after only a few casts of the lead they realised it was too shallow for the ship to approach the shore. *Endeavour* anchored off for the night. The boats went on ahead, and a few miles further on found what they were looking for – an estuary, where a wide river emptied into the sea.

Sandbars partly shoaled the mouth, and high dunes stood watch on the northern shore. But the river had carved a channel to the ocean, and deep water ran along the south bank where *Endeavour* could berth. Beyond were mudflats, where mangroves and crocodiles basked – and where the ship might easily be hauled, careened, and her hull repaired.

Next morning *Endeavour* ran northward under a freshening wind to the entrance. Cook supervised sounding the narrow channel himself. Yet the wind blew up and the sea ran high – and for two days the ship stood off, not daring to risk foundering on the sandbanks within sight of safe harbour.

'Just imagine,' said Molineux, for once giving way to his own fancies, 'what would have happened had this weather struck when we were aground on the reef.'

And it was Isaac who durst not think about it.

It wasn't until Monday 18 June that the wind moderated and the ship made in for the river. Twice she got stuck on the sand: the first time floating free, the second having to be warped off at high tide. But that afternoon, she was safely brought alongside, and her anchors taken ashore.

Next day a stage was built from the deck to the riverbank, and they began unloading her. The four remaining guns were brought up from the hold and mounted on the quarterdeck. The stores and provisions, water casks, ballast, coal, spare anchors, gunpowder, the armourer's forge . . . all were carried ashore to a camp in the dry, browning grass.

Pens were built for the animals. Mr Banks had his tent erected. One was put up for supplies, and another for the sick. No one was seriously unwell – although Tupaia, Taiata, Mr Green and five or six others had symptoms of scurvy, which didn't improve until they got plentiful fresh food.

Once emptied, *Endeavour* was warped up river and dragged onto the mangrove flat, with only her stern in a few feet of water. So anxious was Cook to see the damage, he inspected her by lantern at the first low tide.

As thought, the main problem was at the starboard bow. Four planks were cut to the frame and another three badly damaged: all of them ripped by the coral as if with a saw.

'And see here,' Molineux showed Isaac the most remarkable thing next day. 'When the ship hit the reef, a lump of coral the size of my fist broke off and stuck in the hole. It slowed the water before we fothered her. Without that rock we would have been sunk – literally.'

Part of the false keel had gone; yet it had done its job and protected the main keel, which didn't appear seriously damaged. Some of the timber sheathing had been torn from the larboard bow – important because, studded with wrought iron nails, it helped keep the destructive teredo worm out of the timbers. It would have to be replaced.

'But all in all,' the Master said, 'we were lucky. It could have been worse.'

Endeavour was heeled over, and men were soon at work: carpenters repairing her strakes; armourers making nails, bolts and straps; hands mending her sails and rigging. The ship looked rather forlorn out of her element, as Sydney Parkinson drew her: beached high and pretty dry, like a mangrove pod washed up on the mud. And, just like a pod, she also carried the seed of her own regeneration. The starboard bow was finished in a few days. She was heeled the other way, and men started on her larboard. In little more than a week, *Endeavour* began to come alive again.

Her shattered timbers had been replaced as far as possible. Part of the false keel and some sheathing could not be repaired; but despite the risk of worm, Molineux and John Satterley told Cook all would be well. Empty water casks were lashed to the bows to help refloat her, but the low neap tides kept the ship stranded for a while longer. It wasn't until early July that the water rose high enough to bring *Endeavour* off and warp her down river. Even then, the Captain had her taken to a sandbar for another inspection. Reassured that the remaining damage was of little consequence, the ship was brought alongside the riverbank, ready for her topmasts and rigging.

Thus reinvigorated, *Endeavour* prepared to carry them home. If ever a ship lived up to her name, this one did.

When they were not wanted at the riverbank, the lads were free to explore the country. To climb a high grassy hill behind camp, and watch the onyx-coloured sea break upon reefs as far as their eyes could travel – and to wonder at the dangers still before them. To go hunting through the gum-scented bush, past termite hills taller than a man, the undergrowth kept clear by the fires lit by the Aborigines – their 'fire hunting'. Not that they saw any natives, though their smoke was always on the horizon, or caught much game.

Midshipman Magra, restored to his rank after the incident of Dick Orton's ears, saw something like a wolf.

Nick Young was frightened by a bat. 'Big as a gallon keg it were, and black as the devil wiv two horns on 'is head. Honest.'

Fifteen-year-old Isaac, puffing his pipe on deck, saw a crocodile swim past, innocent as driftwood on the tide. And late one afternoon he spied one of those strange grazing animals they'd glimpsed at Stingray Harbour. Sleek as a greyhound, but with a head like a hare, and mouse-coloured fur. As he approached, the creature rose on powerful back legs and, with heavy tail outstretched, began hopping away like . . . nothing Isaac had ever heard of.

The Captain and Mr Banks soon sighted another. Lieutenant Gore led several expeditions to shoot one. It was almost a month before he managed to do so, however, when the Guugu Yimithirr people said it was called *gangurru*. Kangaroo. Another word that entered the English language via *Endeavour*. And kangaroo tasted splendid.

It was as well that it did, for the land didn't yield them much else by way of sustenance. The berries and wild taro roots they found were bitter, and made some people sick. It was a fortnight before the seine netted enough fish to feed the whole company. And while edible greenstuff was picked, which mixed well with pease porridge, men began to wonder how they'd fare if forced to stay for any time.

Then they discovered the turtles.

In early July, Mr Molineux went out in the pinnace to seek a safe passage to the north. Isaac didn't go with him, as the Captain proposed he help the Midshipmen sound the river entrance and make a proper survey chart – for the lad's willingness had not gone unnoticed.

The Master returned with a boatload of large clams and news that he thought he'd found a way to the open ocean. Cook was sceptical. He'd been up the grassy hill too, and seen shoals stretching to the horizon. So he sent Molineux out again, and this time Isaac went with him.

'High time thee got used to spending long days in a short boat.'

The days were fine, skimming across an opaline sea. Night was dreadful: the boy unable to sleep comfortably on a sandy beach, and wrapped so tightly in his sea cloak against mosquitoes that he almost stifled. Morning and the cool breeze couldn't come too quickly!

It was soon clear that Molineux was wrong in his surmise. They followed his deepwater channel, but as the tide fell it revealed the parapets of yet another reef – with more to the north and east. There was no safe passage that way: and it was the same every other way they looked.

Returning on the afternoon of the second day, Molineux called at a reef ten miles offshore to gather more clams and shellfish for the ship's mess. At low tide the water turned to crystal; and peering over the bow Isaac could see pink and yellow corals, through which drifted fish the colour of topaz and garnets. It was as if nature had strewn the seabed with gemstones.

Strange, that a reef which caused such grief when they ran aground, should here reveal its treasure trove.

Suddenly, across a patch of sunlit underwater sand, he saw a shadow pass: round and reptilian and swimming slowly.

'Turtle!' Isaac cried. 'A green turtle!'

'Where is it, boyo?' Francis Wilkinson rose.

'Just for'ard here . . .'

'Steady there . . . steady on the oars.'

They'd already hauled down the sail approaching the reef, and the boat quickly pulled back.

'Do you see it . . . where I'm pointing?'

'Yes . . . and there's another, look you! And more feeding on the bottom. Turtles everywhere! Oh damme, the things you see when you've not got a harpoon.'

'Coxswain, the boathook,' ordered Robert Molineux. 'Lively now!' Sam Evans passed it to Wilkinson who, leaning out, lowered the long-handled iron hook tipped with a spike into the water and began stalking turtles.

The first one had disappeared among the coral, but another was on the sand, nibbling seagrass. Carefully, Francis came up behind it with the boathook poised like a lance. Ever so gently he drew level with its outstretched head, not letting his shadow frighten the animal.

Easy . . . easy . . . with a sudden lunge the man speared the point into the soft opening between the turtle's shoulder and shell. In as far as he could – and twist!

The startled creature jerked and struggled. A thin stream of blood stained the water, red now with rubies. The turtle tried to draw in its head, and its flippers beat, seeking to escape. Mr Wilkinson pushed with all his strength on the boathook shaft, keeping the turtle pinned to the sand. 'Quick there, mates! Into the water. Bring 'im up.'

Isaac leaped into the sequined sea. It barely came up to his midriff, sharp and cold. And reaching down with two others into the swirling sand, they grabbed the turtle by the carapace and hauled it fighting to the surface.

'Watch it, boyo . . . keep a grip . . .' as eager hands reached over the gunwale to drag their catch into the pinnace.

'It's a big 'un, look you. Near full grown, I'd reckon.'

'We'll feast tomorrow, mates!'

'There'll be hundreds more where that came from.'

Released from the iron point, the turtle tried to heave itself away. It was quickly dragged to the stern and turned on its back. After ten minutes of helpless kicking, the creature ceased to struggle and seemed to resign itself to its fate.

The bloody contest had disturbed the other turtles. Isaac and the men jumped back into the pinnace, to let sea and sand and the grazing prey settle down again, before they resumed the hunt. By late afternoon, they'd caught two more turtles, so that despite unwelcome news about the channel, the boat returned to *Endeavour* laden with fresh food.

Between them, the animals weighed nearly eight hundred pounds: enough to feast the whole ship's company for days on turtle meat – divided equally between every man and boy, as Cook always insisted. The meat was sweet and succulent as plump chicken. Juice and oil ran down chins and beards. And as they wiped greasy mouths and hands, and their bellies groaned, men no longer worried if they'd have enough to eat, were the ship forced to stay at the river for a whole year.

Hundreds of turtles! Isaac whistled on the riverbank with deepest satisfaction.

The Captain sent Mr Molineux back to the reef next day, properly equipped for the hunt. And there were many more expeditions after that.

11

THE BREADTH OF ONE WAVE

Endeavour River to Cape York, July to August 1770

On the day of the turtle feast, the Guugu Yimithirr people first appeared near *Endeavour*.

Crew had already started getting the ship ready for sea: rigging her, stowing ballast, hoisting the water barrels. Satiated by turtle meat, men were lethargically going about their afternoon labours, when seven or eight Aborigines were seen on the opposite bank. Two came onto the sand spit to stare more closely at the spectacle. Cook at once set out to talk to them: but as his boat approached, the natives disappeared – as the Gweagal had done at Botany Bay.

Next morning, however, four men – *bama* – came down with a hollow log canoe and out-rigger, like those seen in the islands. Knowing the season for all things, the Aborigines had returned to the river they called *Wahalumbaal birri*, and were soon spearing fish in the warm shallows.

Isaac was among those aboard *Endeavour* all for going out to them again, but the Captain said nay. 'We shall ignore *them*, and perhaps they will come to *us*.'

Drawn by curiosity about these seeming white *Wangarr* spirits, two *bama* did paddle closer until the canoe was within hailing distance. Greetings were shouted, although the words were not understood. Gifts were more accessible. And while the Guugu Yimithirr knew nothing of the cloth and nails passed down to them, they were sufficiently pleased to bring their two clansmen over for more.

They landed near the camp and stood waiting: black skins painted red and white, chests incised with initiation scars, the eldest with a bone through his nostril. Weapons ready, in case these strangers really were spirits of the dead.

Isaac crowded eagerly with the others on the riverbank. Afraid the visitors would be overwhelmed by numbers, Cook told his crew to stay back. Tupaia alone went to meet them. The Tahitian, in his role of peacemaker once more, advanced across the grass. Then he sat down and gestured to the Aborigines to do the same.

They did so at length, sitting with spears beside them near the priest, and talking softly. Neither knew the others' language: yet human contact was established. The *bama* touched Tupaia's hands and face, and felt his clothes, uttering sounds of wonder. *Yir-ke*. As trust grew, *Endeavour* men drew closer – although the Aborigines became tense if anyone touched their weapons or came between them and the canoe.

They stayed a little while, even allowing Mr Banks to hang a medal about their necks, before paddling back across river. More returned next day – and in the days that followed, they brought gifts of fish for the clothes and beads given to them. They wouldn't eat the *Wangarr* food, however, and were reluctant to exchange their own shell adornments and dilly baskets, for these were useful to them.

Women and children were always kept at a distance. But the men spent much time at the camp, especially with Tupaia, exclaiming *Yir-ke* over the many new objects they saw. In return, they told the men from *Endeavour* the Guugu Yimithirr names for the familiar – though to the Europeans exotic – things in their collections: plants, birds and animals, including Mr Gore's *gangurru*.

Thus, in this first extended meeting between the Aborigines of New Holland and the *Endeavour*, relations seemed to be amicable. Until they suddenly went wrong . . .

In the third week of July Mr Molineux went out in the pinnace once more to look for a passage through the reefs. Isaac wanted to go, but the Master told him to stay behind and help load stores.

'We'll be sailing soon, and every hand is wanted about the ship. Besides, ye've already been out in the yawl hunting turtle again.'

This was true. A dozen fat turtles were now swimming in tubs on deck, just ready for eating. So, while Molineux put to sea and the Captain walked overland to spy out the coast from a high hill to the north, Isaac helped lug the water casks, biscuit, and gunpowder barrels aboard.

Several Aborigines came to the camp that afternoon, and for the first time ventured onto the ship. The *bama* were certainly amazed at what they saw. What interested them most were the twelve captured turtles: *ngawia!*

They left, talking rapidly among themselves. A larger party of ten or eleven *bama* returned next morning, and coming up the gangway they went straight to a tub, lifted out one of the turtles and tried to carry it ashore.

A couple of seamen stopped them.

'Oi! Put that back. That ain't be your'n!'

Oh yes it is. The turtle here are all ours!

But the *bama*'s words had no currency. In such conflicts between cultures, meanings are often lost and only actions signify. More seamen gathered. Tempers rose. And by press of numbers the Aborigines had to return the turtle. They picked up another, however, and were making for the side when they were stopped again.

'Them damned thieves be stealing our dinner!'

We're happy for you to eat our turtle, but you have taken more than you need.

'We caught 'em ourselves!'

By our law you should share them, and so we will take one.

'Oh no you don't!' As the *bama* were once more compelled to replace the turtle in the tub.

Tensions turned into anger. Not only had these *Wangarr* taken turtles from Guugu Yimithirr waters without permission, they were defying the laws of hospitality and the sharing code. Very well! *Bama* could do the same. They seized any loose deck gear – rope coils, casks – and only with difficulty were stopped from throwing them overboard.

Into this scene of jostling confusion, the Captain stepped. Cook was as much bound by his native traditions as were the Guugu Yimithirr. He had no more idea of needing permission to fish the sea, than the Aborigines did of private property ownership. Still, it was clear that the dispute was about food. While he had no intention of giving away his turtles, and dinner was not yet ready, Cook went ashore with Mr Banks hoping to pacify matters by saying the natives could eat as much ship's biscuit as they liked.

The *bama* didn't want any of it! They'd seemed such inoffensive people. Now, they strode off: proud and seething and empty-handed.

But not for long. They plucked fistfuls of dry grass – and lighting them at the coals burning under a pot of caulking pitch, ran upwind of the camp and set fire to the surrounding vegetation.

The tinder brown grassland, high as a man's chest, caught at once. Sickly smoke plumed into the sky. And fanned by strong winds blowing from the sea, scarlet flames leapt and crackled and swept down upon the encampment.

'Make haste!' cried the Captain, as men tumbled off the ship. 'Beat it out with anything you can lay hands to.' The crew grabbed blankets, and sailcloth, and even the shirts from their backs.

'Blimey! How fast it moves. I'd no idea . . .'

'Thank God we brought the gunpowder aboard yesterday.'

'Look to the armourer's forge!'

'My tent!' shouted Mr Banks. 'It will burn. Save it!'

Isaac rushed forward with Nick and Taiata to help dismantle the botanists' tent. A few minutes more and it would be ablaze. Smoke stung their eyes and fouled their breath, and the dirty sun burned fiercely down.

'Quickly! It is nearly upon us!'

But then, through the noise and shouting, Isaac heard a squealing. 'The pigs! Hurry! They'll burn to death!'

Leaving the gentlemen to haul away the tent, the boys ran to the pens. The sheep and goat had already been led to safety, but the sow and her piglets had been forgotten. They were running terrified around their enclosure as the air grew dark with ash, and the livid flames raced closer.

Isaac held open the gate as Nick herded the litter out. The sow and most of her family fled towards the river and safety. But several piglets ran into the fire's path. One of them was later found dead on the blackened stubble; yet perhaps the others escaped, for in this part of the world wild black pigs would come to be known as 'Captain Cookers'.

Mr Cook may have supposed the *bama* would be satisfied. They weren't. He saw the Aborigines move up river, where some of the ship's washing was spread out to dry, and again set fire to the grass.

'Stop!' he shouted, running towards them. 'Cease!'

But they didn't. Once more the grass bloomed like an orange flower, fragrant with smoke. Cook's men were close enough, however, to stamp the fire out; and raising his musket, the Captain fired a round of small shot at the *bama*. They ran to the mangroves – though not before one man had been hit, for a few drops of blood were seen on the linen, and several spears were collected nearby.

Cook shot a musket ball wide to show they were not yet out of range, and the *bama* disappeared among the trees.

Why, Isaac wondered as he had in New Zealand and at Botany Bay, why does it always have to end like this?

The confrontation wasn't over yet. Voices were heard. The Captain and a few men followed the sounds into the bush, where they saw a *bama* elder called Ngamu Yarrbarigo, coming towards them with his warriors.

Both parties stopped, eyeing each other. Then, with great courage in the face of these *Wangarr* with their powerful spirit weapons, the old man approached Cook.

You will come with us, he beckoned.

They followed the Aborigines for over half a mile: past the mangrove flats, then up through the grass to a rise with a rocky outcrop. There Cook sat down, laying the spears beside him in a gesture of peace.

The *bama* sat down a hundred yards away. Waiting.

Cook called to them, and Ngamu Yarrbarigo rose and walked towards the *Wangarr*. He carried a spear without a point, and from time to time wiped the musk-smelling sweat from his armpit and licked it – for strength, and also protection if these *were* spirits of the ancestors.

The Captain rose and handed him the spears.

'We only wish to be your friends,' he said.

And we, too.

The sense was understood. The elder called to his warriors, who laid their spears against a tree and came across. Gifts were given: beads and musket balls, the purpose of which the *Wangarr* explained by sign language. In return, the *bama* promised not to light the grass again. And as there were some who had not yet seen *Endeavour*, they all returned to the ship with her Captain – *which*, as he wrote in his journal that night, *reconciled everything*.

Perhaps not everything, for Isaac and his companions saw little of the Aborigines after that, although the hills burned with their hunting fires for days. Not that the *bama* were hostile. One seaman got lost in the bush, and a family fed him kangaroo meat. They felt him all over, and even had him take off his clothes to show he really was a man. And they guided him back to the ship, as friends. It was just that, after the turtles and the shooting, the Guugu Yimithirr had almost nothing more to do with *Endeavour*, like the people of Botany Bay. Cook even found the shirts he'd given them in a heap by the beach. Nature provided, and they had no need of them.

Endeavour was kept in port for two weeks longer than Cook expected. He was ready to sail and buoyed the channel, but the onshore winds that had fanned the grassfire still blew so strongly that the ship couldn't get out to sea. And what course would it take? For Mr Molineux returned with news that he could find no safe passage through the shoals, and proposed they go back the way they'd come.

'But we've already sailed a thousand miles without the leadsmen ever once being out of the chains,' exclaimed Cook. 'That's unheard of! It would be an endless piece of work to go south again.'

'We may have no choice.' Molineux sounded worried.

'We can't be *that* far from the end of this coast and a strait that Torres claimed lies between here and New Guinea. It's shown on Mr Dalrymple's chart.'

'Other maps show the land extending all the way down to these latitudes.'

'Then we must seek to discover the truth for ourselves. We'll try to find a way north once we're at sea, Robert . . . even if the reefs force us back in the end.'

The winds blew a gale for another fortnight, palm trees streaming ragged against the sky; and it wasn't until early August that *Endeavour* was able to warp over the sandbar and out of the river that the Captain named after his ship. Even then, the weather sometimes forced her to anchor all day: and under sail she could only proceed slowly, the boats always ahead sounding, as they went like blind men feeling for the channels that wound among the maze of shoals and islets that stretched wherever they looked.

The Labyrinth, Cook called it, and he was not wrong.

For a week after leaving Endeavour River the ship crept up the coast, until one morning they saw several small islands fifteen miles to seaward. They stood out for them. Anchored.

And ordering Molineux to sound the lesser isles, the Captain and Mr Banks went in the pinnace to the largest one to see if any way out of the Labyrinth could be spied from its summit. Isaac came with the Mate, Dicky Pickersgill.

It was a stony, rough-grassed island where many lizards lived – and Aborigines, too, from time to time, for fresh water was found, and the remains of shellfish, turtles, and simple shelters.

They climbed the hill on a sultry, hazy afternoon; and to the east, through his spyglass all Cook saw at first was a foaming white ribbon, where the Pacific dashed itself against the outermost reef. No escape there! And yet . . .

'Take a look, Mr Pickersgill. Do you see . . .?'

'I'm not sure, Captain.' But after a little . . . 'There do seem to be an opening in the breakers. Not a large one, mind ye . . . and beyond it, the deep blue of the ocean . . .'

'Quite so. Show the lad. At first light I'll get thee to go in the pinnace and take a look at it. We'll sleep ashore.'

So, next day, Isaac found himself pushing the boat out into the dawn with Richard Pickersgill. It was an easy six-mile sail with the wind: the olivine sea broken and choppy, but a millpond compared to what happened as they neared the outer reef.

Here, the coral rose as a great wall from the deep, like battlements against which the mighty Pacific rollers hurled themselves and broke. The tumult was incessant. The besieging waves roared as they burst upon the ramparts, and foam blew like tattered banners across the protected water behind.

For the most part, the wall held the invaders back. Occasionally there was a gap, through which the ocean poured – and it was towards the largest of these that the pinnace steered. Big enough for *Endeavour*, Mr Pickersgill thought.

'Aye, and deep enough too,' he reported to the Captain, 'though we didn't sound it. We didn't dare enter the channel, sir. The swell was so strong that, once through, I doubt we'd have got back again. We'd have been wrecked on reef.'

Robert Molineux had nothing encouraging to say, when the officers met in the Great Cabin later that afternoon. The openings he'd explored were all perilous, and the shoals seemed to go on for ever up the seaboard.

'I must say, gentlemen, that I'm inclined to quit this coast altogether,' said Cook. 'I'd be sorry not to prove that it ends at the strait Torres discovered – which I believe it does. But if we were to go aground again on these inshore reefs . . .'

'We might be kept a year until we get more favourable winds,' cried Lieutenant Hicks.

'And we've provisions to last us only three months,' reminded the Master.

'There are always turtles and gangurru,' argued Mr Gore, the sportsman.

'We may not be so fortunate again,' the Captain said.

Thus they weighed next morning and headed for the opening Pickersgill had seen. The Master went ahead in the pinnace after dinner to sound: and by mid-afternoon, in the very mouth of the howling breach, he shouted to young Isaac. 'Hoist the signal, lad, for the ship to follow us!'

And they stood into it.

The channel was about three-quarters of a mile wide. The water heaved and slumped as the little craft strove upon the warring sea. Ebb tide and wind were with them, and before long the pinnace, followed by *Endeavour*, was safely through the clashing breakers, and into the open ocean.

Hearts took wing – and voices too when the leadsman cast his line again. *No bottom at a hundred and fifty fathoms!* It was nearly four months since they'd last heard that call.

Captain Cook brought his ship to for the night and men thought, like Theseus, they'd escaped the Labyrinth. All next day, as they sailed north with no land in sight, they reckoned themselves safe.

But the worst was yet to come.

Just after dinner on the second day, the masthead lookout spied land again to the west. Afraid of missing the passage Torres apparently found in 1606, Cook veered a little towards the coast – but by mid-afternoon hostile waves were once more seen crashing on the barrier reef in a battleline that stretched as far as they could see.

Quickly *Endeavour* tacked nor'-east until midnight, when they brought to again. No bottom at a hundred and forty fathoms and no need for a canvas sea anchor, for the Captain believed they were out of any immediate danger. He was wrong.

At four o'clock, as the dawn watch was going up, Isaac was woken by the sound of men talking. The word 'breakers' crept into his consciousness, and sleep vanished. Through the wooden wall of the ship, he could hear surf pounding.

'Nick! Wake up!' And pulling on britches, the boys hurried to the deck.

'Mr Wilkinson, what's happened? Where are we?'

'The ship has drifted in the night, look you. The wind's dropped, and the sea's calm. Yet the current and the flood tide have carried us back to the reef.'

The onslaught could be heard through the darkness, not far away at all.

'What shall we do?'

'Well, you can say your prayers, boyo. But keep them to yourself. To the world you will stand as men, and follow orders. We're not lost yet.'

Cook was already on the quarterdeck and, however fearful he may have felt, as Captain he gave his commands as always with control, decision and example.

The yawl and longboat were ready to lower away at first light to start towing the ship. The pinnace was under repair, but John Satterley and his carpenters were fixing a temporary board to get her afloat again.

Men were heaving on the sweeps, like galley oars through the stern ports, trying to bring the ship's head round and prevent her going broadside onto the swell. And Isaac waited with the linesmen on deck, ready to trim the sails should any wind blow to push them out.

Oh, the wind! After so many weeks of gales, could the sea gods not spare one little puff? The air shook only with the thundering waves as they surged forward, dragging the ship with them, to rise and fall tremendously upon the reef.

Daylight came – revealing their true peril. For *Endeavour* was not two hundred yards from the breakers. Every wave brought them nearer to the coral wall. And once within its tow there was no escape. The ship would inevitably be smashed on the rocks, and every life aboard her lost.

Closer and closer. Isaac thought of Papa – of his brothers and sisters at home in Hatton Garden, not knowing what had become of him. He could picture Mother's face in the silver locket wrapped in his sea chest. Then the image turned into Heimata, glowing iridescent through her pearl. But he dare not leave his post to get his most precious things and hold them close in his last hour . . .

Stand firm my bully boys . . . keep steady, brave souls . . .

Six o'clock, and the boats out towing. They were making no headway. For Isaac saw they were now less than a hundred yards from the reef . . . eighty yards . . . The very roller that lifted them up on one side, bore down and exploded upon the other.

'Between us and destruction was only a dismal valley the breadth of one wave,' wrote the Captain. Yea, the valley of the shadow of death . . .

. . . I shall fear no evil, for Thou art with me . . .

Isaac groped for the words of the Psalm. Mamma . . . Heimata . . . Then all he remembered was the grinning stone skull on the gatepost of St Nicholas's Church at Deptford. The seamen's church, they called it. And now he knew why, when life ended like this . . .

'The wind! There's a breeze!'

All hands to your lines!

The shouts jerked Isaac from his imaginings. He felt a breath on his cheek – a mere billow they wouldn't have noticed at any other time. It was enough to lift every sailor's hope.

On braces and bowlines . . . ease away . . . haul away . . .

And enough, too, with the help of the boats, to take *Endeavour* two hundred yards from the reef.

But then the wind dropped and all fell calm again. Once more the current pulled the ship towards the rocks faster than the boats could tow it away. Mr Banks was dropping paper over the side to see if they were making any progress. They weren't. But as if to assert their disdain in the face of calamity, astronomer Green, Gunner Forwood and a Master's Mate, Charles Clerke, were quite methodically taking the midday readings with their sextants from the quarterdeck.

And Providence seemed to be with them. Their friendly breeze, as Cook called it, visited again, enough to take them a quarter mile off the reef. A little way ahead they saw an opening – not much, but perhaps sufficient to let *Endeavour* through and back into the placid and comparatively safer waters of the inner reef. Mr Pickersgill went to investigate, and the ship followed.

The tide had turned, however, and the ebb was now flowing out strongly through the gap. The ship couldn't make it – thankfully! For they saw rocks, like teeth in its maw. But the rip was enough, with skilful seamanship, to carry *Endeavour* out nearly two miles. There, men ate their dinner meat as if at a funeral wake: relieved they were not yet among the dead, but aware they soon might be when the afternoon tide bore them in again.

Don't give way to thy fancies!

There was another small opening in the reef. Lieutenant Hicks went ahead this time, and returned with news of a slight – but possible – chance.

A light breeze sprang up. Ebb tide turned to flood, and *Endeavour* set her bows to the gap. The towboats showed the way, and the sweeps kept her steady astern as she approached the narrow channel, and was caught by the inflowing current. With a rush the ship was swept through, as if down a millrace, and came to anchor in nineteen fathoms of still, beryl-green waters inside the reef.

Providential Channel, the Captain called it. And rightly so. Two days earlier Isaac and the entire ship's company had cheered to get clear of the shoals. Now, they praised heaven they were back among them. Saved by the breadth of one wave.

The ship moored for nearly twenty-four hours to repair the pinnace, to fish, and to let the nervous energies of all aboard recover. Then, for another four days, it was back to the old work: groping their way through a treacherous sea and the labyrinth of reefs and islets – one of which, many years later, would come to bear Isaac Manley's name.

They anchored every night. At the map table, the spider line on the Captain's chart was growing longer, enclosing the shape of New Holland within its web, as the eastern seaboard narrowed towards that place the Dutchmen Jansz, Carstensz and Tasman had explored and named Carpentaria. Until, on the morning of 22 August, they saw that the mainland ended in a number of islands. Cook had reached the northern cape, which he named for the Duke of York. He had rediscovered Torres Strait for the Europeans.

Later that afternoon *Endeavour* anchored off a small island at the entrance to a channel on the western side. It seemed to lead to the open sea and a route to Batavia in the East Indies. The Captain wanted to get there soon, for supplies were low and the ship was taking water again. But there was one thing more to do.

Several Aborigines were seen on the beach as the longboat came in: most of them naked and armed with spears as the people of Botany Bay and Endeavour River. But one man carried a bow and arrows – like the warriors of the Pacific islands – which the voyagers had not seen here before. The natives didn't oppose Cook, however, but disappeared into the scrub as he landed.

The *Endeavour* men climbed a small hill to spy out the channel: Cook named this Endeavour Strait. Once satisfied, the Captain ran up the Union Jack; fired three musket volleys, answered by three from the ship; and took possession of the eastern coast of New Holland for King George by the name of . . .

What would he call it? He did not of course consult the inhabitants about *their* name for this land, though in some ways it seemed to Cook the Aborigines were far happier than Europeans. They might appear 'the most wretched people on Earth' he wrote, but really they lived in tranquillity, where land and sea provided the necessities of life, and were wholly unacquainted with the superfluous luxuries so sought in Europe. Now he claimed their country for the King . . .

The Captain tried several alternatives of his own, but crossed them out in his journal. New Zealand . . . New Holland . . . New Guinea . . . New Britain . . . were already on the maps. New Wales? Perhaps. But it didn't sound quite right.

After many weeks and much thought, Cook inserted '. . . by the name of New *South* Wales.'

Much better. And thus another phrase of three short words, redolent with their later histories, entered the language.

12

DEAD MEN'S CLOTHES

Java, August 1770 to February 1771

Freed at last from the clutches of the reef, *Endeavour* plunged full of confidence into the open sea. Isaac stood with Young Nick on the foredeck, faces whooping to the wind, as the ship surged, rejoicing with deep, safe water beneath her.

They were out of danger! They were going home! Just a short sail from Possession Island off Cape York to the shipyards at Batavia. A few repairs to *Endeavour's* leaks. And then . . . what tales they'd tell of adventure in the far South Seas when they walked the streets of London again arrayed in robes of triumph!

If only the boys had known they'd come wearing dead men's clothes, for greater perils than the reef still lay ahead of them. If only their Captain knew how damaged his ship really was. Her keel torn; teredo worm in her timbers; two bottom planks almost sawn through by the coral. It was a wonder *Endeavour* hadn't broken up beneath them already. But happy in their ignorance, the voyagers pitched into the Arafura Sea – and even detoured out of curiosity to see something of New Guinea.

The coastal waters were shallow, however. The pinnace only

made one brief landing: and then the gentlemen had to wade two hundred yards ashore. They had time, like Robinson Crusoe, to see a human footprint in the sand, and look at the coconuts, before they were attacked and chased back to the boat by armed warriors.

They left New Guinea alone after that. Besides, the Dutch and Portuguese had already explored these parts, and after two years away almost everyone aboard *Endeavour* was yearning for home. Even Mr Banks started to calculate the distance to Old England and fame.

So Cook set his course for Java, for men were also feeling the want of fresh food. They hooked a couple of sharks, which Henry Jeffs butchered and one-handed John Thompson turned into a stew. Everybody ate it with gusto – a far cry from those early days when old Ravenhill had warned against 'man-eaters' as vittles.

'We've met *real* cannibals in New Zealand,' Isaac whispered to Nick, and the whole mess table sniggered.

Supplies remained a problem for the few who were sick. Tupaia, after so long on a ship's diet, was constantly ill – and began to irritate everyone with his complaints and demands. He even abused Taiata, when the boy was himself suffering. Astronomer Green had long fought symptoms of scurvy, which he exacerbated by drinking more heavily than usual: but then, most of them did, overcome with fatigue or homesickness. Isaac more than once had to help a drunken Molineux into bed.

'By the mark . . . shoal water. Eh, boy?'

A hungover steersman one afternoon set the ship on a wrong tack and the sheet lines, which held the corners of the sails, went slack so that the canvas flapped uselessly about.

'Look at 'im!' Young Nick nudged Isaac in the ribs. 'Letting the ship drift like that, three sheets in the wind, just like them boozy tars down below.'

Nick was calling himself a 'tar' now, letting his hair grow long like the adult sailors, with a pigtail plaited and dabbed with tar to keep it in place. Isaac had a plait too – but without the tar. Mother wouldn't have liked it.

Endeavour passed Timor, but when the ship reached the small, fertile island of Savu, the temptation to go ashore could not be resisted. Lieutenant Gore was sent ahead, and returned with word of safe anchorage. The local chief or rajah was hospitable. He gave the gentlemen and officers a feast of pork and rice (with enough left over for Isaac and the other servants), and offered to sell them buffaloes if the Dutch Governor agreed.

The Governor was willing – at a steep price. But when Sydney Parkinson innocently asked if any cloves or nutmegs grew on Savu, the Dutch became very defensive about 'their' spice islands and tried to stop trade altogether. Only when Captain Cook presented an old broadsword to the rajah, who began waving it at the native troops, did business resume: and *Endeavour* left Savu with nine buffaloes, a crate of fowls, and a stock of sweet palm wine syrup.

Thus provisioned they ran with the trade winds, fragrant with cinnamon, until they reached the southern shores of Java. And just before sighting Java Head on 1 October, the Captain collected their logbooks and journals, and swore everyone to silence.

'The right of our discoveries belongs to King George,' he said. 'But the Dutch are suspicious. If they hear we've been to New Zealand and New Holland, they might well make claims of their own, and detain us at Batavia longer than I wish.'

'And those of us who were there with the *Dolphin* know that Batavia is *not* a place to stay a moment longer than necessary,' remarked Dick Pickersgill.

To which Molineux added, 'The air is most unwholesome, and the people sickly with fever. The only way to survive is to lay in a plentiful store of arrack liquor.'

'What's that?' asked Isaac.

'Rather formidable native spirits, boyo,' said Francis Wilkinson, 'made from palm or rice wine.'

'Sounds good,' cheeked Young Nick. 'More sheets in the wind.'

'Aye, and we are mostly in the pink of good health,' observed Cook. 'I hope to repair *Endeavour* and leave as soon as possible. Meantime, say nowt to anybody.'

They saw Princes Island, lying like a pulled tooth at the entrance to Sunda Strait. Before making the passage, a boat went ashore to get fresh coconuts for Tupaia and feed for the buffaloes. *Endeavour* was hailed by several Dutch ships. Zachary Hicks, who went aboard, was circumspect – saying only that they'd come 'from Europe'. Yet he returned with much news of his own. 'They tell me that Captain Carteret in the *Swallow* called at Batavia nigh two years ago!' he exclaimed to cheers in the wardroom.

The *Swallow* had sailed in company with Captain Wallis and the *Dolphin* in '66; but the ships had become separated off Cape Horn, and *Swallow* was feared lost. Now, the *Dolphin* men who knew her – Molineux, Gore, Pickersgill and Wilkinson – celebrated to think she'd survived.

'Why, she might have reached home!' cried Robert Molineux. 'Come Isaac, bring another bottle to drink her health!'

Swallow did get safely home, six months after *Endeavour* left England. And Mr Hicks brought other news. The American colonists were refusing to pay their taxes, and King George was proposing to send a force to suppress the rebels. It was the first time that Isaac – or any of them – got wind of the conflict in which, years later, he would serve as a Lieutenant and be promoted to command his own ship.

Endeavour spent the best part of a week making her way along the north Java coast, until she came to anchor in Batavia roads – the city's outer harbour – on 10 October. Where they discovered it was actually 11 October.

'Why the difference?' Isaac wondered.

'We forgot,' explained Mr Molineux. 'Sailing westward around the world we gained an extra day.'

After paying his respects to the Governor-General, Cook sought leave to have *Endeavour* properly heaved down in dry dock.

The Dutch were everything the Portuguese authorities at Rio were not. Permission was readily given to repair the ship in the yards at Onrust Island across the bay. Fresh supplies were sent aboard, including a cask of arrack. It went down a treat as Molineux foretold, and they later took on a hundred and fifty gallons more.

The Indies were heading into the rainy season, and as a precaution Cook had the crew attach a lightning chain to the masthead. It was as well he did, for an electrical flash split the topmast of a Dutch ship, and one night *Endeavour* was shaken by a thunderbolt. Isaac later came to see it as a premonition – a warning of what was to happen: though at the time Batavia seemed to promise all they wanted.

A vessel was about to sail for Holland, so Cook wrote a brief letter to Secretary Stephens, informing of their safe arrival. Also at anchor were three British ships, and his crew had much joy drinking with their fellow jack tars again.

It was impossible not to say something over the arrack of the Venuses at Tahiti or the terrors of the reef. But what struck Isaac and all *Endeavour* men was the pallid, spectral look of the sailors – and of every other European they saw at Batavia.

'Look at us, hale and bonny after two years at sea!' Nick jeered. 'But you're as thin and white as ghosts, like dead men waiting for your shrouds.'

'Fever,' they replied in mournful voices. 'The ague. This place be rife with it, mates. Stay here too long, and ye'll be haunted by it y'rselves.'

It seemed nonsense to Nick and young Isaac. True, the night breeze carried foul smells and mosquitoes from mangrove swamps along the coast. But apart from Mr Green, Lieutenant Hicks was the only crewman who ailed, and he was allowed to take quarters in Batavia. Mr Banks and Dr Solander also took lodgings with their servants, and soon sent for Tupaia and Taiata to join them.

The Tahitians revelled in their first experience of a town. They wandered amazed among crowds on paved streets beside broad canals, staring at fine churches, mosques and pagodas. Taiata trotted with delight beside small horse-drawn carriages, stopping outside rich shops and houses. People riding animals! Never had the boy imagined it! He stood marvelling with Tupaia at the fortress guarding the entrance to the canal. No *marae* was ever built like this!

Such a variety of people and costumes! Wealthy Europeans in velvet brocades and full powdered wigs. Chinese merchants, clothed in white taffeta. Javanese artisans and Malay slaves in sarongs and coloured cotton shirts. Tupaia insisted that he, too, appear in proper Tahitian dress, and a length of *tapa* cloth was sent ashore from *Endeavour*.

Thus attired, Tupaia was walking with Mr Banks one day when he was stopped by a man who came running from his house to ask the priest if he'd not been in Batavia before.

'No, sir, he has not,' Banks replied. 'Why so odd a question?'

It turned out that, some eighteen months earlier, the French commander de Bougainville had been in Batavia with his two ships. On board was a Tahitian man, Aotourou, who appeared very similar to Tupaia.

'I mistook your Indian for him, sir,' the Dutchman responded. 'I do apologise.'

At least it explained the mystery of the strange ships that had visited Tahiti before Cook. And it gave the Captain something else to think about as he wrote a longer report for the Admiralty, to be sent with a copy of his charts and journal by the next ship to Europe. The French were busy in the Pacific, too! Their Lordships would be most interested.

Cook was modest enough about his own achievements. *Altho' the discoveries made in this Voyage are not great . . .* Their Lordships' heads must have been spinning when they looked at his work for the first time. Yes, and read that no one, other than Forby Sutherland, had died of sickness during the voyage. In that, however, James Cook spoke too soon.

They had to wait two weeks before bringing *Endeavour* alongside the Coopers Island wharf. Stores were unloaded; tents pitched for the crew; topmasts and rigging taken down. There were further delays before the ship moved to the careening yards at Onrust. Still . . . all seemed well.

But Batavia deserved her reputation as one of the unhealthiest places in the East. The Dutch may have built the town with pristine memories of Holland, yet into its canals the citizens poured all their filth. Human excrement, garbage, offal, even dead animals were tipped into waterways which became like cesspits, choked with silt. They constantly had to be dredged, and the black, oozing muck was piled in heaps to dry, before being carted off.

The stench in the monsoonal heat was appalling. It hung over Batavia like a sickening vapour – a miasma – that everyone thought was the cause of disease. Mosquitoes swarmed in stagnant backwaters, attacking soft human flesh by night.

Malarial fever quickly spread. Every year, some three thousand people died of it – mainly Europeans who had no immunity, half of them within twelve months of their arrival.

No wonder they had a spectral look. And no wonder that, within a fortnight, *Endeavour* men also began to sicken.

Dr Monkhouse, at his quarters in town, was the first to suffer. Then Taiata and Tupaia became ill: seized with a sudden shaking cold, followed by violent sweating that lasted for hours. They seemed to improve for a day or two. But the fever returned, and Tupaia pleaded to be taken back to the ship.

'I do not think a town is good for Tahitian people,' he said. 'We need to breathe fresh winds blowing off the sea.'

So Joseph Banks took them out to Cooper's Island, and pitched a tent near the *Endeavour* crew. Tupaia seemed happier, as if he could sense faint perfumes borne from Ra'iatea to the east. Better in mind but not in body, for fever recurred to grip him and Taiata, as it did young Isaac Manley.

He was in the tent, writing a letter home. 'Dear Mamma and Papa, I trust this finds you well as it leaves me . . .' But Isaac hadn't got far when he realised that he wasn't very well at all. His head began to throb. The lines on the page blurred, the ink turned into dark pools, and his words lost all meaning.

He was cramped, and every limb felt as if it had turned to lead. Isaac lay in his hammock for days, alternately shivering and burning. His letter had fallen to the ground and was trampled into the mud, unfinished and forgotten, until at last it blew into the sea and was lost.

Isaac wasn't alone. Almost every voyager was struck by malaria. Even Mr Banks was seized with such pain at his lodgings he could barely crawl downstairs.

His people were bled by physicians, trying to rid the body of malignant humours: purged with strong emetics, and their skin blistered with a hot glass. Banks was fortunate to have with him some bark of the South American cinchona tree, known as a remedy for the ague, when drunk as an infusion like tea. Others were not so lucky. Dr Monkhouse grew worse: and even as *Endeavour* was taken to Onrust in early November, the ship's surgeon died and was buried at Batavia.

He was succeeded by his assistant, William Perry, only in his early twenties, and barely able to cope with the number of sick. Nick Young was appointed his servant – the lad's first proper job on *Endeavour*'s muster book. Apprentice to the doctor. In truth, with nearly all her crew ill, those between bouts of fever did what they could to nurse their fellows. Some days there were not twenty men fit for duty. And when the full extent of the damage to the ship's keel was revealed, the Captain was glad to let the skilled Onrust workmen do the repairs. His own crew were just too sick . . .

'Isaac . . . Issy . . .' The boy heard Young Nick's voice through a feverish dream.

'What is it?' Isaac sought to rouse himself.

'It's Taiata. He's got worse . . . he says he's dyin' . . .'

'He can't!'

'Come and help me . . .'

Nick got Isaac to his feet, and the lads made their way to another tent. It had been raining again, but in the cool dawn there were a few hours respite from the steamy heat. Isaac's aching body felt some relief – as if this would be a better day.

He would need his strength. For they found Taiata crying out in delirium, 'Tupaia . . . master . . . save me . . .' Just as he had done that day he'd been seized at Cape Kidnappers. Then, as now, the boy struggled for his life – floundering in a sea of memory, until he fell back exhausted into the arms of the astronomer, Charles Green.

The man had been close to the boy: had taught him English and even a little science during those long days at sea, when the other lads were about their duties. Now he sponged Taiata's brow, and encouraged him to drink the medicine Young Nick held to his lips.

'Laudanum . . . Mr Perry says it will do you good.'

'Aye, and we'll soon be out together on the beach again collecting coconuts, as we did at Tahiti. Remember . . .?'

The name conjured such visions of home. Taiata swallowed the opiate, as if the taste of it would carry him there; and for a moment Isaac saw his eyes dance as they had when playing his flute at a *heiva*.

'Purea . . . Tutaha . . .' More names on Taiata's breath, before the light in his eyes faltered and he sank cold as morning ashes on the straw mattress.

Fever was followed by more chill spasms – and Mr Green, who had been up all night and felt his own ague returning, asked Isaac to hold Taiata for him. So were the sick attended by those in remission. And so Isaac sat during the torrid day: through the boy's incoherence, and brief moments of lucidity talking in his native tongue . . . *Te pohe nei au e tou mau hoa . . .*

'I am dying, my friends.'

'No, Taiata! Look, here's Nick with more laudanum. We'll see Matavai Bay again . . . and the spangled lagoon.' Yes, and in Isaac's heart the hope of whole being rose again with remembrance of Heimata, radiant in pearl shell.

'For you maybe, Tire. Not for me. I wanted to see the world with Tupaia, and tell them all at home. But I will not journey now beyond this place.'

Their tears fell together with the night, and the rain, and the veil on Taiata's brief sum of years. For the boy died during the dark hours, as Isaac and Nick Young sat watch with him – and travelled with him, too, next day, to a cemetery where they buried prisoners on nearby Eadam Island.

Tupaia was distraught when told of Taiata's death, for he loved the boy and felt responsible for his passing. The priest had refused all William Perry's remedies; but now not even the scented winds brought any help for his sickness, or comfort for his sorrow. They made it worse, reminding Tupaia of all he had lost.

He lay in his tent weeping, 'Taiata! We should never have left our islands with Toote. Oh, Taiata!'

Becoming weaker and more inconsolable, until he was beyond anyone's help. Two days later Tupaia himself died, and was interred near the boy.

There was little time to mourn them, for others were also dying. Green farewelled Taiata, then buried his own servant, John Reynolds. Tim Reardon went, lamenting his native Cork. Even as the ship was finished and returned to Coopers Island, Cook himself went down with fever.

Here was disaster in the making, for what if the Captain should also succumb? Mr Banks sent what help he could, and Cook slowly recovered his health. It was intermittent, however, like all of them:

a day or two of wellness, followed by periods of cold and terrible fever. Sometimes a mere dozen men were able to muster for duty, and the business of reloading the ship was painfully slow.

The only one who showed no symptoms of disease was old John Ravenhill, the sailmaker, who was almost perpetually drunk on arrack. Not that the others were especially sober; but they struggled to carry stores aboard, haggard as the walking dead they'd mocked among their fellow British tars. And the silent dead as well, for two more *Endeavour* men went to their graves.

It wasn't until the second week of December that the ship was ready and they stood into Batavia to take on water and fresh supplies. The fourth pump still wasn't working, and the Captain wanted it repaired before facing the lonely wastes of the Indian Ocean. That took another fortnight: and only on Christmas Day was Mr Cook able to take his leave of the Dutch Governor-General and Council.

They'd arrived so well and hearty! Now, as *Endeavour* weighed, she was leaving like a hospital ship. Seven of her company had died at Batavia – and nineteen new men were signed on to replace them and those lost earlier in the voyage.

Another one went before they departed. Still brooding on the unresolved challenge to his authority six months earlier, Captain Cook offered a reward of fifteen guineas to anyone who could prove who'd cut the ears of his clerk, Richard Orton – and fifteen gallons of arrack if anyone could show who'd cut his clothes. The reward was never claimed; but on Christmas Day Pat Saunders took advantage of a shore boat and deserted, never to be heard of again. Most men took that as an admission.

Mr Banks also hired another servant, for Jim Roberts and Peter Briscoe were still sick, and he was missing Tupaia. Still, the Tahitian's death brought him some consolations. The finest dog skin cloaks from New Zealand, the most important carved and *pounamu* treasures the Maori had given to the priest of *Oro*, now entered Banks's own collection – eventually to adorn museums throughout Britain.

For the rest, as *Endeavour* made her way along the Java coast, sad little auctions were held on deck as crew bid for the dead men's clothes and personal effects. It was a way of raising money for the families of the deceased.

'What'll ye gi' me, mates, for Tim Reardon's red neckerchief?'

'Fourpence,' from Nick Young, who'd long admired it.

'And Johnny Woodworth's sea knife, good as new.'

'A shilling.' Isaac bid high, to replace the knife he'd given Heimata.

'One shilling and threepence!' from the back.

'One and sixpence, then.'

''Tis your'n, Master Manley.'

'A nice pair o' canvas britches . . . and two shoe buckles, belonged to young John Reynolds . . .'

The pathetic little sums were entered in the dead men's pay books.

So they went, Isaac thinking his lot unhappy enough as the year turned. But it was only a rehearsal for what was to follow. His health grew worse, as did the health of them all. Dr Solander even saw mosquitoes breeding in the drinking water of the scuttlebutt on deck, though he did not realise the significance. So many were sick, it took *Endeavour* a week to get through Sunda Strait and anchor off Princes Island, for the Captain wanted to load more water before the long voyage to Cape Town.

It's unclear why he stopped there. He'd been warned the water was bad, though good on the Java side. Yet the ship stayed at the island for nine days. And every morning Cook gave his weakened shore crew their orders: 'You must take particular care to avoid brackish water near t' coast, and fill your casks from higher up t' stream.'

Whenever Isaac told the story in after years, he always said, 'We did try. I *know* we did.' Whether the blame for what was to happen lay at Princes Island, or with foul water taken aboard from the sewers of Batavia, no one ever knew. Yet Isaac's heart broke anew with the thought of it.

Endeavour left Java Head on 16 January 1771, carrying dysentery – the bloody flux – as an extra passenger.

The symptoms showed themselves within a few days of putting to sea. Fever. Vomiting. Agonising pain. Diarrhoea running crimson with blood.

Isaac was stricken. Seized with a burning in his gut he doubled over, feeling as if his bowels had been ripped from him. He struggled down to his hammock, and lay in his own mess. Stinking, helpless, expecting any moment to die.

'Nick . . .' he whispered, as his friend came by with laudanum, and a wet cloth to sponge him. 'Nick, I want . . .'

'Don't distress yourself, Issy . . . The medicine helps . . .'

'In my sea chest . . . under the shirts . . . a small black bag . . . give it to me . . .'

'Later, Issy. There's a lot for Mr Perry to attend. Let me clean you up a bit.'

'*Now*, Nick. Please . . .'

So Nick brought Isaac his little bag of treasures. The boy lay clutching it, as Nick wiped him. He was frightened and barely conscious – yet found some comfort in sensing his mother's locket and Heimata's dark pearl beside him.

The people he loved *were* there. He could feel them, enclosed in velvet. Safe. Present. And gradually through his darkness, Isaac glimpsed a small candleglow of will to see them again. He was young. And strong. He *would* survive.

And in truth, as time passed the lad did begin to recover. He was able to keep down water. It was the likely cause of their ailment . . . but you had to drink! Isaac sipped a little broth that Nick brought him in a mug, and ate a slice of beef, without his bowels splitting. Slowly the nausea eased, his head cleared, sensation returned to his limbs. At long last Isaac could crawl up on deck to wash himself again with seawater, and buy clean clothes from the slops store.

He even borrowed Mr Molineux's old razor to shave himself. For at fifteen, a downy beard and stubble had grown during his illness; and it was time to begin a man's ritual.

Others also had the will to live. But that didn't save them. One by one they began to die. Corporal Truslove of the marines was the first, on 24 January – 'a man much esteemed by everyone,' the Captain said, as he read the burial service.

High or low alike, they were not spared. The next day Herman Spöring died, an assistant naturalist in Mr Banks's party. Two days later Sydney Parkinson went to his maker, bequeathing to posterity his artist's record of the voyage and the first beautifully accurate paintings of botanical species unknown in Europe.

Hard liquor didn't preserve old Jack Ravenhill in the end, or the astronomer, Charles Green. Bloody flux killed them both. Cook admired Green's skill, but sniffed like a Quaker at his boozing and erratic way of life – which seemed to promote his disorders, in the Captain's view! As if getting dysentery was the man's fault!

For the disease was quite undiscriminating. Drunk or sober. Virtue or vice. Some lived. Some didn't. By the end of the month six more seamen died, among them the one-handed cook, John Thompson, and Archie Wolf who'd been flogged at Tahiti for stealing spike nails to buy love – and never told on the others.

'A calamitous situation!' cried the Captain, as well he might. Sometimes they could muster barely enough hands to tend the sails. Watches were reduced to only four men; and those who were well enough shared every duty.

Isaac went aloft with the call. He served his trick at the wheel, and stood to his lines as *Endeavour* hauled herself seaward. Below, on a putrid mess deck, he became by turn cook and nurse, patient and orderly. They scrubbed the ship with vinegar, and tried to sweeten her water with lime. To no avail. The muster of the dead went on . . .

Dan Roberts, the gunner's servant. John Thurman, press-ganged at Madeira, flogged at Rio and Tahiti, and now never to see home again. John Gathrey, the Boatswain. Midshipman John Bootie, who once called Nick Young 'a son of a bitch', comforted in his last hours by the self-same lad.

We therefore commit his body to the deep . . . Cook reading his Bible. And always the same grieving auctions of dead men's clothes.

'Sam Moody's blue jacket, mates, what's it worth . . .?'

'A straw hat Frankie Haite got at Rio . . .'

Isaac bid his small shillings and sixpences. Then on the fifth day of February he was called to the Great Cabin. Cook was there, with his Lieutenants and the Master, each as wasted as the other. Molineux in particular had been very ill, and taken to drinking even more heavily.

'You sent for me, Captain.'

'Mr Manley, I don't have to tell you our plight. So many dead . . . and more to come, I fear. Mr Bootie died yesterday. I doubt Mr Monkhouse will recover. We need another Midshipman, and Mr Molineux speaks highly of you.'

'Aye, sir, I do,' said Molineux, unsteady in his voice, but managing. 'I told him to learn his ship. He has been a good pupil. And . . . he has looked after me well.'

'The young gentleman's mathematics are still weak. Nevertheless,' the Captain smiled thinly behind his table, 'I can help him there. I remember telling you on your first day aboard to show willing and jump to thee orders. You have done that, Isaac. I am pleased with you. Do you accept the promotion?'

'Captain, with all my heart!' A heart that was bursting.

'Let it be recorded. Now, Mr Manley, on the quarterdeck if you please. We have a ship to steer for Africa.'

The Captain was right about Jon Monkhouse. The young man, who had saved them on the reef, now joined his brother, the surgeon, on the ledger of those who would not come home. The same muster book enrolled Isaac in his stead. And it showed that Mr Manley spent the very large sum of fifteen pounds eighteen shillings and sixpence from his wages buying the deceased Midshipmen's uniforms . . .

A royal blue frock coat, with white lining and cuffs, detachable velvet collar, and brass buttons. Two pairs of white breeches. Silk stockings. An embroidered waistcoat. And a proper naval three-cornered hat with gold trim.

Dead men's clothes, indeed.

13

MR MIDSHIPMAN MANLEY

To Cape Town and England, February to July 1771

For five more weeks *Endeavour* bore like a coffin ship across the Indian Ocean, her track on the chart marked with crosses as if for those who died. The carpenter, John Satterley. Henry Jeffs, the butcher. A young marine. More seamen . . .

If nothing else, a burial service at least gave Mr Midshipman Manley an opportunity to appear in his complete new uniform. That, and the occasional flogging.

Overcome with alcohol and fear one evening, the marine drummer, Tom Rossiter, started beating up the sick in their hammocks. ''Tis thy fault!' he shouted. 'Thee brought the bloody flux on this ship!' When the watch tried to stop him, Tom fought until he was subdued and put in irons.

Next morning, as Isaac stood on the quarterdeck in his frock coat and cocked hat, among those officers well enough to attend, Tom was given twelve bloody lashes. His outbreak was a symptom of the dread that hung over all of them, for no one knew who'd be next to die. Squalidly. Horribly.

As Isaac came on watch one day, a seaman was seized by a pain in the guts and began screaming, 'The gripes have got me! I'll die. I'll die!' He collapsed hysterically and was carried below. In time, he began to recover, as did many of those who, like Isaac, survived the first awful bout.

It was a long business, however. More than once Isaac was brought low by recurring sickness; and even when things improved as *Endeavour* found the cooler trade winds, often a mere dozen hands were able to work the sails.

At such times the Midshipman's blue coat was laid aside, and Isaac climbed aloft to help brace the yards or set the canvas as the Captain ordered. Cook expected it. And far from lowering Isaac's standing in the eyes of the topmen, his willingness to work alongside them actually increased it.

'Tha'll know what orders *mean*, lad, when day comes t' give 'em y'rself.'

Even so, Isaac *was* now a petty officer, and this meant all kinds of shifts in his status. He had his sea chest carried from the low berth amidships to the slightly less cramped quarters for'ard he shared with the other Midshipmen, James Magra and the Captain's young relative, Isaac Smith. He slept in a cot: slung like a hammock, but the sides stretched with timber to make it more like a bed.

'Goodbye, Issy,' said Young Nick, for the two had been friends from the start. 'Don't let fings change too much between us.'

''Course not.'

But of course they did. Rank mattered. It was Isaac who dined in the wardroom, and Nick who waited on him with the Master's new lad, Dick Hill, and the other servants.

It was Isaac who took his turn as an officer of the watch. Who did the rounds of the sleeping ship with his lantern at night: treading softly through the numinous shadows, concerned to know that all was safe with *Endeavour* as she rode in his care.

As a Midshipman, Isaac had charge when the logline was streamed on the hour. The weighted 'chip', on a line knotted at every seven fathoms, was trailed over the stern, and the number of knots running out from the spool was counted as the sand ran through a half-minute glass.

Three . . . four . . . five knots, sir . . .

Isaac would note it in the logbook. 'Dead reckoning', as they called it, was a rough way of measuring the ship's speed and of estimating the distance sailed, allowing for the currents. But it was also liable to considerable error.

Not long after his sixteenth birthday in early March, Isaac was on deck one evening when he thought he saw land to the northward. Africa! He pointed it out to several others, but when the Captain was informed, he dismissed it.

'I believe you were mistaken, Mr Manley. You probably saw a cloudbank. The log shows we're a hundred leagues from landfall – forty corrected by lunar observation.'

Dawn showed it was Cook who was mistaken. The coast of Natal was a mere two leagues off, and a steady wind was blowing *Endeavour* straight onto the rocks. They tacked about; yet Isaac was not alone in wondering what would have happened had it still been dark.

Thereafter, the Captain stood well out as they followed Africa down to the Cape and rounded it. At noon on 14 March the officers were taking their midday readings off Cape Town, the flat top of Table Mountain spread before them. Latitude and longitude were almost exact. Even Isaac was surprised at his accuracy.

''Tis practice, Mr Manley . . . th' art improving.'

Gales forced *Endeavour* to anchor in the outer harbour, the roadstead; but an East Indiaman, the *Admiral Pocock,* saluted with eleven guns, and her captain sent a basket of fruit aboard. Next morning, with the wind easing, *Endeavour* headed into port, Mr Manley at his place on the quarterdeck as they saluted the Governor's castle.

The Dutch at Cape Town were as accommodating as they'd been at Batavia – and the place didn't have fever! *Endeavour* was taken to her berth; arrangements were made to refit her for the last leg home; and lodgings were taken for the sick at a cost of two shillings a day for each man.

There were twenty-eight sick taken ashore – among them Lieutenant Hicks whose consumption was daily getting worse, and Robert Molineux still suffering from dysentery and drink. With Lieutenant Gore up country to shoot game, the burden of supervising the loading of supplies and *Endeavour*'s overhaul fell on the Midshipmen and Mates. It was a responsibility Isaac's training had equipped him for, and under the watchful eyes of Dick Pickersgill, Frank Wilkinson and Charles Clerke, he grew into it.

'Careful, Tunley, with that water cask . . . Well done, Littleboy. The fresh beef and greens are to be eaten now – take them to Tom Matthews in the galley.'

Still, there was time to enjoy the town. There were no playhouses, and an epidemic of measles stopped those private parties to which young Midshipmen might have been invited. Yet the busy port, where sixteen ships lay, had many taverns. And while ordinary seamen roistered in the front bars, their superiors sought upstairs rooms to drink and exchange gossip with others from distant parts. French, Dutch, Danish, Britons: mariners all, finding common understanding in the language of the sea.

'We lost twenty-three men to sickness in our voyage from Batavia,' Isaac said to one of the Mates from an East Indiaman, just arrived from Bengal. 'It was dreadful.'

But his words found little sympathy.

'I'd say that was pretty good. We lost nigh on forty during our time in the East, and more went down with scurvy.'

'How long out from England?'

'Not quite a year.'

'We've been away two and a half.'

'How many lost altogether?'

Isaac counted them. 'Seven in Batavia from fever. Eight before that.' He could see their faces drifting in the tobacco smoke. Alex Weir with his foot caught in the buoy rope . . . Peter Flower plummeting from the shrouds . . . Forby Sutherland buried at Botany Bay. 'About a third of us dead, I suppose.' Isaac paused, then added, 'No one to scurvy, though.'

'Then I'd say you were dead lucky. I've known ships lose twice as many people in half the time.'

'We took on bad water at Princes Island. That probably caused the flux.'

'*Neen*, *neen*,' broke in a Dutch sailing master. 'Ve sailed straight from Batavia, no stop at Prinzen, still many die of bloody bowel.'

'Is that true?'

'*Ja*, *ja*. Is bad air and vater at Batavia. Whole place is no bloody good . . . Vere else did you say you haf been in two years and a half?'

But that was a subject about which Isaac knew to keep silent.

Of course it wasn't only nautical business. Released from months of celibacy aboard an all-male ship, men sought the company of women for pleasure and reassurance. Cape Town was well provided there, too.

Rich Dutch burghers may have lived behind the pious facades of white gabled houses, sheltered from Africa's wind and dust. But the town existed to meet the needs of seafarers: and down at the waterfront their noisy demands spilled from the taverns and into the streets. Here berthed sinful mankind from around the world. And the girls who served them.

Maria . . . and Francine . . . and Amber . . . and Tabitha . . . Sounds of drumming, and singing, and dancing, and quarrelling, and the clinking of silver. Here was the pulsing, portside life Isaac had glimpsed as a boy at Rio, and been too sick to enjoy at Batavia. Now, entering his manhood at Cape Town, Isaac became part of it: life asserting itself, for he'd come near to death on the ocean.

Sometimes he and Isaac Smith would dress themselves in their finery, hair curled and ribboned, and walk to the Company Gardens, a green oasis in the bare township. They'd stroll among the trees, or look at zebras and ostriches in the zoo, keeping their eyes open for pretty Dutch maidens.

The young gentlemen doffed their hats with sweeping bows – and the young ladies, coquettish behind fans, would curtsey, sending out little sparks of flirtation. Mr Banks always said Dutch women made the best wives in the world. The two Isaacs never really discovered much about them, for the girls were always chaperoned, and the Midshipmen inevitably returned to their dockside nymphs.

That Amber! Looking at the gents across the room with eyes dripping honey. And Tab like a princess in the new silk shawl Isaac bought her . . .

Not surprising, perhaps, that those eternal vows Isaac had sworn to Heimata on a Tahitian beach began to disappear. Nor, as March turned to April, that the few sovereigns left in his purse also vanished. He had clothes to buy. Francine wanted an ivory hair comb. There was no chance a letter to Papa requesting more money would be answered in time. And Mr Molineux started to make demands . . .

The Master had taken lodgings with the sick, but he wasn't helping his recovery by continuing to drink far more than he should. Whenever Isaac went to visit him of a late afternoon, he'd find Molineux sprawled on his bed, surrounded by bottles and calling drunkenly for more.

'You're a good lad, Mr Manley. Be a better one, and bring me a flagon of this good Constantia wine.'

'It costs very dear, and I've almost run out of money.'

'So have I, son. It's what comes of long voyages.' He laughed stupidly. 'You're a young gentleman with a rich papa. I'll pay thee back when we get to England.'

'But you're still sick, Master. More liquor won't help you.'

'Don't you tell me!' Molineux bellowed. 'It's the only thing that *does* help. Laudanum, too.' He slumped on his pillow and whined. 'I've been good to thee, boy. Taught you well. Why don't ye return the kindness . . .?'

'If you put it like that . . .'

'So I do. And bring another bottle of Mr Perry's medicine! I'm in shoal waters . . . eh?' He giggled to himself again.

Pressed by the competing calls of self, obligation and guilt, Isaac's reserves at last ran dry. And the day came when, kneeling by his sea chest, he found himself opening a small black velvet bag and looking at the two treasures he might sell to raise a little cash to farewell Cape Town in style.

Mother's locket, with her picture painted on ivory in a silver frame. No. That was for ever. Put it back. Now.

But the translucent South Seas pearl Heimata had given him . . . had taken from her ear . . . its teardrop sheen like the violet sands of Matavai Bay. He might . . . she might not . . . *would* not mind if it was to help Isaac . . .? Surely she'd part with it as willingly again, to make him happy . . .?

Thus Isaac also found himself in a pawnbroker's shop exchanging the pearl for a handful of dollars. Solemnly promising to redeem it before *Endeavour* sailed.

Naturally he didn't. Isaac wasn't the first sailor boy to spend all his money, or to find a new love in another port. And in the end it didn't really matter. Isaac had no need of the pearl to remember Heimata in the moonlight, or rising from the forest pool. She was his first sweetheart. His first love. He never forgot her.

Endeavour was ready for sea by mid-April. Almost as many sick were brought back on board as had gone ashore: indeed, three had since died and few of the others had yet recovered. Certainly not Mr Molineux. He was carried down to his cot and lay wasting away – his duties as Master taken over by Richard Pickersgill.

They'd taken on ten new hands, and Isaac was fully occupied helping to settle them into the routine of the ship as they stood out of Table Bay. It wasn't until the night of the fifteenth, anchored off Robben Island, expecting the arrival of a ship with news from England, that he went down to see Molineux.

Nick was there with medicine and sponges: but it seemed the Master was drifting beyond human help. Sickly jaundiced in the lantern light, he tossed and mumbled to himself.

'By the mark . . . three fathom, Captain . . .'

Catching sight of Isaac, he cried out, 'Keep ears and eyes open, mouth shut, and any light fingers to thyself, young gentleman.' Just as he had that first morning at Deptford – though now everything had changed. Here, the two lads gave *him* commands: it was Mr Molineux who wavered on the brink of an uncharted journey.

'Don't concern yourself, Master.' Isaac wiped his sweating brow. 'Keep calm, and hold onto me. Nick's brought a draught for you. We weigh tomorrow.'

'Aye, aye. Right enough . . .'

He calmed. Though as Isaac left, the man started to cry again, 'By the mark . . . two . . . and tide's running out.'

As it was for Robert Molineux. Next day the English ship still hadn't been sighted, and Cook would wait no longer. *Endeavour* departed just after dinner; and at four o'clock that afternoon, as they headed into the Atlantic, the Master died. All his worldly goods he left to his sister, Ellen, back home in Liverpool.

'A young man of good parts,' the Captain judged him in his journal, 'but had unfortunately given himself up to extravagancy and intemperance, which brought on disorders that put a period to his life.' Much as he'd said about Tupaia and Mr Green.

But for Isaac, removing his hat as the late Master's corpse slid into the sea, it seemed more than that. Perhaps the strain of navigating *Endeavour* for months through the labyrinth of the reef had proved too much for Molineux. He'd been all right until then. But once back in known seas, maybe his nerve had simply failed. He was young. Only twenty-five years old. He was human. No one at Java was immune from sickness. And he had taught his servant boy all he knew.

By the mark . . . shoal water, Captain.

Or possibly he'd just been at sea too long. Molineux had been around the world once in the *Dolphin*, and barely been home a month before he signed with *Endeavour*. He'd have circumnavigated the globe for a second time had he lived another fortnight, for they crossed the Greenwich meridian of zero degrees at the end of April, completing the circuit.

Other *Dolphin* men saw their second circumnavigation – Gore, Clerke, Pickersgill and Wilkinson – not forgetting the goat. Whereas Robert Molineux . . . Isaac sighed. Who could tell where a man's weakness lay?

Besides, death hadn't finished with them yet.

In early May, they anchored off the island of St Helena to take on water and stores, and fell in with a fleet of twelve East Indiamen being escorted home by HMS *Portland* and the sloop *Swallow*. It was the same *Swallow* that sailed with the *Dolphin*, and now happy re-acquaintance! A chance also to join the convoy, for *Endeavour*'s rig was daily getting weaker; and for twenty days she kept company with the fleet as they sailed into the tropics.

We'll rant and we'll roar like true British sailors,
We'll rant and we'll roar across the salt seas.

But *Endeavour* couldn't keep up with the other ships, and lost sight of them soon after crossing the equator: though not before Cook gave logbooks and journals to the *Portland*, thinking it would be home sooner. And not before a surgeon examined Lieutenant Hicks, whose consumption made him no longer fit for duty.

There was nothing to be done, for his illness was in its final stages and, on the afternoon of 26 May, Zachary Hicks also died.

John Gore took his place and Charles Clerke was promoted to Lieutenant, for the life of the ship had to continue.

That evening Hicks' body was committed to the deep: another young man, only thirty-two, whose name still resonates with those who see, from a sailing ship, the blurred point of land he first sighted in the dawn off New South Wales.

Mourning. And ceremony. And Mr Midshipman Manley, with *Endeavour*'s complement, saluting his passing as the sun set.

Yet grief could wait. Anticipations of home and loved ones could not. Every day brought them closer – and if thoughts and whispers could have filled *Endeavour*'s sails, they'd have been there sooner. Faces and voices that had lain dormant in memory during the voyage, now reawakened as they'd been three years ago. Isaac began to wonder how much his brothers and sisters would have changed? John must be in the army by now. And Mother and Father? Would they see the changes in *him*?

He gazed more frequently on Mamma's portrait in her silver locket, as if to remind himself, 'Not long!'

Weather eyes scanned for ships that might bring news. A Rhode Island whaler was hailed off the Azores, whose Master told them that England's quarrels with the American colonists had been made up. For the time being. So that was well.

Straining and heaving with curling wind and waves, *Endeavour* hurried homeward as fast as she could. But the Whitby collier was weary. Every day something else gave way. A patched t'gallant sail split again. A pair of weather stays broke, and the main topmast cap sprang . . .

They sailed through the summer days of June, north-easting with fair winds for the most part. Higher into northern latitudes. Off Spain. The Bay of Biscay. And heading towards the English Channel.

Not far, little ship, and we'll all be in safe harbour!

Into July, and more vessels to bespeak in the sea lanes. A Dutch cargo boat bound for Riga. A Boston brig heading to Falmouth. Do they know at home about us? Do they know we're nearly there? Sing lustily, bullies!

Until we strike soundings in the Channel of old England,
From Ushant to Scilly is thirty-five leagues.

Sunday 7 July. They hailed a Liverpool brig, and another out of London for the West Indies.

'Be you the *Endeavour* bark what sailed with the Royal Society gentlemen for the South Seas?'

'The same.'

'But they're saying you be lost with all hands.'

'No. Have our dispatches not arrived from Batavia?'

'Don't know, Captain. Men are laying bets you're all drownded.'

'And letters sent by the *Admiral Pocock* from Cape Town? Have they not reached England?'

'Can't say. I do know people are wanting to collect on their wagers.'

'Well, I'm very glad to say they'll be disappointed.'

'Me too, Captain. God speed you, *Endeavour*. Only three day's sail to the Scillies and the Chops o' the Channel.'

Three days! With mothers and wives thinking they might be dead.

'Mr Gore, give orders to put on every inch of canvas *Endeavour* will bear.'

There was no need to give orders – or offer rewards – for the man who first saw Land's End. That challenge was taken for granted by everyone aboard.

So it was, at two o'clock on a clear afternoon four days later, that Nick Young was standing at the masthead. And just as he'd done when he first spied New Zealand, Nick suddenly cried from above –

'Land! Land ho!'

And with every immense *Endeavour* heart beating, Old England's southernmost promontory – the Lizard – hove into view.

So we rounded and sounded, and got forty-five fathoms,
We squared our main yard, up channel steered we.

By nightfall they were abreast of the lighthouses, and all through the next day continued their run along the green, beckoning coast-line. Past Portland and Peverell Point. A cutter came alongside, asking if they'd seen the East India fleet? So Isaac knew *Endeavour* wasn't far behind!

The signal was made for the grand fleet to anchor,
All in the Downs that night for to meet.

Ever eastward beyond Beachy Head and Dungeness. By noon on Saturday 13 July, *Endeavour* was nearing Dover's white cliffs. At three o'clock that afternoon, she came to off the Downs and anchored once more in English waters.

Then it's stand by your stoppers, see clear your shank-painters,
Haul all your clew garnets, stick out tacks and sheets . . .

Home.

FINALE. FULL CIRCLE

London, July 1771

The Captain and Mr Banks went ashore at Deal and took coach for London and glory. Cook went straight to the Admiralty where he found that his letters from Batavia had arrived, and laid before their astonished Lordships his charts and journals. Yes, and a proposal for another voyage to prove if the southern continent really did exist in as yet unexplored oceans.

'I suggest, gentlemen,' Cook observed, 'you go by way of Africa and Van Diemen's Land, to Queen Charlotte Sound. Spend a whole summer searching the far South Pacific and Antarctic seas. Then north to Tahiti, perhaps, to refresh and discover those islands Tupaia told us of. And then home with the westering trade winds.'

Their Lordships listened to the Captain – and within four months *Resolution* was purchased and a new expedition was getting ready, in which Midshipman Isaac Manley was entered as number four in the muster book.

For Cook knew merit where he found it. Just before he went ashore that Saturday afternoon at Deal, he stopped for a word with his young Midshipman.

'You have done well, Mr Manley. Your father will be pleased, and I shall say so in my report t' Admiralty.'

It was over a week, however, before Isaac had the chance to tell that to his father in person, though he sent a short note home. A week during which the sick were taken on shore, fresh supplies carried aboard, and the pilot navigated *Endeavour* – creaking in every joint – around North Foreland and into the estuary of the Thames.

At last, on 20 July 1771, she came to her berth at Woolwich. There was much work still to be done: to secure and unload her, to pay off her crew, and to send what was owing to the families of the dead. Days of labour to lift the crates of specimens from *Endeavour*'s dark hold, and send them into the light of public adulation.

Thousands of wonders! The strangest plants and animals, birds and fish, paintings, drawings, pieces of rock and native curiosities from places people had barely heard of. It was as if the *Endeavour* men had returned from another world altogether.

But it was *this* world they most desired. More than anything. And Isaac begged a couple of days leave to go home to see his family. Which Mr Gore agreed.

Thus on Sunday morning, Isaac stowed his gifts into the sea chest. Lengths of *tapa* cloth and woven flax for Mamma, Louisa and Maria. Maori carving for Papa. A stone *patu* and whalebone club for John and Robert. A throwing stick and spearhead from New Holland. A greenstone pendant, shaped like Maui's fishhook, that Te Horeta had given him. The blue leaf tattooed on his arm . . .

There was, of course, an empty space in the black velvet bag where Heimata's pearl had been. But they would not know that at home: and Isaac felt no regret.

A seaman carried his chest up to the deck, and Young Nick helped him load it into a waiting ferryboat.

'Fare ye well, Issy,' he said. 'It was a good sail.'

'To be sure it was, Nick.'

'Your family of landlubbers will hardly recognise you.'

Isaac laughed.

'I'll be back in a day or two. I'll let you know.'

Nick held out a hand to steady him.

'Careful as you get in the boat. Right foot first. We don't want to lose our Midshipman now.'

'Indeed not.'

'We might even go voyaging together again one day, sir.'

'Perhaps, Mr Young. Who can say?'

Isaac took his place on the thwart, and the ferryman cast off. The tide was running up river, and quickly it carried them past the wharves and shipping. Up beyond Greenwich – the elegant symmetry of the Seamen's Hospital, and the Observatory high on its hill, where the Astronomer Royal was collating readings of the Transit of Venus, and awaiting the results from Cook and Mr Green.

Through Deptford and the dockyards, where Isaac had joined *Endeavour* three years before. 'Now I have truly come full circle around the world,' Isaac said to himself. But as they passed the hulls and figureheads of great ships swinging on their cables, he thought, 'No, I have journeyed further than that.'

Further *into* the world – into a deeper understanding of himself and his fellow creatures – than the boy who'd been ferried down river ever dreamed. Carried by *Endeavour* to undiscovered places of the heart and intellect, in a voyage whose significance for the future world had only just been glimpsed. That was the truth of it.

And Isaac's own journey didn't end here. He'd berth awhile in home waters, like these ships at anchor, to refit and replenish.

Then one day he'd slip his cable, and leave safe haven to embark on the questing sea again. For the world had much more to show.

Swiftly the flood bore their boat up stream. The boatman tried to engage him in conversation, but Isaac was lost in his own reveries.

'They say what *Endeavour*'s been to Tahiti, where love be free,' the man ventured. 'Is that true?'

'Yes.'

Isaac could see palm trees, and the waterfall, and Heimata rising lustrous from its depths.

'And fearsome warriors.'

'Aye.'

Isaac grabbing the yawl as Taiata ran for his life along the shore at Poverty Bay.

'Cannibals?'

A boy's smashed skull, still in its pickling jar.

'And reefs far as ye can imagine.'

'That too.'

Where death held out its hand across a valley the breadth of one wave. And was cheated. Though it caught them at Batavia.

'And somefing called a kan-goo-roo they say . . . like a greyhound what 'ops . . . though I don't believe it meself.'

'It is so.'

The boatman sucked in his breath.

'What marvels! They say every voyage is the first time for someone. But you really *was* the first.'

He drew on his oars.

'All London's talking about 'ee.'

Well, not quite at this moment. When they entered the city that Sunday morning, all London was going to church. Merchants and dowagers, shopkeepers, tradesmen and scrubbed-up apprentice boys . . . As they rowed past Wapping and the Tower, bells were pealing from steeples across town as if welcoming Isaac home.

By the Customs House and Billingsgate. Even now his family would be hurrying to Saint Giles-in-the-Fields to remember him in their prayers. How surprised they'd be to return to Hatton Garden, and find Isaac already there!

Past Dark House, and Lyons Quay, and into the shadow of London Bridge. Where, even through the chiming bells, Isaac could hear the cataract roar as tidal water rushed between the arches.

Danger. He could feel it as the boat began to catch in the swirl and eddy. He could see it churning in the foam on the other side.

'What do you say, young sir?' asked the ferryman. 'Will you have some adventure and shoot the bridge with me?'

But this time Mr Midshipman Manley chose wisely.

'No,' Isaac said. 'Pull over to the stairs, if you please. I'll walk around the bridge, and meet you on the other side.'

He had no need to do anything else.

AFTERWARDS. ADMIRAL ISAAC

December 1771 to October 1837

James Cook was as good as his word. A few weeks after *Endeavour* returned, he wrote to Secretary Stephens requesting the Admiralty confirm the promotions he'd made, and advancing the names of those who had performed well. Of his two younger officers the Captain wrote, 'Mr Isaac Smith and Mr Isaac Manley, both too young for preferment, yet their behaviour merits the best recommendation . . .'

Isaac Smith had already become a Master's Mate after Robert Molineux died, and as such sailed on *Resolution* for Cook's second voyage. And within a few days of that ship, another Whitby collier, being commissioned with Cook as its Commander, Isaac Manley was entered as Midshipman.

Yet he did not sail on her. The muster book shows Manley joined the crew on 3 December 1771, and was discharged on 8 April the following year, when he became a Midshipman on the guardship HMS *Terrible* at Spithead, off Portsmouth.

It is unclear why Isaac left *Resolution*: but the most likely explanation seems to be that Cook kept him on the pay books as an act of generosity, until such time as the young man got a permanent berth.

Midshipmen didn't get paid unless they belonged to a ship. As a second son, Isaac had to make his own way in the world. Perhaps his father felt he had a better chance of advancement and of earning prize money in the regular navy, than by undertaking a second voyage of exploration.

However that may be, Isaac Manley was not the only prospective member of *Resolution*'s company who failed to make the voyage. Joseph Banks also did not sail with her. When *Endeavour* returned, it was Mr Banks who got most of the popular attention; who received an Honorary Doctorate from Oxford University; who was presented first to the King; and who was spoken of as if it had been his expedition. Certainly Banks later presented Cook to King George, and the monarch in turn handed Cook his commission as Commander. But in the public mind Cook was at first rather ignored – though not by his mentors at the Admiralty, who knew where responsibility for success really lay.

Perhaps this wasn't surprising, given that *Endeavour*'s voyage had largely been undertaken at the request of the Royal Society, Banks had put up a large sum of his own money, and the scientific results in so many fields – astronomy, geography, navigation and natural science – were truly breathtaking. It was among the most important voyages of exploration ever made.

Nearly forty islands had been discovered by Europeans. New Zealand and the east coast of New Holland had been mapped with remarkable accuracy, and gaps in the major habitable portions of the Earth filled in – apart from some Pacific islands, many of which Cook found in his later voyages. More than a thousand species of plants unknown in Europe were brought home, and seventeen thousand botanical specimens not seen in England. Animals, birds, fish and insects hitherto unheard of were introduced to the nascent science of zoology. Even the goat shared the fame: the celebrated Dr Johnson wrote a Latin verse in her honour for having twice circumnavigated the globe, and Mr Banks had it inscribed on nanny's silver collar!

The collections of artefacts brought back by Banks and Cook from the South Seas, together with their detailed descriptions of native societies, laid the ground for the discipline of anthropology. The observations of the Transit of Venus at Tahiti were critical for astronomers. The wonder and beauty of South Seas culture was opened to popular, no less than refined, imagination.

Given all this it's understandable that, when Banks announced he would go on the second voyage, some thought of it as *his* expedition. He proposed a party of seventeen scientists, artists and musicians, and demanded substantial modifications to the ship to accommodate them. The result was that *Resolution* became top heavy and threatened to capsize. The pilot refused to sail her down river. The Admiralty ordered the superstructure dismantled. And in a fit of temper – which he must have regretted for the rest of his life – Banks had his equipment taken off *Resolution*. He chartered another ship, and went to Iceland instead.

Interestingly, Charles Clerke sailed as Second Lieutenant on *Resolution* for Cook's second voyage to the Antarctic, and again as Captain of the sister ship *Discovery* for the third voyage to find the North-West Passage around the top of North America. In fact, he took over command of the expedition after Cook's murder at Hawaii in 1779. But following Clerke's death from tuberculosis six months later, Lieutenant John Gore brought *Resolution* home and took over Cook's offered position as Captain of the Royal Hospital for Seamen at Greenwich.

Gore had sailed to Iceland with Joseph Banks when he quit the Antarctic expedition – as did Nick Young. After which Nick disappears from the historical record, although a statue of the boy can be seen near the beach at Gisborne, New Zealand, looking out across Poverty Bay to the point which bears his nickname: Young Nick's Head.

As for Isaac Manley, history shows he went on to prosper both in his naval career and in private life. Six months after joining HMS *Terrible,* he transferred as a Midshipman to HMS *Thames* of the Channel Service, patrolling home waters. Another eighteen months, and in 1774 Isaac sailed for the West Indies and the Jamaica Station on the *Antelope* – where, having served his time as a Midshipman and passing the examination, he was promoted as Lieutenant Manley to HMS *Ostrich* in May 1777.

That same month Isaac's father wrote to Mrs Elizabeth Cook, ordering volumes of the Captain's *Resolution* voyage, and giving news of his son in Jamaica. Isaac was starting to earn his fortune by taking part in the capture of eight enemy prize ships. In letters home, 'he spoke with much acknowledgement of both yours and Captain Cook's kindness to him, and desired to be remembered to you both.' Proof of the bond that had grown between the families.

Isaac returned to England the next year, and spent twenty-one months ashore on half pay. But the rapid build-up of enlistments following the outbreak of the American War of Independence, saw him appointed to HMS *Inflexible* in 1780. A year later Isaac sailed for New York on the *Lion* – and in November 1781 he became Second Lieutenant on HMS *Prince George*, flagship of Rear Admiral Digby who had taken command of the America Station in the closing stages of the war.

It was an opportunity for a young Lieutenant to shine before the eyes of his superiors, and Isaac took advantage of it. In April 1782, *Prince George* was part of a combined fleet under Admiral

Rodney that defeated the French at the Battle of the Saintes, in the Caribbean. A French fleet had been blockading the British army trapped at Yorktown, leading to the surrender of Lord Cornwallis (Isaac's brother John was a Captain on his staff), and the end of the land war. Now the French ships tried to seize the British-held island of Jamaica, but were decisively beaten at the Saintes.

Isaac must have performed well, for in December he was promoted to Master and Commander and took over his first ship, HMS *Britannia,* based in New York. He held several brief commands of escort ships over the next year. As Captain of the *Otter* he read the proclamation of peace; and with the establishment of the United States of America, Isaac sailed for home in command of the sloop HMS *Hound*.

There followed nearly three years ashore on half pay. But Isaac was rising in the world, and in 1786 he was given command of the sloop HMS *Fairy* out of Falmouth, then Leith in Scotland. It was pretty mundane work – patrolling the northern coast, chasing smugglers, even pressing seamen from passing brigs – but he was lucky to get the appointment. With the end of hostilities, the navy had been reduced from one hundred and ten thousand to only eighteen thousand men. It's a sign of Isaac's ability – as well as, in that age of patronage, his family's continuing influence with the Admiralty through Secretary Stephens – that he was offered the post at all.

And it wasn't all routine. In late 1788, even as an infant colony was struggling to establish itself at Port Jackson in New South Wales, *Fairy* was ordered to join a British squadron sailing for the west coast of Africa. Beyond the peak of Tenerife, which Isaac knew from his *Endeavour* days, they protected the seas used by the slave ships carrying their human cargoes across the Atlantic to the West Indies. Shades of Tom Richmond and George Dorlton, indeed!

The *Fairy* even made a crossing to the familiar waters of the Caribbean. The logbook shows that Commander Manley ordered his share of floggings for insolence, misbehaviour and drunkenness (of which he seems to have been much less tolerant than Cook). Then Isaac was stricken with fever, and in June 1789 he discharged himself as captain, his place taken by the Lieutenant.

So ill was he that it was a year before Isaac returned to England . . . 'Being at the time in so indifferent a State of Health that it was utterly impossible for me to do the duty of the ship,' he wrote to Stephens. The Admiralty must have understood, for on 22 November 1790 Isaac was promoted to the substantive rank of Post-Captain, and immediately went on half pay. Upon recovery, he wrote saying he was ready for service; but apart from some months raising troops in Oxfordshire after the outbreak of the French Revolutionary Wars, Captain Manley was not given another command.

It was an adequate career – but hardly a glorious one, given his magnificent start with Captain Cook and *Endeavour*. Yet fortune continued to smile on Isaac. Three months after becoming Post-Captain at the age of thirty-six, he married an heiress, Frances Pole, and they bought the estate of Braziers near the village of Checkendon in Oxfordshire. The house was remodelled and a front wing added in the Strawberry Hill gothic style: a lovely, late eighteenth century confection of battlements, arched doors and windows, overlooking the park and farmland.

Braziers is still standing, like a little fairy castle. It now belongs to a community, and visiting the house that Isaac built you have the impression it must have been a happy place for the family who grew up in it. There were two children: a daughter Ann (after Isaac's mother), and a son John Shawe (both family names) born in 1794.

He matriculated from Oxford and studied law at Lincoln's Inn; but for much of his life lived as a gentleman on the family lands in Staffordshire, the father of Isaac's five grandsons, and built a mansion of his own called Manley Hall.

It was to Isaac's good fortune that his elder brother John died in 1799 without children. So, when his father died two years later, Isaac inherited the bulk of the estate: properties in London, near Litchfield, and in Cheshire, with gold and silver plate. His unmarried sisters came to live at Braziers, and Captain Manley prospered as a landed gentleman. At a large ceremony in 1810, Oxford University conferred an Honorary Doctorate of Civil Laws on Rear Admiral Manley, as he had become.

For Isaac was also blessed with a long life. In those days, a Post-Captain on half pay continued to be promoted according to seniority. In 1790 there were some four hundred and thirty officers above Isaac on the Navy List. As one man died, so Isaac advanced up the ranks. And as he kept on living through the years of war with France and Napoleon, he rose to be appointed Rear Admiral in 1809; Vice Admiral of the Blue in 1814, of the White in 1820, of the Red in 1821; and in 1830 he was appointed Admiral of the White, all the time continuing to draw the appropriate half pay. In January 1837, Isaac became an Admiral of the Red, with only fourteen officers more senior to him.

Yet life was drawing to a close. In March he turned eighty-two. In July his wife Frances died, two years older than him. And as he sat at Braziers, telling the story of the *Endeavour* voyage to his grandsons for one more time, Isaac knew there would soon be no one to tell it again. He was the last of those still alive who could remember.

His namesake, Admiral Isaac Smith, had died in 1831. The Captain's widow, Elizabeth Cook, who almost outlived them all, passed on in 1835 at ninety-four, having burnt her husband's letters. Given his regard for Mrs Cook's kindness to him as a youth, it is likely that Isaac stayed in contact with the Captain's widow throughout their long lives. With Elizabeth's death, there was nobody left now from *Endeavour* days but Isaac Manley . . .

Such a long time ago . . . So much had happened since then. Wars and revolutions. Change and reform. The boy, who learned to sail with Captain Cook, had lived to see the first steamships cross the Atlantic. British colonies and new civilisations had been planted in those lands of the magical South Seas that Isaac had been among the first Europeans to see . . .

Aye, and could see them still in the embers of his fire and the piquant memories of wood smoke. Heimata, crowned with flowers, coming to him through the palm grove with gifts of coconut milk.

Tire . . . Tire . . .

The boy Te Horeta, standing proud on the high rock of the *pa* at Whitianga.

I will be a great warrior myself when I grow up.

And as the fair green promise of a new adventure rose on the sea's horizon, Isaac could still hear Nick Young calling to him from the very masthead of His Majesty's Bark *Endeavour.*

Land! Land ho!

On 17 October 1837, Admiral Isaac George Manley himself died. And the first thing that was said of him on the memorial at Checkendon Church, and in his obituary published in the

Gentleman's Magazine, were these words about the greatest event of Isaac's life:

> *He was the last survivor of the crew who sailed with Captain Cook during his first voyage around the world.*

HISTORICAL NOTES

The best part of writing any book is the research journey one has to undertake: and the best part of this book was the eight-day voyage from Melbourne to Sydney I made as a supernumerary on board the *Endeavour* replica. It was a pretty ghastly start, to be sure, hit by a violent storm as we left Port Phillip and laid low with seasickness. I sprawled on the deck, clipped to a safety line, pouring my innards into Bass Strait and wanting only to die. But I came good the next day, having the only firm bunk on board in 'Banks's cabin' (everybody else, including the captain, sleeping in those awful swaying hammocks).

In any case, you have to know the depths in order to appreciate the poetic heights of a sailing ship: of standing on deck in the fair, grey dawn; the wind luffing in the sails; the light just beginning to slip above the eastern horizon. It was on such a morning, on the fourth day into our voyage, that Captain Ross Mattson pointed to a smudge on the distant shoreline and said, 'That's Point Hicks over there.' Cook's first landfall on the east coast of New Holland. And I had one of those moments of epiphany that sometimes occur in life. Here, I thought, for me and my family – and for all whose families have migrated over the past two-and-a-quarter centuries to the country we now call Australia – here is where it all began: from such an early morning sighting in April 1770 on the quarterdeck of a ship just like this.

It was the beginning of the story of European settlement: one that actually commenced eighteen years later with the colony at Sydney Cove, largely at the promptings of Sir Joseph Banks and James Matra [Magra] who'd both been aboard *Endeavour*. And of course from there it has developed over the generations into the free, prosperous nation we know today.

But I was also conscious that for the indigenous people encountered by *Endeavour* men and later voyagers – in Australia, New Zealand, Tahiti and islands across the Pacific – it marked the beginning of the destruction of societies, cultures and very often the people themselves. Not just by invasion, dispossession and superior weapons. For along with their material goods and knowledge, much of which was highly desirable, Europeans also brought more insidious things: smallpox, measles, venereal disease, even the common cold wrought havoc among people who had no resistance to them. Within a few years of colonisation, the Aboriginal population around Sydney had declined by some 70 per cent, largely the result of infection – not to mention the effects of introduced alcohol, which have devastated many indigenous communities around the world.

It's undeniable, I think, that we're still living with the consequences of that original European incursion. We cannot change the past: but we can attempt to right the wrongs that occurred, to accommodate all citizens within the societies *we* are creating. And the movements for indigenous cultural and political recognition, which have been such a feature of South Pacific countries in recent years, not least Australia, are very much part of that imperative. Certainly, throughout the writing of this book, I also tried to present a view as it might have seemed to those 'on the other side of the beach'.

Recent controversies over the inscriptions on statues of Captain Cook claiming that he discovered Australia or other territories, for example, show how potent a symbol he remains to all people touched by the subsequent history of his voyages. Personally, I think there's a good case for placing an addendum on such statues. Cook did not discover Australia or New Zealand, Fiji, Tonga or Hawaii. These lands were discovered by their first indigenous inhabitants, and their descendants have every right to feel they've been rendered invisible by those who give that honour to the Captain. Yet to replace the original inscriptions – or even to remove the statues entirely – would be folly. They speak to their time and the people who created them. 'Historical understanding proceeds through a process of accretion, not erasure,' as the director of the National Museum of Australia, Dr Mathew Trinca, wrote in a fine article on Cook and Indigenous Australians. Quite so. The challenge we have today is to incorporate *both* indigenous and immigrant perspectives in our telling of the nation's story.

Even Captain Cook recognised that, whatever advantages might accrue to Britain and the world from his explorations and contact with indigenous people, they came at a dreadful cost. The tropical climate, the easy life, the sexual favours granted to the visiting sailors on Tahiti in return for a scrap of metal, made it seem like some earthly paradise. Yet the discovery that venereal disease was even then rife among Tahitians filled him with dismay. It would, Cook confided to his journal, be to 'the eternal reproach' of those who brought it there. And it was of little comfort to be told by the people there that it had been first introduced by the crews of either Captain Wallis or de Bougainville's two ships. The worm was already in the fruit of this apparent Eden.

The French were also active in the Pacific at the time of the *Endeavour* voyage – as the Spanish and Portuguese had been in earlier centuries, claiming countries for their respective monarchs and establishing colonies. Indeed, Cook and de Surville passed each other's track in heavy weather, rounding the north cape of New Zealand in December 1769. Within days of the First Fleet arriving at Botany Bay they were visited by La Perouse, and in following years d'Entrecasteaux and Baudin, among others, visited the Australian coast.

It's clear that European migration into the South Pacific would have occurred eventually, even without Cook's three great voyages. The significance of Cook's expeditions lay in the extraordinary accuracy of his navigation and the charts he produced. If a satellite image of the east coast of Australia is overlaid on Cook's chart, the correlation with those sections he actually mapped is remarkable. Certainly, there are blanks that were later filled in by others, but at the very least the scope and accuracy of Cook's achievement helped ensure that the region was opened to European trade and settlement earlier than might otherwise have been the case. And because of the *Endeavour* voyage, it's to our good fortune (though Indigenous Australians and Maori might disagree) that the two principal land masses Cook charted – New Zealand and the eastern part of New Holland that he named New South Wales – were occupied by the British rather than another European power. The colonists brought with them English common law and British notions of political and economic liberalism; and the territories thus became self-governing and ultimately independent, democratic nations sooner than they might otherwise have done.

James Cook was undoubtedly an immensely gifted seaman. But in that age of patronage and distinction between the social classes, this son of a Yorkshire farmhand was also extremely fortunate in the opportunities that came his way, his capacity to take advantage of them, and the support he received thereby from the great men of influence in the Royal Navy, the Admiralty, the Royal Society and at court.

Cook learned his trade sailing merchant colliers from Whitby to London: robust, deep-waisted, shallow-draught barks. *Endeavour* (and *Resolution*) became the most famous examples of this type of ship, because of the skill with which Cook used them in his Pacific exploration. Indeed, the discovery of *Endeavour*'s likely last resting place off Newport, Rhode Island, where she was sunk in 1778 as part of a blockade during the American War of Independence, is a noteworthy aspect of these 250th anniversary commemorations.

Transferring to the Royal Navy, Cook rose quickly from master's mate to master. He took part in the survey of the St Lawrence River that facilitated the capture of Quebec in 1759; and for the next decade Cook honed his abilities in navigation, mathematics and astronomy by charting the coasts of Newfoundland and Nova Scotia. The work brought Cook to the attention and patronage of the then governor and subsequent Admiral, Sir Hugh Palliser. This, together with the published charts and his paper on the observation of a solar eclipse, brought Cook to the notice of the Admiralty and the Royal Society. And that in turn led to his appointment to command the scientific expedition to observe the 1769 Transit of

Venus at Tahiti (only recently discovered for Europeans by Captain Wallis in the *Dolphin*) and thence to search for the unknown continent believed to exist in the South Seas.

It was the Royal Navy's – and one of the world's – first voyages to carry a complement of scientists: something the Portuguese governor of Rio refused to accept, ordering them to remain on board *Endeavour*, believing them to be spies. Remarkably, Cook was dissatisfied with the results of his observation of the Transit, for there was over half a minute's difference in the times his three teams recorded between the planet entering and leaving the sun's limb. It had to do with the distortions caused by the sun's 'halo' or penumbra; though when combined with observations taken at the same time from various parts of the globe, the Earth's distance from the sun was calculated pretty accurately at ninety-five million miles.

The Captain was modest about his geographical achievements – proving that Tasman's New Zealand was in fact two large islands and not part of any great southern continent, and mapping the east coast of New Holland – believing them to be no great discoveries, though of some service to navigation and human knowledge. The Admiralty thought rather more highly of Cook's accomplishments and quickly had him preparing for a second Pacific voyage, which he'd suggested: a nice example of the man making and seizing his own opportunities.

Even on the *Endeavour* Cook had begun to doubt the existence of any large undiscovered landmass in habitable latitudes, and the second voyage proved him correct, when he twice entered the Antarctic Circle – the first mariner with his crew to do so. Cook was rather less self-effacing about this feat. Indeed, at a time when European sailors had to depend either on the unreliable method of 'dead reckoning' or complex lunar observations and mathematical formulae to fix their longitude (though Cook came to realise the Polynesians had traversed vast stretches of the Pacific using the stars and currents as their guide), the second voyage contributed another mighty service to human knowledge. Cook had with him Larcum Kendall's copy of Harrison's chronometer – 'our trusty friend' Cook called it, 'our never-failing guide the Watch' – and by proving its worth revolutionised the practice of navigation and safety at sea.

To which we should add the remarkable pains he took to care for the health of his crews. By insisting – to the extremes of the lash if necessary – that his men ate fresh meat and vegetables wherever possible, Cook did as much as any eighteenth century sea captain to eradicate scurvy from his ships. He introduced sauerkraut and concentrated lemon juice to Royal Navy diets, constantly collected greenstuff such as scurvy grass and native 'celery' at his landings, and made 'spruce beer' from local ingredients. It's true that, during the three years *Endeavour* was at sea, she lost a third of her crew: but that was due to other diseases, mostly contracted at Batavia, or accidents. Not one man died of scurvy: an extraordinary thing in that age, after such a long voyage.

Cook was no less fortunate that the *Endeavour* expedition brought him into the company and friendship of that wealthy young gentleman, Joseph Banks – a passionate student and patron of natural history, a genuine spirit of the Enlightenment, and at twenty-three already a Fellow of the Royal Society. In fact, he put up some £5000 towards the cost of the expedition, a vast sum in those days. Along with his own enthusiasm and knowledge of the world, the quality of the scientific and artistic talent Banks brought on board contributed significantly to the astonishing success of the voyage in both popular and cultured European opinion.

The Royal Society had appointed a former assistant Astronomer Royal, Charles Green, to observe the Transit in company with Cook and his fellow officers. The novelty was that Banks had in his civilian retinue the celebrated Swedish natural historian Dr Daniel Solander, a student and protégé of Linnaeus, together with his assistant, Herman Spöring, to identify and classify the tens of thousands of botanical, zoological and mineral specimens the expedition found: many of them, from New Zealand and New South Wales, hitherto unknown in Europe. One of the plants, the genus *Banksia*, was later to bear its collector's name. But there was also an extraordinary animal, like a greyhound that hopped, called a *kongouro* [kangaroo]. And eucalyptus trees that, defying nature as the Europeans knew it, kept their leaves and shed their bark!

Accompanying the scientists were two artists: Alexander Buchan, employed to draw and paint the landscapes that the expedition visited and the people they met, and Sydney Parkinson, a young natural history draughtsman of great talent, to record for posterity the specimens they collected. As it turned out, Buchan died at Tahiti and Parkinson had to assume almost the entire artistic workload – a challenge to which he rose wonderfully. In the course of the voyage, before his own tragic death from dysentery and malaria on the way home, he produced over 1300 drawings and sketches, an average of more than two a day. They are of superb quality, depicting the ship, the landscapes, the people, the flora and fauna they encountered. Banks had 743 of Parkinson's finished botanical watercolours engraved at great cost under Dr Solander's supervision, intending to publish them. Curiously he never did. It wasn't until 1980 – two centuries later – that the complete *Banks' Florilegium* began to be published, and the full extent of Sydney Parkinson's artistic achievement was revealed. Even so, from prints made at the time after Parkinson's drawings, Europeans saw for the first time the tattooed head of a Maori, and the two Aboriginal men, armed with shield and spear, who confronted the landing party at Botany Bay.

There was more than just the *depiction* of a Maori. In his vast collection, Joseph Banks also had the severed head of a boy – acquired by trading his underwear with a local chief at 'Cannibal Bay', as the crew called their anchorage in Queen Charlotte Sound. Very gruesome . . . but undoubtedly very fascinating. And it was this fascination with recording the local customs, social mores, structures, languages, beliefs and behaviours of the native inhabitants – collecting artefacts, items of clothing, weapons, utensils and objects of veneration – that further enriched the importance of the *Endeavour* voyage. Indeed, the great ethnographic collections brought back by Banks – and later by the Forsters, father and son, from the second voyage – laid the foundation for the modern discipline of anthropology. Much of the material was dispersed – even lost – over the years, though there have lately been some splendid touring exhibitions bringing many of the artefacts together again. More are planned for the 250th commemoration years; and the reopening of the Banks collection at the Pitt Rivers Museum in Oxford is yet another cause for celebration.

Nor were the new vistas opened up by *Endeavour* confined to the academies: they had a huge effect on the public imagination. The idealised accounts of life in Tahiti, and the return to Europe of a Tahitian man named Aotourou with de Bougainville and another called Omai, from Cook's second voyage, fed into those concepts of the 'noble savage' so popular at the time. They were believed to epitomise the seemingly happy innocence of humanity in the state of nature before we were corrupted by political institutions, as supposed by some Enlightenment philosophers. 'Man was born free, and he is everywhere in chains,' wrote Jean-Jacques Rousseau in the opening lines of *The Social Contract*. These were influential ideas in the growing resistance to autocratic government in the later eighteenth century, culminating in the American and French revolutions. They resonated again in the slogan of the communist Karl Marx during the following century, 'Workers of the world unite! You have nothing to lose but your chains.' And who could argue those words don't echo down to the present day? Of course the *Endeavour* men, who had seen the piled-up bones of warriors killed during a recent war in Tahiti and observed the remains of a Maori cannibal feast, could have told them that life in the state of nature was not all tranquillity and bliss. Human beings were prone to conquest and violence everywhere. Indeed, Thomas Hobbes's view of life in such a condition as 'nasty, brutish and short' might be considered as closer to the mark.

Still, that didn't stop exotic notions of a tropical paradise from influencing artists, players and writers down the generations, from Robert Louis Stevenson to Paul Gaugin. To be sure, they had their own reasons for moving to Samoa and Tahiti: but idyllic imaginings of the sweet and plenteous life, brought to Europe with Wallis, de Bougainville and Cook, were very persuasive. As they still are. I've been smitten with them since I first read *Treasure Island*.

Given the vast amount of material brought back by Banks and his party, it's not surprising that public opinion initially saw the *Endeavour* voyage as his expedition and credited him, rather than Cook, with responsibility for its success (though the Admiralty knew better). After all, Banks was a rich young gentleman who'd invested heavily in the venture, and was rightfully due all the accoutrements of celebrity in that deferential age. He was presented first to the King, and he subsequently introduced Cook and

Solander, whom he'd appointed his secretary and librarian. Banks became lionised throughout London society, his collections the magnet of the educated world in Britain and Europe.

His decision, then, to withdraw from Cook's second expedition – to the Antarctic – in a fit of temper, was surely one of the most foolish dummy-spits in scientific history. Still, Cook remained on cordial terms with Banks. He was always the 'humble and obedient servant' in their correspondence, for he knew his place in the social order. He sent Banks several casks of preserved birds, fish and a box of plant specimens from the Cape on his return from the second voyage. And when Cook was killed in 1779 at Hawaii – the group of islands he discovered for the Europeans during his third voyage, trying to find the North-West Passage over the top of America – Banks did as much as anyone to ensure the Captain's achievements became fully known to the world.

It wasn't until after his death, indeed, that Cook became immortalised as the great and humane navigator he was, and he took his own place in the firmament of celebrity. Where his star continues to shine brightly (if not uncritically) during these 250th commemorations, that of Joseph Banks has dimmed somewhat by comparison in the public mind. Perhaps, in this transit of personalities and endeavour, it has something to do with the radiance of Cook's own 'halo'.

Anthony Hill
Canberra, 2018

CHAPTER NOTES

INTRODUCTION

Sincere thanks to Professor Adrian Horridge, and to Michelle Hetherington, Senior Curator, Australian Society and History at the National Museum of Australia, for reading the introduction and historical notes in draft, and for their valuable comments and suggestions.

Endeavour. I sailed on the *Endeavour* replica from Melbourne to Sydney in April 2006. A more complete account of the research journey is on my website www.anthonyhillbooks.com/ideaofisaac.html. There are many photos of the replica ship on the National Maritime Museum of Australia website www.anmm.gov.au/whats-on/vessels/hmb-endeavour.

CHAPTER 1

Black hand. The Manley family dates to the Norman Conquest, and the crest to medieval times. John Manley's shield can still be seen in Middle Temple Hall.

London Bridge. The first stone bridge over the Thames was opened in 1209 and stood for over six hundred years. The second

London Bridge opened in 1831, and the most recent in 1973. Baldwin's *Guide* of 1768 gives the watermen's rate from London to Deptford as two shillings and sixpence (half a crown). *Shooting the Bridge*. The dangers were very real, see Jackson, pp 70–1.

Manley family. Isaac was descended through the younger branch of a landed family from Erbistock, in Wales. His great-great grandfather, John, fought for Cromwell and was an MP. His great-grandfather, Isaac, was Postmaster-General in Ireland, and grandfather, John (d. 1743), was a Commissioner for Customs and lived at Hatton Garden. His father, also John (c. 1716–1801), was called to the Bar in 1739 and became a Bencher (senior member) of the Middle Temple in 1768. In 1750 he married Ann Hammond and they had five children.

Isaac George Manley. Baptised St Giles-in-the-Fields, London, 3 March 1755. His elder brother, John (d. 1799), and younger brother Robert Kenrick (d. 1843), both entered the 33rd [Lord Cornwallis's] Regiment. Isaac had an elder sister, Maria, and a younger, Louisa, both apparently unmarried. It's not known where the children went to school: possibly the family had a tutor. A coloured print of Admiral Manley in later life by Richard Dighton can be seen at the Greenwich National Maritime Museum website.

Servant. It is unclear how Isaac got a place on *Endeavour*, but his father had connections with the Royal Navy. In 1790 Isaac wrote to the Secretary of the Admiralty, Sir Philip Stephens, *My father desires his compts* [compliments] Adm 1/2126. It was the age of patronage, and Stephens had begun his career at the Navy Office, near the Customs House where Isaac's grandfather was a Commissioner.

London. I have used the facsimile of John Roque's *Plan* of 1746.

Tahiti. The modern spelling. Cook and others used the archaic *Otaheite*.

Endeavour. Built in 1764 as a collier at Whitby, Yorkshire. A cat-built (deep-waisted) bark of three masts, square rigged, she weighed 368 tons, had an extreme length of 97ft 7in (29.7m), and was 29ft 3in (8.9m) at her widest (measurements Parkin, p 4). She drew about 14ft of water (less than 2.5 fathoms) laden. Originally the *Earl of Pembroke*, she was renamed HM Bark *Endeavour* when bought by the Navy in 1768.

James Cook. One of the world's greatest navigators. Born in 1728 at Marton, Yorkshire, son of a Scottish farm labourer. At seventeen he was apprenticed to a Staithes grocer, but subsequently transferred to a Whitby coal-shipper, the Quaker John Walker, where Cook learned his seamanship. In 1755 he joined the Royal Navy, and received high praise for his survey of the St Lawrence River in Canada during the Seven Years' War. His later survey of Newfoundland and observation of an eclipse brought him to the attention of the Royal Society, the Admiralty, and his appointment as Lieutenant to command *Endeavour. Cook's description.* Dr David Samwell, surgeon on *Discovery.* The John Webber portrait of Cook at the Australian National Portrait Gallery can be seen online, and the Nathanial Dance portrait, considered a good likeness, at the National Maritime Museum, Greenwich.

Nick Young. Described by Molineux's *Journal*, October 1769, as about twelve years old. Gore calls him 'a little boy'. He does not appear on the muster roll until 18 April 1769 after Alexander Buchan died at Tahiti, but was clearly on board.

HMS *Dolphin.* The *Dolphin* made two voyages around the world. The first was with Captain Byron (1764–66). The second, under Captain Wallis (1766–68), discovered Tahiti; and his glowing accounts encouraged the Royal Society to select the island for the Pacific observation of the Transit of Venus.

Master. One of the most important roles on an eighteenth-century ship. The modern equivalent would be that of navigator, although a Master's responsibility for the internal management of the ship was much broader. Isaac would have learned his trade from topmast to keel. Otago University has a fine portrait of Molineux. Otago Harbour and the Clutha River, New Zealand, were originally named after Molineux by Cook.

Larboard. Easily confused with 'starboard', and subsequently charged to 'port.'

CHAPTER 2

Endeavour. My descriptions of life aboard the ship are based on an eight-day sail I made as a supernumerary on the *Endeavour* replica from Melbourne to Sydney in April 2006, and visits to the ship at the Australian National Maritime Museum, Sydney. I thank Captain Ross Mattson, his officers and crew for their kindness in helping to teach this landlubber his ropes. See the Australian National Maritime Museum for photos of the ship.

Hammock. I had one night sleeping in a hammock in the 4ft 6in section of the deck. It was enough.

Joseph Banks. The son of a wealthy Norfolk landowner. Born in 1743, he was educated at Harrow and Eton, where he developed his love of botany. He furthered his studies at Oxford and, after inheriting his father's fortune in 1764, pursued his natural history interests with a visit to Newfoundland and Labrador, and tours of Europe. Elected to the Royal Society in 1766, it asked that Banks be allowed to join the *Endeavour* expedition to the South Seas. His reputation established by the extraordinary collections he brought back from the voyage, Banks became one of the most important figures and patrons in the British scientific establishment, a friend of

King George III for many years, and was created a baronet and a Knight Companion of the Bath. Banks was elected President of the Royal Society in 1778, a position he held until his death in 1820. Banks gave his support to the establishment of a penal colony at Botany Bay, though he long believed that the merino sheep, which he was breeding for the king, wouldn't thrive in the new colony. The latter opinion was to prove as wrong as the former was correct.

Storm. Cook, *Journal*, 1 September 1768.

Weather sayings. From a collection at the Maritime Museum, Falmouth, UK.

Net. Banks, *Journal*, 5 September.

Weir. Cook, 14 September. *Flogging.* 16 September. A photo of the cat-o-nine-tails can be seen online at the National Maritime Museum, Greenwich. Pickersgill was himself made to 'Stand before the mast' in disgrace the following month, for refusing to help scrub the deck.

Scurvy. See Brown, Rodger, pp 100–103; Beaglehole, *Life*, pp 135–6. The physician James Lind wrote in 1756 on the value of citrus in preventing scurvy, but little notice was taken at first.

Lord Anson. George Anson (1697–1762), First Lord of the Admiralty. Circumnavigated the world 1740–43, his fleet of six ships reduced to one. Less than 200 men returned. Of the 961 men who died, 90 per cent perished of scurvy. Brown says, 'This terrible loss heralds the golden age of scurvy research in England.'

Funchal. Parkinson (p 2) says the hills above Funchal were cultivated with vines and orange trees, and it 'appears like one wide, extended, beautiful garden'. As distinct from the uncultivated floggings taking place on board *Endeavour*.

St Nicholas. Author visit October 2006. The skull and crossbones can still be seen on the gateposts, also the charnel house.

Thurman. Beaglehole, *Journal*, vol I, p 600, 'The Ship's Company'. *Press gang abroad*. See Rodger, pp 180–2. I assume Thurman was taken ashore; press gangs also boarded merchant ships.

CHAPTER 3

Tenerife. Banks, 23 September.

Spanish Ladies. The shanty dates to the 1690s. It recurs throughout this book. I have used a version found with three different tunes at www.ingeb.org/songs.

Shark. Banks, 29 September.

Bully boys, Bullies. 'Fine boys, hearties.' Originally a term of affection or comradeship, and used in this sense. No doubt actions such as the press gangs led to its current tyrannical meaning.

Sauerkraut. Keeps well and retains much of its vitamin C, a vital ingredient in overcoming scurvy during long sea voyages. Though Cook did not know the science, he received the Copley Medal in 1776 for demonstrating its efficacy. See Cook, *Journal*, 13 April 1769, for his psychology in getting the crew to eat it. Cook's other remedies against scurvy included malt wort, portable soup, and concentrated lemon juice (rob of lemon), but boiling or vinegar removed most of the vitamin C and they were largely ineffective. Apart from sauerkraut, the real antiscorbutics were fresh food, greenstuffs, and above all citrus fruit. Once this was understood, every British ship carried lemons and limes – hence the term 'Limeys'.

Crossing the Line. Banks, 25 October, describes the ceremony.

Rio. Cook, 13–30 November.

Sneaking ashore. Banks, 22–26 November. *Jails*. 20 November.

Portuguese. My thanks to the Embassy of Portugal, Canberra, for the translations.

Flogger flogged. Cook, 30 November.

CHAPTER 4

Flower. Cook, 2 December 1768.

Watches. A continuous watch must be kept on a ship to ensure safety and readiness for duty. This requires a proportion of the crew to be 'on watch' at any one time. Usually, all watches are four hours, except the first and last 'dog watches', which are each two hours long. 'Dog' may be a shortened term for those said to be 'dodging' a full four-hour watch.

A ship's twenty-four-hour day formerly ran from noon to noon. Before chronometers, this was a known time with the sun at its zenith. In a three-watch system (red, white and blue), crew serve every third watch. If the dog watches were not split, each watch would be on duty at the same time every day. This typical three-day roster shows how the time of watches rotates for each watch:

Watch	Day 1	Day 2	Day 3
Noon–4pm	Red	White	Blue
4–6pm (dog watch)	White	Blue	Red
6–8pm (dog watch)	Blue	Red	White
8pm–midnight	Red	White	Blue
Midnight–4am	White	Blue	Red
4–8am	Blue	Red	White
8am–noon	Red	White	Blue

With a two-watch system (Port watch and Starboard watch) the crew is divided into two rather than three groups. They are 'on watch' for four hours and have only four hours off. There are no dog watches. The system means more crew are available for each watch, but they have less rest.

The watch is not only necessary for the safe passage of the ship: it provides structure, meaning and occupation for the daily lives of sailors, helping to prevent minds from becoming idle, bored or mischievous.

Giants & pigmies. See Hawkesworth, 'Introduction'; also Byron and Wallis sections.

Indians. The *Endeavour* journals usually refer to any native peoples as Indians. I have kept the practice here in direct speech.

Fearnought jackets. Cook, 6 January 1769.

Guanaco. Animal similar to a llama.

Deaths. Based on Banks, 16–17 January. Buchan's painting of *Endeavour's* watering place at Terra del Fuego can be seen online at the British Library. Also search the National Library of Australia's Trove online pictures archive for Buchan's view of a native hut.

Slaves. It is estimated nine-and-a-half million African slaves were transported to the Americas during the eighteenth and early nineteenth centuries. England stopped its slave trade in 1807 and abolished it altogether in its colonies in 1834.

Albatross. Banks, 5 February.

Nails. See Wallis, July 1767, in Hawkesworth. *Goat. Ibid*, p 313.

Greenslade. Cook and Banks, 26 March.

CHAPTER 5

Search the National Library of Australia's Trove pictures archive for illustrations of Cook and *Endeavour* at Tahiti. Search also Matavai Bay, Fort Venus, Transit, Parkinson, etc.

Plantain. Tropical fruit, similar to a banana.

Rules. Cook, 13 April. *Thieves.* 14 April. *Shooting.* 16 April.

Buchan. Banks, 16–19 April. *Nick Young.* Mustered, 18 April; Beaglehole, *Journal I*, p 600.

Flags. Cook, 12 June.

Dog. Cook, 20 June; Parkinson p 20.

Heiva. Banks, 'Manners and Customs of South Seas Islands', *Journal*, 14 August.

Flytrap. Banks, 22 April.

Doll. Cook, Banks, 28 April. *Quadrant*. 2 May.

Mutinous talk. Molineux, 5 May, and also trip around island, 8 May.

Surfing. Banks, 29 May, the first European description of the sport. I assume Isaac also saw it.

Rats. Molineux, 26 May; Parkinson, p 21.

Transit. Cook, 3 June. The Transit occurs in pairs, eight years apart, separated by approx. one hundred and twenty years. It occurred in 1761 and 1769, 1874 and 1882, 2004 and 2012. It was hoped to calculate the Earth's distance from the sun using the principles of parallax – i.e. to measure the slight apparent shifts in the track of Venus across the sun as seen from different parts of Earth. Hence the importance of the Tahiti sighting. See Lomb.

Observation. I can find no primary source description on how the observation was done. I have assumed that direct observation through the reflecting telescope (with dark filter glass) and projection onto a card or screen were both used. I thank Dr David Jauncey, Dr Nick Lomb, and Margaret Morris for their advice. Part of Cook's report on the observation can be seen online in the NLA's Trove pictures archive: search 'Cook Transit'.

Note: It cannot be stressed too strongly how dangerous it is to observe the sun with the naked eye. Even using a dark glass is no longer acceptable. Always make an observation under proper supervision and with correct equipment.

Tupaia. Banks, 5 June.

CHAPTER 6

Continent. See *Alexander Dalrymple* note next chapter.

Teredo. A shipworm which bores into timber hulls, piers, etc.

Mourner. Banks, 10 June.

Tattoo. Cook, 'Description of King George's Island', *Journal*, 13 August; Banks, 5 July and 'Manners and Customs'; Parkinson, p 25.

Wolf. Cook, 4 June. *Banks & Monkhouse*. Parkinson, 19 June, p 32.

VD. Cook, 6 June. It seems that gonorrhoea was the particular venereal disease brought to Tahiti. The widespread tropical disease of yaws can give some immunity to syphilis. I have used 'pox' as period slang to include any form of VD: 'distemper' is Cook's word. As he foretold, it spread through the Pacific with other diseases introduced by Europeans – measles, smallpox, even the common cold – that devastated indigenous communities. Beaglehole, p 188; Salmond (2004), p 69.

Arioi. Banks, 'Manners and Customs'.

Thurman. Cook, 12 June. How Thurman must have regretted going to Madeira!

Marae. Banks, 13 & 18 June.

Boy chief. Cook, 21 June.

Rake. Cook, Banks, 14 June. *Island tour*. 26 June–1 July.

Marines. Cook, 10–11 July. Despite his punishment Gibson had great respect for the Captain, as Cook did for him. Gibson sailed as Corporal on Cook's second voyage in the *Resolution*, and as Sergeant on the third voyage. He was with the Captain when Cook was killed by natives at Hawaii in 1779.

Tupaia. Banks, 12 July, writes, 'I do not know why I may not keep him as a curiosity, as well as some of my neighbours do lions and tygers . . .'

Heimata. A popular Tahitian name, it means 'crowned with eyes'; a clairvoyant. I thank Tehani Fiedler-Valenta of Tahiti Tourisme Australie for her assistance.

Quarrel. Bootie, *Journal*, July 1769. The torn-out page has been re-inserted in the wrong place. *Evil communications* is from the Bible, *1 Corinthians*. It is uncertain if Nick wrote the words himself, as the hand seems very mature for a twelve-year-old.

Orders. Beaglehole, *Life*, pp 147–9.

INTERLUDE

Tupaia's map. Cook's drawing based on Tupaia's map is at the British Library. See Aughton, pp 132–3. Drawings by Tupaia can be seen online at the British Library site. The Wikipedia entry for Tupaia has the map he drew for Cook showing the islands around Tahiti.

Alexander Dalrymple. Scottish geographer (1737–1808), a believer in the southern continent. In 1767 he published *An Account of Discoveries in the South Pacifick Ocean previous to 1764* including a map, a copy of which he gave to Banks. The Royal Society proposed Dalrymple command the *Endeavour* expedition, but as he was not a Royal Navy officer the Admiralty gave the post to Cook, and the two thus became rivals. See Robson, and also *Torres* note in Chapter 11.

Mat sails. Could be tilted fore and aft, much like a modern windsurfer.

Ceremony. Cook, 17 July. *Possession.* 21 July.

Taiata. Parkinson did a fine drawing of the boy, see Aughton, p 113, also online.

Smoking. The muster book shows Isaac was first charged nineteen shillings for two months' tobacco in September 1769.

By February 1771 it had increased to twenty-eight shillings and sixpence.

Reading. Cook, 28 August. *Comet*. 29 August.

Sextant. I thank Captain Jim Cottee, navigator during my sail on the *Endeavour* replica, for his patience in showing me how to use a sextant.

Supplies. Banks, 23 September, also *weevils*. He notes they have seventeen sheep, four or five fowls, as many Muscovy ducks and Tahitian hogs, an English boar and sow with litter. The goat is not mentioned. The sauerkraut is as good as ever.

Reward. Parkinson, p 85. He says Cook offered *two* gallons of rum if land were discovered at night! *Land of Promise*. Banks, 1 October.

CHAPTER 7

Poverty Bay. Account based on Salmond (2004), Cook, Banks and esp. Monkhouse, 9–12 October. Cook does not name the four boys with the yawl. I assume Isaac was there.

Maori names. See Salmond (2004), pp 116, 119. *Tattoo*. Monkhouse.

Rock. Called *Toka-a-Taiau*, it has been removed for navigation. A fine memorial at Gisborne, in the form of a Maori canoe prow, overlooks the site of these encounters.

Homeland. The first canoes carrying the Maori ancestors reached New Zealand around AD1000 from central Polynesia, which includes today's Society, Marquesas, Cook and Austral Islands. The homeland is now generally known as Hawaiki. Banks spelt it Heawye, and the name Hawaii has the same origin. The island of Ra'iatea was also once known as Havai'i, Salmond (2004), p 37.

Maori. The first Maori settlers lived by fishing, gathering, cultivating sweet potato (*kumara*), and hunting the large ostrich-like moa bird that became extinct. The second phase of settlement from about 1350 was marked by more intense agriculture and fortified settlements (*pa*) especially in the North Island, reflecting greater population pressures and violent competition for resources. Bellwood, p 416. An online search for 'Parkinson Maori' will yield good results.

Maori boys. Banks, 10 October, gives their names as Taahourange, Koikerange and Maragooete, aged about eighteen, fifteen and ten.

Censure. Cook's defence, 10 October.

Arse. Monkhouse, *Journal*, in Beaglehole, *Journals*, vol I, p 576.

Kidnappers. Cook et al., 15 October. I thank Paul Tapsell of the Auckland War Memorial Museum for his insights into the motives behind the seizure of Taiata, and also for the importance of Tupaia (symposium 'Discovering Cook's Collections', National Museum of Australia, July 2006).

Whitianga. Author visit, May 2006, and Salmond (1991). The video *Twelve Days*, produced for the Mercury Bay District Historical Society, gives an interesting Maori and Pakeha perspective on Cook's time at Whitianga. I climbed to the *pa* site on Whitianga rock. I thank Peter Johnston of the Ngati Hei people for his illuminating advice.

Shooting. Cook, 9 November.

Te Horeta. See Beaglehole, *Life*, p 206; Salmond (2004), pp 131–2, with painting.

CHAPTER 8

Kauri. Cook, 21 November. *Bay of Islands*. 30 November.

Terrors of shipwreck. Banks, 5 December.

De Surville. Jean de Surville (1717–70), commanded the *St Jean Baptiste.* Landed his damaged ship at Doubtless Bay on the west coast of New Zealand, but left after conflict with Maori. Drowned off Peru. Beaglehole, *Life*, p 211. See also www.history-nz.org.

Cannibal Bay. Cook named it 'Ship's Cove', as it is still known. The name 'Cannibal Bay' appears in several log books and Parkinson, p 117. I had a magical day on the Sound with Peter and Takutai Beech, who told many tales from the past.

Topaa. Banks, 29 January 1770, gives his name; see also Salmond (2004), pp 145–6.

Human arm. Banks, 16 January, records the conversation. *Topaa's forearm.* Cook, 17 January.

Heads. Banks, 20 January. *Buys one.* Banks, 'Account of New Zealand', *Journal*, 31 March.

Upper arm muscles. I thank Professor Adrian Horridge for this interesting detail. He got it from an old lady in New Guinea who apparently spoke from experience. In his later visits, Cook landed goats and South Seas hogs in New Zealand to provide meat. They thrived, and provided the Maori with an alternative source of protein to human flesh. Betty Rowe had some of their descendants at her sanctuary on Arapawa Island in Queen Charlotte Sound when I visited in 2006.

Cook Strait. Banks, 6 February. *Possession.* Cook, 31 January.

Portuguese. A probable sixteenth-century Portuguese or Spanish helmet has been found in Wellington Harbour. Peter Beech tells of the *Rewharewha* sickness, possibly measles, caught by Maori from the sailors of a ship which visited the Sound long before Cook, maybe one of Christopher de Mendonça's fleet in the 1520s, see note in Chapter 9. Some say the spotty symptoms resembled the pattern found on pottery from this ship, others that it was like the flecked grain of the rewarewa tree. Many sailors are said to have been killed after trying to steal Maori women as their ship left. An epidemic of *Rewharewha* (coughing sickness) killed many Maori in the nineteenth century.

Cape Turnagain. Cook, 9 February.

Longitude. I commend Sobel's book to all interested readers. By general agreement, the *prime meridian* from which longitude readings are made runs through the Royal Observatory, Greenwich. Visitors to *John Harrison's* three sea clocks at the Royal Observatory are conscious of a great man. Cook's chronometer, made by Larcum Kendall after Harrison, is displayed at the National Maritime Museum, Greenwich. The *Nautical Almanac*, first published in 1767 by the Astronomer Royal Nevil Maskelyne, halved the time it took to work out a 'lunar' – but it only contained tables to the end of 1769. Those for 1770 and 1771 were not completed until after *Endeavour* left England. See Howse and Sanderson.

Airy fabric. Banks, 10 March. *Regret.* 14 March.

Westward route. Cook, 31 March.

CHAPTER 9

Whistle. Falconer writes in 1769 of superstitious seamen being 'afraid of the dreadful consequences of whistling in a storm' (entry on midshipmen). Whistling is still prohibited on Her Majesty's ships, as it can be confused with piped orders by the Bosun: the Bosun's call. Many other vessels also frown on whistling as bad luck.

Point Hicks. The date is sometimes given as 20 April, to account for the modern International Date Line. Parkin offers a splendid narrative of *Endeavour* and its journey up the east coast of Australia.

East Coast. It is possible that other European navigators explored the east coast of Australia in the centuries before Cook.

Trickett, among others, supported by some archaeological evidence, argues that it was charted by the Portuguese captain Christopher de Mendonça in 1522–23, but that his purloined maps were wrongly aligned by French cartographers working at Dieppe in the mid-sixteenth century. Mendonça may also have charted Australia's west coast and much of the North Island of New Zealand. Knowledge of these maps was limited, and they tended to be overlooked by later explorers or ignored by other colonial powers. Some think Cook may have seen a Dieppe map in the British royal collection, but surely he would have said so! He credited the Dutch explorers with their earlier discoveries.

Many traditional cartographers, it should be said, strongly contest the Mendonça connection with the east coast of Australia, New Zealand, or the Dieppe maps, and offer alternative explanations for the few pieces of material evidence. The Spanish helmet, for example, might have fallen from a ship visiting Wellington Harbour in the nineteenth century.

Whatever the truth, it remains the case that, before Cook, few published maps showed an east coast of New Holland: after Cook they all did. And the modern histories of Australia and New Zealand still begin with Cook's *Endeavour* voyage, the territorial claims he made for the British Crown, and their subsequent colonisation.

Station pointer. I thank the State Library of NSW for showing me the many Cook and *Endeavour* relics in the collection, including navigational instruments and the Captain's Bible. It brings one into immediate contact with the voyagers.

Leadline. The line was marked as follows: 2 fathoms, two strips of leather; 3, three strips of leather; 5, a piece of white duck [material]; 7, red bunting; 10, leather with a hole; 13, blue serge; 15, white duck; 17, red bunting; 20, a piece of line with two knots, and so on. The depths between the marks were estimated as 'deeps'.

Fathom. A fathom is 6 feet. *Endeavour's* draught was about 14 feet, and she thus drew over two fathoms.

Isaac Smith. Born London 1752. Post-captain 1787, superannuated Rear-Admiral 1807. He lived in London and at Merton Abbey with his cousin Elizabeth Cook, and died 1831. Mrs Cook died in 1835 at the age of ninety-four.

Gamay. Sometimes spelt Kamay, the Aboriginal name for Botany Bay. I thank Les Bursill of the Dharawal community, and Ron and Margaret Simpson, for their advice, friendship, and a memorable day on the Hacking River looking at Aboriginal Australia. See the website *The Archaeology of the Dharawal People of NSW* at www.lesbursill.com. Search also 'Parkinson Aborigines' and 'Parkinson Endeavour'.

Punishment. Being made to stand in the rigging or at the masthead were common punishments for the boys and young gentlemen – short of being tied over a cannon and beaten with a cane or a cat-o-five-tails: 'kissing the gunner's daughter'.

James Magra. Born New York 1746, died 1806. Later changed his surname to Matra, joined the British diplomatic service, and in 1783 produced a pamphlet proposing a settlement in NSW. The Sydney suburb of Matraville is named after him.

Orton. Cook, 23 May 1770.

Reef. Parkin is excellent on the hazards of sailing the 'chameleon sea'.

CHAPTER 10

Aground. Parkin provides an authoritative commentary on the events of 11–13 June.

Fothering. Parkinson gives the detail that the fothered sail was lowered over the bows and hauled aft by ropes until it was sucked into the leak.

Bower anchor. The small bower anchor was recovered in 1971, and is now on display at the fine James Cook Museum, Cooktown, with one of the cannons raised in 1969.

Sheathing. See Parkin, p 71, and commentary for 22–24 June.

Mangrove pod. Alan Gould in his poem 'The Great Circle' gives a lovely image of *Endeavour* on the river mud like a cast-up pod. Search 'Parkinson Endeavour' for a print of the scene after Parkinson's drawing.

Kangaroo. Cook and Banks spelt it *kanguru*, I used *gangurru* from today's Guggu Yimithirr spelling. Gore shot his first specimen on 14 July. Paintings based on the skin and also a dingo brought back by Banks were done by George Stubbs. Search 'Stubbs kangaroo' and 'Stubbs dingo'.

Turtle hunt. Cook says only that a boathook was used. I thank Trevor Nicholson and Sam Dibella of Cooktown for their advice on how it may have been done.

CHAPTER 11

Bama. I acknowledge the written statements by Eric Deeral displayed at the James Cook Museum, giving a Guggu Yimithirr perspective on *Endeavour's* time at the river. I have drawn upon them in my version of the story. Margie Callaghan also gave much assistance.

Yir-ke. I have used the spelling given by Beaglehole, *Journals*, vol I. Banks and others note a number of expressions used by the Aborigines to denote surprise, including '*charco*'. See Brunton (ed.), p 64. Hicks calls the river 'Charco Harbour'.

Sharing code. I acknowledge helpful conversations with Roy

McIvor, Willie Gordon, Helena Loncaric and other members of the Hopevale and Cooktown communities for an Aboriginal perspective on the sharing code and the incident with the turtles.

Ngamu Yarrbarigo. Eric Deeral gives the name of the elder.

Reconciliation. Cook, 19 July.

Pickersgill. I assume he went to the opening, still called Cook's Passage, as none of the journals say which Mate it was. See Robson p 178.

Quit this coast. Cook, 13 August.

Sweeps. Once again, see Parkin's detailed commentary on the events of 16–17 August.

Readings. Ibid p 414.

Manley Island. Named much later for Isaac. It is among the small Cockburn Islands off Cape Grenville in Far North Queensland.

Torres. Cook does not name the Portuguese navigator in his journal. Nor does Cook mention his rival Dalrymple (see note in Interlude), on whose chart Torres's 1606 track south of New Guinea appears. Banks had a copy of Dalrymple's map on *Endeavour*.

Bearings. It is extraordinary how close to the true position the latitude and longitude given by Cook was; see the historical notes in this book.

New Britain. An island off the north-east coast of New Guinea, named *Nova Britannia* by Dampier in 1700. Cook named the south-eastern archipelago New Caledonia (the Latin name for Scotland) in 1774.

New South Wales. Cook's first names are illegible. He called it 'New Wales' for quite some time. Beaglehole, *Life*, p 249, notes that 'South' was added after a copy of the *Journal* was sent to the Admiralty from Batavia in October.

CHAPTER 12

Swallow. The sloop HMS *Swallow* reached England in May 1769.

Date. In July 1769 Cook crossed what is now the International Date Line east of New Zealand, but did not adjust his tally of the days.

Batavia. Parkinson gives an excellent description of Batavia. Search 'Dutch Batavia' online for images of the old city and shipping, also the Trove pictures archive at the National Library of Australia.

Bougainville. Louis Antoine de Bougainville (1729–1811) led the first successful French circumnavigation of the globe. He was in Tahiti early in 1768, and Batavia later that year. The island of Bougainville and the tropical plant bougainvillea are named after him. The Tahitian who sailed with him, Aotourou, was feted in Paris, stimulating European ideas of the 'noble savage', Salmond (2004), p 53. See also the historical notes to this book.

Malaria. The term literally means 'bad air'. It was not until 1898 that Sir Ronald Ross proved the disease was spread by female *Anopheles* mosquitos. In his paper on malaria in Batavia in the eighteenth century, van der Brug suggests fish ponds were the most likely breeding grounds, but stagnant canals and the mangrove swamps also contributed. The figures quoted are from van der Brug. Banks gives a graphic account of the filth dredged from the canals.

Cinchona. Banks, 13 November. From the 1640s, bark of the Peruvian tree had been known in Europe as effective against malaria or 'ague'. The active ingredient, quinine, was finally extracted in 1820. Cinchona trees were not grown in Java until the 1850s.

Nick Young. Remustered as Perry's servant on 6 November 1770.

Laudanum. Tincture (weak solution) of opium, used to relieve pain and diahorrea since the seventeenth century. Its addictive properties were recognised in the nineteenth century.

Taiata. His death is based on Parkinson. I thank Tehani Fiedler-Valenta of Tahiti Tourisme Australie for the translation. Search 'Parkinson Taiata' online for a lovely print of the boy in native dress playing his nose flute, after Parkinson's drawing. The site also shows Tupaia's painting of a Maori presenting a lobster to either Banks or Cook.

Tupaia. 'He was a Shrewd Sensible, Ingenious Man,' wrote Cook on 26 December, 'but proud and obstinate which often made his situation on board both disagreeable to himself and those about him, and tended much to promote the deceases which put a period to his life.' Search 'Tupaia Tahiti' for paintings by Taiata, including one of canoes and a longhouse.

Ravenhill. Cook, 26 December.

Dead men's clothes. Chris Donnithorne says that even until recently the clothes were sometimes sold several times over to raise more money. Ordinary seamen couldn't bid for officers' uniforms 'above their wear' or spend more than was due to them on the pay book. The Purser got 5 per cent of the sum raised for handling the transaction. *Regulations*, 1790 ed., Part II.

Princes Island. Both Cook and Banks note the warnings about the brackish water.

Green. Cook's comment, 29 January, that Green's manner of living 'greatly promoted the disorders [. . .] which put a period to his life,' is similar to his remark about Tupaia. Censoriousness of his dead is one of the Captain's less admirable traits.

Calamitous situation. Cook, 31 January.

Promotion. Muster roll shows Isaac became a Midshipman 5 February 1771 (Adm 36/8569).

CHAPTER 13

Rossiter. Cook, 21 February. *Gripes.* 15 March.

Midshipmen. See Elliot for a young midshipman's account of how Cook trained him.

Log line. A knot tied at every seven fathoms is based on the length of a nautical mile converted to feet per second. The number of knots passing over the stern in thirty seconds (later twenty-eight seconds) as measured by the sand glass give the ship's approximate speed, not the distance travelled. Thus, three knots are equivalent to three nautical miles per hour. A *nautical mile* is one second of arc on the sextant at the equator, and is 1.15 times longer than a land mile.

Natal. Cook, 5 March.

Cape Town. Banks gives an excellent description of life at Cape Town in 1771.

Water. Cook, 15 March, notes ships from Batavia all had flux yet none had taken on water at Prince's Island. Many arrived in a worse state than *Endeavour.*

Molineux. Cook, 16 April. The details of the Master's decline are imagined.

Pickersgill. Cook admired his seamanship and appointed him Third Lieutenant on the first *Resolution* voyage. He commanded the *Lyon* sent to the east coast of Canada to meet *Resolution* should Cook have found the North-West Passage during his third voyage. Pickersgill's leadership was questioned and he was court-martialled on his return. He drowned when he fell into the Thames while boarding a ship in 1779. He was described as a good officer, but (like his friend Molineux) 'liking ye Grog'. See article by Ian Boreham in Robson p 178.

Circumnavigation. Endeavour crossed longitude 0 degrees on 29 April.

Swallow. See Captain's logs (Adm 51/956 and Adm 51/4562).

Hicks. After Hicks died, John Gore became Second Lieutenant and Charles Clerke Third Lieutenant. Both sailed with Cook on his third voyage, and both commanded the *Resolution* after his murder at Hawaii in 1779. Clerke was Captain until his death from tuberculosis off Petropavlovsk, Siberia, and Gore brought the ship home.

Whaler. Cook, 19 June. *Weather stays.* 22 June. *Bets.* 7 July.

Nick Young. Banks, 10 July.

Woolwich. Parkinson.

AFTERWARDS

Cook letter. 8 August 1771, Beaglehole, *Journals*, vol 1, p 736 (Adm 1/1609).

Isaac on Resolution. Beaglehole, *Journals*, vol 2, p 874 (muster roll Adm 36/7672).

Endeavour results. See Beaglehole, *Life*, p 273. Robson, p 45, says about thirty thousand botanical specimens returned in *Endeavour*, and one hundred and ten new genera and thirteen hundred new species had been identified. Approximately fifty thousand specimens were brought back altogether, including ethnographic, zoological, geological and marine examples.

Goat. It apparently went to Cook's house at Mile End, London. *Dr Johnson's Latin verse* in translation reads: 'The globe twice circled, this the Goat, the second to the nurse of Jove, is thus rewarded for her never-failing milk.' Beaglehole, *Life*, p 291.

Resolution. Cook sailed *Resolution* as Commander on his second circumnavigation (1772–75) with HMS *Adventure*; and again as Post-Captain on a third Pacific voyage (1777–80) with HMS *Discovery*, during which Cook was murdered at Hawaii, 14 February 1779.

Banks's temper. See Elliot, p 7. 'He swore and stamped upon the Wharfe like a Mad Man, and instantly ordered his servants and all his things out of the ship.'

Endeavour. After Cook she was used to carry freight to the Falkland Islands, and was sold by the Navy about 1775. There are several versions of her fate. Most recently it is thought she was renamed *Lord Sandwich*, used to transport troops to New York during the American War of Independence, became a prison ship, and was scuttled with twelve other ships off Newport in 1778 to protect shore batteries from an approaching French fleet. A number of these wrecks have been found. Although *Endeavour* has not yet been identified from particular features of her timber construction, researchers from the Rhode Island Marine Archaeology Project (RIMAP) believe she is among a small group of wrecks located in Newport Harbour. Whether she will ever be raised is a subject of continuing discussion. See the website www.rimap.com.

Gore & Young. Beaglehole, *Journals*, vol I, 'The Ship's Company', pp 595, 600.

Isaac's Career. Isaac George Manley, *Memorandum of Services*, Adm 9/1, p 53. See also references under 'Manley, Isaac George' for Captain's Letters and ships' logs.

The Saintes. 9–12 April 1782. See Hannay, pp 276–280, also entry online on Wikipedia.

Isaac's letters. Captain's letter 7 July 1790, Adm 1/2126. See also references under 'Manley'.

Isaac's marriage, Burke's *The Landed Gentry*, p 1268.

Braziers. See Cross for an excellent account with photographs of Braziers' history, including the Manley years. A stone in the cellar is dated 1688. Drawings of Isaac's gothic additions were displayed at the Royal Academy in 1799. Isaac's son sold the property in 1851.

The author Ian Fleming, creator of James Bond, grew up at Braziers. Since 1950 the property has been owned by the Braziers Park School of Integrative Social Research. I acknowledge with gratitude three happy days as a visitor in October 2006. It is still a working estate.

Captain John Manley. Died 1 March 1799, without issue. His father records in his will that he laid out £1250 to equip his eldest son as an officer in Lord Cornwallis's 33rd Regiment: a vast sum of money for those days. As a lawyer, John Manley senior seems to have had a professional association with the Cornwallis family. He died 5 September 1801. His very detailed will and codicils can be seen online at www.nationalarchives.gov.uk.

Doctor of Civil Laws. Jackson's Oxford journal, 7 July 1810.

John Shawe Manley. See Burke; also Joseph Foster's *Alumni Oxonienses.* I acknowledge the assistance of Oxford University Archives.

Admiral Isaac. Isaac's promotions are recorded in the Navy List, also in his obituary. See entry under *Isaac George Manley* in Chapter 1 for details of Richard Dighton's portrait of him in later life.

Steamships. The US ship *Savannah* was the first sailing ship with an auxiliary steam engine to cross the Atlantic, to Liverpool, in 1819. The Dutch-owned but British-built vessel *Curaçao* was the first to cross using mainly steam in 1826. The Canadian *Royal William* in 1833 was one of the first to make a transatlantic voyage using steam only. The British *Great Western* began the first regular steam service in 1838. See www.curassow.com.

Obituary. The Gentleman's Magazine, December 1837.

Memorial. Plaque above the pulpit at St Peter & St Paul's Church Checkendon, author visit 2006. Isaac's will can be seen online through the Captain Cook Society, www.captaincooksociety.com.

HISTORICAL NOTES

Banks and Matra. For their role in the decision to establish a colony at Botany Bay see O'Brian, *Banks*, pp 264–9.

Smallpox. A good account of the effects of the disease that devastated the Aboriginal community near Sydney can be found in an article by Craig Mear, 'The origin of the smallpox outbreak in Sydney in 1789' in the *Journal of the Royal Australian Historical Society* June 2008 edition.

Trinca. 'Informed and rounded perspective incorporates view from ship and shore', *The Australian*, September 16–17 2017, p 19.

Venereal disease at Tahiti. See Cook's *Journal* for Tuesday 6 June 1769.

Cook's naval background. See notes to Chapter 1. A short account is in O'Brian, *Banks*, pp 71–2. For a full account see Beaglehole, *Life of Captain Cook*, Chapters III and IV.

No great discoveries. Cook twice used similar words in correspondence to the Admiralty. From Batavia, whence he sent a copy of his journal, he wrote, 'Altho' the discoveries made in this voyage are not great, yet I flatter my self that they are such as may merit the attention of their Lordships…' (Beaglehole, *Life*, et al. p 259). And upon arriving home, when he sent in his charts and drawings, Cook wrote to Secretary Stephens hoping they would convey 'a Tolerable knowledge of the places they are intended to illustrate, & that the discoveries we have made, tho' not great, will Apologize for the length of the Voyage' (Beaglehole, p 272). As Beaglehole remarks, Cook's unwillingness to claim more than minimal credit must have seemed incomprehensible to their Lordships.

Chronometer. Dava Sobel's *Longitude* is a marvellous book about John Harrison's clocks and the solution to the longitude problem. The three sea clocks can be seen at the Royal Observatory,

Greenwich, and the prototype chronometer (H4) at the Science Museum, London. Kendall's copy of Harrison's chronometer, known as K1, went on Cook's second and third voyages. It also arrived at Botany Bay with the First Fleet in 1788, before being returned to England. It is now on display at the National Maritime Museum, Greenwich.

Florilegium. See, for example, a discussion on the National Museum of Australia website www.nma.gov.au under 'European Voyages to the Australian Continent'. Gooding et al. have recently published a fine single-volume edition for the general reader.

Resolution. For Banks's 'dummy spit' see O'Brian, pp 187–90. He includes an exchange of letters between Banks and his friend the Earl of Sandwich, First Lord of the Admiralty, but only extracts. As O'Brian remarks, '. . . passion does tend to grow intolerably wordy.'

Isaac Manley. The single sentence on Isaac is in Beaglehole, pp 139–40.

Admiral Manley's Map. For a longer article about the map and the family to whom it was given, see my website http://www.anthonyhillbooks.com/isaacs-map.html.

ACKNOWLEDGEMENTS

A great many people helped me during my own voyage of discovery for this book, and I thank them all. Each piece of information, however small, contributed to my understanding of the subject.

I would like to acknowledge the assistance given by The Australia Council for the Arts, which enabled me to visit sites of importance in the *Endeavour* story and complete the writing. Mr Graeme Powell, formerly manuscript librarian at the National Library of Australia, generously allowed me to sit with Cook's journal.

Pete and Takutai Beech, Ruth Boreham, Margie Callaghan, Chris Donnithorne, Captain Ross Mattson and the company of HMB *Endeavour*, Alexandra Fullerlove, Alwyn Peel, Margaret and Ron Simpson, and Cliff Thornton were of special assistance during the research. Les Bursill, Dr Alan Cowan, Rear Admiral Ken Doolan, Michelle Hetherington, Professor Adrian Horridge, Dr David Jauncey, Michaela Jerome, Peter Johnston, Dr Nick Lomb, and Anthony Longhurst were among those who read the manuscript in whole or in part and suggested many improvements, although any errors are my own. I thank everyone.

Canberra: Sue Clarke; Dr Alan Cowan; Director and staff, National Library of Australia, particularly Andrew Sergeant of the Petherick Reading Room; Rear Admiral Ken Doolan who helped on all matters nautical; Embassy of Portugal; Peter Filmer; Alan Gould; Michelle Hetherington; Professor Adrian Horridge who gave much advice on the South Seas voyages; Dr David Jauncey who assisted with the Transit; Michaela Jerome; David Kaus, and the Director, Dr Mathew Trinca, and staff, National Museum of Australia; Robert King; Sea Power Centre; Huub Schwartz.

Sydney: Les and Robyn Bursill; Dr Nigel Erskine and staff, Australian National Maritime Museum; Associate Professor John Faulkner; Cameron's Management; Dr Nick Lomb; Captain Ross Mattson, Anthony Longhurst, staff and crew of HMB *Endeavour* who taught this landlubber his ropes, and Captain Jim Cottee who showed me the sextant; State Library of NSW and staff who gave access to the Cook material; members of the Captain Cook Society; Margaret and Ron Simpson, who with Les Bursill gave me a splendid day on Port Hacking looking at Aboriginal Australia.

Cooktown: Dr Judy Bennett; Margie Callaghan; Helen Crampton and staff, James Cook Museum; Eric Deeral, an elder of the Guugu Yimithirr people; Willie Gordon, Helena Loncaric, Roy McIvor and members of the Hopevale community who gave me an Aboriginal perspective on Cook, the sharing code and the incident with the turtles; Trevor Nicholson (Nicho) and Sam Dibella who suggested how a turtle might be caught with a boathook.

New Zealand: Pete and Takutai Beech with whom I had a wonderful day on Queen Charlotte Sound; Peter Johnston of the Ngati Hei people, who gave much valuable advice; Betty Rowe; Don Thomson; Mercury Bay District Historical Society museum; John Robson; my editor, Suzanne Wilson.

Tahiti: Walter Demmayer; Tehani Fiedler-Valenta, formerly of Tahiti Tourisme Australie; Alberts Tours.

Britain: Anne Batchelor, who kindly made her Manley research materials available; The British Library; Ruth Boreham, an invaluable research assistant; Maurice Roth, Cliff Jordan and residents of the Braziers Park School of Integrative Social Research; Cliff Thornton, Alwyn Peel, Ian Boreham and members of the Captain Cook Society; Joyce Cook; Chris Donnithorne who shared his knowledge of the Royal Navy; staff at the National Archives; Alexandra Fullerlove, Bernard Bryant and staff of the National Maritime Museum, Greenwich, who made me welcome; Michael Manley, a direct descendent of Isaac; archives of the Honourable Society of the Middle Temple; Margaret Morris; R and D Nuttal of Dodleston; Oxford University Archives; Oxfordshire Record Office; Noel Stevens of Cheltenham; my dear family Brenda and Bob Blewitt, and Gail and Edward Mann.

I would also like to thank Noel Hall of Brisbane; Jane and Paul Mangion, and Tony Radford of Melbourne; and Cathy Manly Sockol, who runs an online Manley family history site, for their assistance and advice.

Finally I acknowledge my friend, Jane Tanner, who has given her literary encouragement throughout this adventure; and of course my loved wife, Gillian, who has been with me for the whole of the journey.

REFERENCES

Aughton, Peter. *Endeavour, the Story of Captain Cook's First Great Epic Voyage* (Cassell & Co., London, 2002). A beautifully illustrated account of the voyage.

Banks, Joseph. Ed. Paul Brunton. *The Endeavour Journal of Joseph Banks: The Australian Journey* (Angus & Robertson with State Library of NSW, Sydney, 1998). Also Banks's *Journal* at southseas.nla.gov.au.

Beaglehole, J.C. *The Life of Captain James Cook* (Stanford University Press, 1998). The definitive biography.

Beaglehole, J.C. (ed.). *The Journals of Captain James Cook on his voyages of discovery* (Vols I & II, The Hakluyt Society, London, 1955–61).

Brown, Stephen. *Scurvy: How a surgeon, a mariner, and a gentleman solved the greatest medical mystery of the age of sail* (Penguin, Melbourne, 2003).

Burke, Bernard. *Burke's The Landed Gentry* [1914]. See entry for Manley of Manley Hall & Shenstone Park; also Isaac's wife Frances, Chandos-Pole of Radburne.

British Library: *Endeavour Log*, May–August 1768 MS89598; Isaac's grandfather a Commissioner of Customs 1720 MS61605 ff 187, and living at Hatton Garden Add 1394 ff 28–30; folios of drawings by and engravings after Alexander Buchan, Sydney Parkinson, et al., from *Endeavour* voyage Add 15508 & Add 23920.

Cook, James. *The Journals* (Penguin, London, 2003, selections ed. Philip Edwards from Beaglehole's editions). Also Cook's *Journals* at southseas.nla.gov.au.

Cross, Clarence. *Braziers Before the Community* (Braziers Research Communications, 1982). See 'The Manley Era'.

Elliott, John, and Richard Pickersgill, ed. Christine Holmes. *Captain Cook's Second Voyage* (Caliban, London). Journals of two Lieutenants.

Endeavour Journals. Manuscript journals of the following *Endeavour* crew held at the National Archives, London: Anonymous Adm 51/4547; John Bootie Adm 51/4546; Charles Clerke Adm 51/4548; John Gore Adm 51/4548; Zachary Hicks Adm 51/4546; Robert Molineux Adm 51/4546 and Master's Log Adm 55/39; Richard Pickersgill Adm 51/4547; Francis Wilkinson Adm 51/4547. Extracts from some are printed in Beaglehole, *Journals*, Vol I.

Falconer, William. *A universal dictionary of the marine* (Cadell, London, 1769). See plates at www.nla.gov.au.

French, Jackie. *The Goat Who Sailed the World* (Angus & Robertson, Sydney, 2006).

Gooding, Mel; David Mabberley & Joe Studholme. *Joseph Banks' Florilegium, Botanical Treasures from Cook's First Voyage* (Thames & Hudson, London, 2017). A handsome abridged volume of highlights from the complete *Florilegium*, at an affordable price.

Hawkesworth, John. *An account of the voyages undertaken by the order of His present Majesty for making discoveries in the Southern Hemisphere* (Byron, Wallis & Cook [*Endeavour*] voyages, London, 1773). Also at southseas.nla.gov.au.

Hetherington, Michelle. 'Cook's voyages to the Pacific' in exhibition catalogue *Cook's Pacific Encounters* (National Museum of Australia, Canberra, 2006).

Jackson, Peter. *London Bridge* (Cassell & Co., London, 1971).

Lomb, Nick. *Transit of Venus: The scientific event that led Captain Cook to Australia* (Powerhouse Publishing, Sydney, 2004).

Macarthur, Antonia. *His Majesty's Bark Endeavour: The story of the ship and her people* (Angus & Robertson with the ANMM, Sydney, 1997).

Manley, Isaac George. *Captain's Letters* 1784–95 (Adm 1/2124 to 1/2129), National Archives, London. Also the logs during his command of HMS *Britannia* [Dec 1782–Mar 1783] Adm 51/139; *Otter* [Mar–Apr 1783] Adm 51/664; *Hound* [Apr–Aug 1783] Adm 51/463; *Fairy* [May 1786–June 1789] Adm 51/333).

O'Brian, Patrick. *Joseph Banks: A life* (1987 [2016], Folio Society, introduction by Peter Campbell).

Parkin, Ray. *H.M. Bark Endeavour* (Melbourne University Publishing, 2003). A masterly book.

Parkinson, Sydney. *A Journal of a Voyage to the South Seas in* HMS *Endeavour* (Caliban, London, 1984 – a facsimile of the 1784 edition). Also at southseas.nla.gov.au.

Robson, John (ed.). *The Captain Cook Encyclopaedia* (Random House, Sydney, 2004).

Rodger, N.A.M. *The Wooden World: An anatomy of the Georgian navy* (Fontana, Glasgow, 1988).

Salmond, Anne. *The Trial of the Cannibal Dog: Captain Cook in the South Seas* (Penguin, London, 2004). See the Polynesian sections of the voyage.

—. *Two Worlds: First meetings between Maori and Europeans 1642–1772* (Viking, Auckland, 1991). See Chapter 5, 'Goblins from the sea', esp. Whitianga section.

Sobel, Dava. *Longitude: The true story of a lone genius who solved the greatest scientific problem of his time* (Fourth Estate, London, 2005). The remarkable tale of John Harrison (1693–1776), who invented the chronometer.

Thomas, Nicholas. *Discoveries: The voyages of Captain Cook* (Penguin, London, 2004). A contemporary anthropologist's account of Cook in the Pacific.

Trickett, Peter. *Beyond Capricorn: How Portuguese adventurers secretly discovered and mapped Australia and New Zealand 250 years before Captain Cook* (East Street Publications, Adelaide, 2007). A fascinating story. The theory is contested by many traditional cartographers.

Van der Brug, P.H., 'Malaria in Batavia in the 18th century' in *Tropical Medicine & International Health*, Vol 2, Sept 1997, p 892). Also available on the internet.

INTERNET

Australian National Maritime Museum. www.anmm.gov.au. Home of the *Endeavour* replica. A great resource for the maritime exploration of Australia.

Braziers. www.braziers.org.uk. Home page of the Braziers Park community in Oxfordshire, with information about the house where Admiral Isaac Manley lived.

British Library. www.bl.uk. One of the world's greatest libraries. Check out the online image collections, including drawings by Sydney Parkinson, Alexander Buchan and others.

British Museum. www.britishmuseum.org. Another of the world's amazing institutions with wonderful collections of South Seas material brought back to England by Cook, Banks and others.

Captain Cook Society. www.captaincooksociety.com. A worldwide society of people interested in the life and work of Captain Cook. Isaac's will is online.

Dharawal people. www.lesbursill.com. The website of Les Bursill, an Aboriginal man of the Dharawal nation. An excellent resource for words, images and traditional lore of the area around Botany Bay.

Journals of Cook, Banks and Parkinson. southseas.nla.gov.au. An excellent National Library of Australia site, including voyaging accounts, maps, a South Seas Companion, cultural atlases, indigenous histories and European reactions.

National Maritime Museum, Greenwich. www.nmm.ac.uk. A magnificent site for all things associated with Cook, *Endeavour*, and British maritime history. Also check out the Royal Observatory for Harrison's sea clocks and chronometer.

Royal Navy. www.royal-navy.mod.uk. A fascinating site full of information and pictures of the Royal Navy.

Royal Navy biographies. www.navylist.org. A UK database maintained by Chris Donnithorne of people and ships associated with the Royal Navy since 1660.

State Library of NSW. www.sl.nsw.gov.au. The Library has a splendid collection of objects associated with Cook, Banks and *Endeavour*, including the Captain's Bible, navigation instruments, personal items, Banks's journal and other manuscripts. Many of them can be seen online.

Also by Anthony Hill

The dark clouds returned and gathered about the boy. His eyes grew distant, and he began to tremble. He heard not only shells exploding, but the cries of dying men . . . He was stumbling over churned earth, looking into the face of an officer, bloodied red as the poppies, ripped apart in the Flanders mud . . .

A small boy, an orphan of the First World War, wanders into the Australian airmen's mess in Germany, on Christmas Day in 1918. A strange boy, with an uncertain past and an extraordinary future, he became a mascot for the air squadron and was affectionately named 'Young Digger'. And in one of the most unusual incidents ever to emerge from the battlefields of Europe after the Great War, this solitary boy was smuggled back to Australia by air mechanic Tim Tovell, a man who cared for the boy so much that he was determined, however risky, to provide Young Digger with a new family and a new life in a new country, far from home.

At the close of the First World War, and after surviving a gas attack on the Western Front, Captain Walter Eddison moved his family from war-ravaged Britain to start a new life in Australia. The Eddisons were offered 'land fit for heroes' under the Australian government's soldier-settlement scheme, but the grim realities of life in the remote bush were not easy for a family used to the green pastures of England.

Walter and Marion made the best of their limited prospects, but as they raised their young family on the outskirts of the nation's newly established capital, tensions were again simmering in Europe. When the Second World War broke out, they were forced to confront their worst fears as their three sons headed back to the battlefields they'd tried so hard to leave behind.

Anthony Hill expertly weaves military history and gripping accounts of frontline fighting into this intimate portrait of a family who sacrificed everything for their country, showing how the global conflicts of the twentieth century came home to Australia, with tragic consequences.